Susannah glared at Cooper,

but he knew her growing fury was directed solely at the man who had dared to violate her home and leave his mark on it. The bastard's biggest mistake, however, was daring to order her to leave. That was something Cooper knew Susannah took from no man.

"You can't stay here alone, sweetheart," Cooper said. "You can either come home with me or I'm spending the night."

She wanted to tell him not to call her *sweetheart*. She should have demanded that he quit giving her ultimatums. But when he looked at her like that, as if he could see into her very soul, her knees weakened and she couldn't seem to catch her breath. And that was just from a probing look. If he stayed the night, and it was just the two of them, in the darkness . . . alone together . . .

D0027805

Dear Reader,

It's March, and spring is just around the corner. To help you through the last of the chilly days and nights, we've got another lineup of terrific books just waiting to be read. Our American Hero this month is Linda Turner's *Cooper,* the next hot hero in her miniseries called "The Wild West." He's a man you won't want to miss.

The rest of the month is equally irresistible. Justine Davis is back with *Wicked Secrets,* a tale every bit as enticing as its title implies. Lee Magner's *Banished* makes it worth the wait since this talented author's last appearance. And then you'll find Beverly Barton's *Lover and Deceiver,* Cathryn Clare's *Sun and Shadow,* and Susan Mallery's debut for the line, *Tempting Faith.* Each one will have you turning the pages eagerly; this really is what romance is all about.

And in coming months, keep looking to Silhouette Intimate Moments for all the passion, all the excitement and all the reading pleasure you're seeking, because it's our promise to you that you'll find all that—and more—in our pages every month of the year.

Yours,

Leslie Wainger
Senior Editor and Editorial Coordinator

Please address questions and book requests to:
Reader Service
U.S.: P.O. Box 1325, Buffalo, NY 14269
Canadian: P.O. Box 1050, Niagara Falls, Ont. L2E 7G7

AMERICAN HERO

COOPER

Linda Turner

FROM THE LIBRARY OF CARMEN LOPEZ BUSTOS

Silhouette® INTIMATE MOMENTS®

Published by Silhouette Books New York

America's Publisher of Contemporary Romance

If you purchased this book without a cover you should be aware
that this book is stolen property. It was reported as "unsold and
destroyed" to the publisher, and neither the author nor the
publisher has received any payment for this "stripped book."

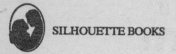 SILHOUETTE BOOKS

ISBN 0-373-07553-7

COOPER

Copyright © 1994 by Linda Turner

All rights reserved. Except for use in any review, the reproduction
or utilization of this work in whole or in part in any form by any
electronic, mechanical or other means, now known or hereafter
invented, including xerography, photocopying and recording, or in
any information storage or retrieval system, is forbidden without
the written permission of the editorial office, Silhouette Books,
300 East 42nd Street, New York, NY 10017 U.S.A.

All characters in this book have no existence outside the imagination of
the author and have no relation whatsoever to anyone bearing the same
name or names. They are not even distantly inspired by any individual
known or unknown to the author, and all incidents are pure invention.

This edition published by arrangement with Harlequin Enterprises B. V.

® and TM are trademarks of Harlequin Enterprises B. V., used under
license. Trademarks indicated with ® are registered in the United States
Patent and Trademark Office, the Canadian Trade Marks Office and in
other countries.

Printed in U.S.A.

Books by Linda Turner

LINDA TURNER

began reading romances in high school and began writing them one night when she had nothing else to read. She's been writing ever since. Single and living in Texas, she travels every chance she gets, scouting locales for her books.

To my uncle, Buddy Whiteley, who made
going to my grandparents' an adventure
when I was a kid. Even when that
meant trying to ride a pig bareback.
Thanks for all your help with this
series.

Chapter 1

Standing head and shoulders above his sister-in-law, Josey, and his sister, Kat, Cooper Rawlings glared down at the two of them in affectionate exasperation. He loved them both to death and knew they only had his best interests at heart, but he was, he promised himself, going to kill them both just as soon as this potluck Sunday dinner they'd arranged was over. He was up to his ears in women, and it was all their fault!

"Dammit, you've got to quit doing this to me," he said fiercely in a lowered voice that wouldn't carry to the rest of the guests. "*I don't need a wife.*"

Watching the flock of women flitting through the house like colorful birds trying to get Cooper's attention, Josey only grinned cheekily and patted his arm. "Of course you do. You're just not ready to admit it."

"Anyone would think we were arranging your hanging," Kat teased. "If you'd just relax, you might enjoy this, you know."

He groaned, wanting to shake them. They'd had this same discussion countless times over the past two weeks, always with the same results. It was enough to drive a man to drink.

"You need a wife."

Josey had made the announcement weeks ago over breakfast, shocking him and amusing the hell out of the rest of the family. Ignoring the others' laughter, she'd calmly related how she'd noticed the restlessness that plagued him lately, the loneliness that haunted his brown eyes when he thought no one was looking. And as the only doctor in the family, she'd decided there was only one cure for what was plaguing him. He was thirty-one, still living in the home he'd been born in and in danger of becoming a crusty old bachelor while all his friends had settled down with wives and babies and spreads of their own. He needed a wife to shake him up a little.

He'd almost choked on his coffee and flatly denied that he needed anything of the kind. What he *hadn't* said was that he'd only been in love once in his life, and like a fool he'd fallen for a girl on the rebound from another man. She'd eventually gone back to her old love without ever knowing that he'd been crazy about her, and he'd vowed that he was never going to give another woman a chance to hurt him.

He'd told Josey the whole story and would have sworn she understood that just because she and his brother, Gable, were happy as clams didn't mean he intended to follow in their footsteps. He should have known when she gave in so easily that he was headed for trouble.

The ambush she'd planned with his sister came out of nowhere. Kat, the rat, had given her the names of every single woman in the county, then the two of them had put their heads together and set about coming up with ways for him to meet them. In a matter of days, they'd organized dinner parties and barbecues and card games, innocently claiming that they were just trying to make the long, slow winter days more interesting by entertaining. And since Kat would soon be going back to college now that the spring semester was about to start, she wanted to have some friends out to the ranch before she left. It sounded good, but Cooper wasn't fooled. He knew a setup when he saw one.

For the past two weeks, he hadn't been able to turn around without tripping over a strange woman. Another man might have been flattered; hell, he'd have been amused himself if it had been anyone else but him standing in his boots fending off a half dozen flirting females. If he'd been less experienced, all the attention might have gone to his head, but he hadn't fallen off the stock trailer just yesterday. He'd seen the dollar signs in the feminine eyes perusing him and knew it wasn't him the women were after, but the ranch.

Oh, it wasn't that he was ugly or anything, he was as good-looking as the next fellow and certainly didn't have any trouble getting a date when he wanted one. But he could have been as homely as a cedar fence post and still drawn women like flies to honey with the Double R. For generations, men and women had fought over it and connived to steal it out from under his family simply because it had the best water in southwest New Mexico.

And nothing had changed when he and his brothers and sister inherited the ranch at their parents' death. He and Flynn had only been teenagers at the time, and Kat just a little girl. They would probably have lost everything through mismanagement if it hadn't been for Gable. Only twenty-two himself, he'd fought to keep the family together and the ranch out of the hands of the vultures just waiting to pounce on it like a road kill.

They'd won that struggle, but the time had yet to come when they could relax their guard. Just two years ago some of their neighbors, suffering from a drought and envious of the Double R springs, had conspired to get control of the ranch by sabotaging their efforts to make a mortgage payment. Luckily, the plot had failed, but the family had all learned a valuable lesson. When it came down to trust, blood was thicker than water.

And the women who had come running the minute the rumor leaked out that he might be looking for a wife weren't to be trusted. Even if they didn't have any ulterior motives, a man liked to do his own picking!

"Dammit, Josey, you know I'm not good at this kind of thing," he growled, trying to reason with her one last time. "Before you came along, all Gable had to do was crook his little finger to get any woman he wanted. And Flynn, hell, he's been flirting since the day he was born. I'm not like that. I've got to have time to get to know a woman, see what makes her tick, before I let her know I'm interested."

"Then take your time," she said simply, giving his arm a reassuring squeeze. "I just want you to have a chance to meet someone other than those loose skirts who hang out at the Crossroads."

At the mention of the bar where local cowboys met after work for a beer or two, a game of pool, or a fast squeeze with a willing woman, Kat grimaced, "Yeah, why don't you go talk to the Carson sisters? They've been trying to get your attention all evening. Come on, Josey, let's go check with Alice and see how the food's holding out."

They were gone before he could stop them, leaving him alone in the middle of the living room and fair game. The Carson sisters, thin as sticks and two of the most aggressive women in the county, saw their chance and started toward him.

And, like a coward, he ran. Giving them a grimace of a smile, he headed for the bar in the den. He needed a drink.

Gable, acting as bartender, took one look at him and poured him a shot of whiskey, neat, just the way he liked it. "You look like you could use this, little brother. What's the problem?"

Cooper sipped at the liquor, letting the bracing heat seep through him. "Do you even have to ask? I know you can't do anything about Kat—we spoiled the little brat rotten from the moment she was born—but when are you going to do something about Josey?"

"I thought I already had." He chuckled, laughter skimming across the hard, weathered lines of his face. "I married her."

"I know," he grumbled. "That's the problem." At his brother's arch look, he scowled. "Don't look at me like that. You know we're all crazy about her. But there's nothing worse than a happily married woman. The minute she gets that ring on her finger, she turns into a matchmaker. And I don't want to be matched! Can't you talk to her?"

Gable wanted to laugh, but Cooper looked so miserable, he just couldn't. "Sure," he agreed easily. "But I won't get any further with her than you did. You know she can be stubborn as a mule when she sets her mind to it."

He spoke nothing less than the truth, but that was hardly what Cooper wanted to hear. "I never thought I'd see the day you were wrapped around a woman's little finger," he said with a rueful shake of his head. "How the mighty have fallen."

Unperturbed, Gable only grinned. "Don't knock it till you've tried it. You might like it." Glancing past Cooper's shoulder to the group of women converging on the bar, his light blue eyes began to dance. "Looks like you've got trouble heading your way. If I were you, I'd head for the hills.''

Alarmed, Cooper glanced over his shoulder...and lost the chance to run. Before he could take a step, he was surrounded.

"Did you try the chocolate cake I brought, Cooper? I know how you like chocolate and I baked it myself.''

The soft purr of the woman hanging on his right side drew Cooper's eyes to Sharon Thomas. Her big blue eyes smiling with invitation, she gazed up at him with a sweet smile, looking for all the world like an angel. But Cooper knew from the loose talk of the men she had dated that she was anything *but* an angel. Lord, how had he gotten himself into this mess? Feeling the walls closing in on him, he pulled at the string tie he'd worn to church with his pressed white shirt and jeans. "Actually, I didn't," he choked. "I wasn't very hungry.''

"That's because he filled up on the smothered steak I brought," Liza Carson retorted, tightening her hold on his other arm as she shot Sharon a triumphant glance that was guaranteed to set her teeth on edge. "Everyone knows a man likes meat and potatoes. And that old cake of yours is probably heavy as lead. You never were much of a baker.''

"Why you—''

A cat fight, Cooper thought in disgust. Great. Just what he needed. "Ladies—'' he began sternly, only to stop when he saw his younger brother, Flynn, step out of the kitchen into the hall, dragging on his sheepskin coat as he headed for the front door. With a murmured excuse, Cooper hurriedly extricated himself from the women pulling at him. "Hey, what's going on?'' he asked, intercepting Flynn as he reached the front door. "Where you going?''

"To the springs," Flynn retorted, settling his gray felt cowboy hat on his dark brown hair. "We just got a call in on the CB from Red. A gust of wind knocked down that old cottonwood we used to swing on as kids and it fell on the fence between the Double R and the Patterson place. Red would have fixed it himself, but with this storm coming, his arthritis is really giving him fits, and the rest of the hands have the day off. So I thought I'd run out there with the chain saw and take care of the problem myself. It shouldn't take me too long."

"No!" Jumping at the chance to escape, Cooper jerked open the door to the hall closet and pulled out his own jacket. "I'll go. You stay here and try some of Sharon Thomas's chocolate cake. I'm sure she's just dying to know what you think of it."

Flynn stopped in his tracks and cocked a brow at him, a slow grin spreading across his boyish face. "You've got the look of a fox two steps ahead of the hounds," he said, mischief sparkling in his sapphire eyes. "Are the ladies getting to you or what?"

Cooper gave him a withering glance. "Don't start with me, Flynn," he warned. "I'm not in the mood."

Not the least daunted, Flynn's grin only broadened. "I can't imagine why. You've got every available female in the county drooling over you. You ought to be in hog heaven."

"So you stay and entertain them," he tossed back. "I've had all I can take. I'm getting out of here."

Grabbing his battered cowboy hat from the rack near the front door, he strode outside, the sound of his brother's amused laughter ringing in his ears. That's all right, he told himself smugly, a grin tugging at his mouth as he headed for the barn where the chain saw was kept. Flynn could laugh himself silly, but Cooper was the one with the last laugh. That fallen cottonwood was huge. Cutting it up would take the rest of the afternoon.

* * *

Shutting the front door of her father's house. Susannah Patterson stepped outside and caught her breath as the cold wind snatched at her hair and sent a shiver racing down her spine. Grabbing at the dark brown strands of her hair with one hand, she used the other to pull the collar of her coat tighter around her throat. It wasn't the best day for a walk, she silently acknowledged to herself, taking in the dark, bruised clouds gathering on the horizon like an invading army. The Arctic front that had been forecast for later that evening was already racing unrestricted across the barren New Mexico desert, bringing with it the very real possibility of freezing rain. If she had any sense, she'd stay inside where it was safe and warm.

But she'd never been one to play it particularly safe when there was a whole world outside her door, just waiting to be explored and drawn into her books. And she'd always loved days like this, days when anticipation whispered on the wind like a lover, stirring her blood and tempting her past bearing. The air itself seemed to buzz with electricity, just as it did whenever she started writing a new book, whenever she left on a research trip and found herself racing down an open stretch of highway.

And right now, she'd have given anything to be packing her car for parts unknown. As the author of the popular Ace MacKenzie books, a men's adventure series that had done amazingly well over the past few years, she answered to no one. She didn't have to stay here, struggling with elusive memories she'd spent years forgetting. She could simply get in her car and drive away. Within a matter of hours, she could be out of the state and on her way to another book destination, where she could plot out her next story, then immerse herself up to her earlobes in research.

Tempted, she hesitated. But when it came time to actually write the book? the voice of reason reminded her. What then? Would she once again race full tilt into the writer's block that had stymied her ever since her mother had died two months ago?

Hurt stabbed her in the heart at the thought, but the tears she needed to cry just wouldn't come. Her mother had been her best friend, and her unexpected death from a heart attack had devastated her. Still, she'd thought she was handling the loss all right... until she'd tried to write again.

Then, much to her horror, she'd gotten nowhere. Unable to concentrate, her creativity seemed to have died with her mother. All she'd been able to think of was that she had no one now. No parents, no family, only bittersweet memories she wanted nothing to do with. And that, a psychologist had told her, was what was causing her problems with her writing. She couldn't go forward until she dealt with the past and the pain she had successfully repressed for years. Until she went home and faced her childhood, there was a good chance she wasn't going to do anything but spin her wheels.

So three days ago, she'd come home to her father's ranch in New Mexico, convinced her stay would be a short one. After all, there was nothing here for her now. There hadn't been for seventeen years, ever since her father had cut her out of his life because she'd chosen to live with her mother instead of him after they divorced. She'd been twelve at the time. So completely had he made the break that, when he'd died in prison two years ago—incarcerated for having shot one of his neighbors—she hadn't even known he was in trouble!

She'd quickly discovered, however, that the solution to solving her writer's block couldn't be found in a matter of days any more than her ambivalence regarding her father could be dealt with the moment she was surrounded by his things. Neighbors had come in after his arrest to clean out the refrigerator, but except for that, the house was exactly the same as the last time her father had walked out of it. And from the looks of the place, he hadn't thrown out a single book, magazine, or scrap of paper since the divorce. She'd tackled years of dust and dirt, and so far, the only room she'd touched was the kitchen.

Weeks, she thought. She was going to be here weeks. Disturbed, she tucked her head down against the wind, buried her cold hands in the pockets of her jacket, and struck out walking.

The ranch, like the house, hadn't changed much in the seventeen years that had passed since she left with her mother. The barn and outbuildings were still faded and in need of paint; the windmill still creaked out a lonely tune with every turn of its blades. As a child, the sound had scared her in the middle of the night, but now she found it reassuring, a symbol of the fact that some things never changed.

She didn't know how long she'd been walking, but when she finally stopped to catch her breath, she found herself nearly a mile from the house and standing on a small rise that overlooked the springs of the Double R. When she'd first started out to get a little exercise and clear her head, she would have sworn she had no particular destination in mind. But the memories that reached out and grabbed her by the throat told her she'd been heading for this spot from the moment she left Dallas for New Mexico. It was home to the few memories she allowed herself to remember.

The cold wind buffeted her, flushing her cheeks and chilling her blood, but she hardly noticed. Her vision directed inward, she saw herself at seven, snagging her shirt as she slipped through the barbed wire fence that separated her father's ranch from the Double R. On a hot summer day, she hadn't been able to resist the temptation of the cool, crystal-clear springs bubbling among a stand of cotton-woods, their green leaves whispering to her in the hot wind. She'd been caught, of course—her torn shirt had given her away and she'd had to confess where she'd been—and her father had ordered her to stay on their side of the fence, away from the Rawlingses. But the lure of the water had been too much for her, and she'd snuck over the fence every chance she got.

She started down the rise and only then noticed the half dead cottonwood that had fallen across the barbed wire, knocking down a hundred foot stretch of fence. Her hands balled into fists in her pocket, she stared at the open gap that beckoned, the need to see the springs again drawing her nearer. She wasn't a child, she told herself. If she stepped across the fence, she would be trespassing.

That fact didn't bother her nearly as much as it would have yesterday, before she'd read her father's journal. She knew he'd made it a practice to write down his thoughts—prison officials had turned his last reflections over to her after he died—although she still hadn't been able to bring herself to read them. She hadn't intended to read the journal she'd found on his desk, either, at least not until she had time to brace herself emotionally. But the roughly scrawled words had caught her attention before she could walk away.

The drought is killing off my cattle one by one, and the Rawlingses are thrilled. I always knew they were just biding their time, waiting for me to lose this place. The greedy bastards won't be happy till they own the whole southwest corner of the state.

The words were etched in her mind with a branding iron, impossible to ignore, impossible to forget. Stunned, she'd

sat in her father's study and read the journal from beginning to end, caught up in the distrust and resentment her
father had spilled out in his private writings one long winter night when he'd had no one to talk to.

As a child, she'd always known her father disliked the
Rawlingses, but only now did she know why—they'd
wanted his ranch. Then they'd stood by, with their bubbling springs, during the worst drought in half a century and
watched as his cattle dropped like flies. Not once had they
offered to help. Agonized by his animals' suffering, her father had only been trying to get water for his herd when
Gable had unintentionally been shot. And for that, an un-
fortunate accident, the Rawlingses had had her father sent
to prison.

Resentment churned in her gut, turning her eyes as hard
as smoked glass. The Rawlingses were one of the most
powerful families in New Mexico; they could have stopped
her father from going to jail if they'd wanted to. But they'd
granted him no mercy. Intent only on revenge, they'd put
him through the stress of a trial and then coldly allowed his
incarceration. For an accident, for God's sake! Less than
two months later, their thirst for vengeance had finally been
quenched. Her father's weak heart hadn't been able to take
the strain, and he'd had a heart attack and died. Alone.

And for that, she would never forgive the Rawlingses.
Granted her father had never been a saint. He'd always been
a hard, domineering man with a driving need to control, and
her own feelings for him had been a confusing mixture of
love and hate. Over the years, however, she'd held onto the
hope that one day she'd be able to make peace with him.
Now, thanks to the Rawlingses, that chance was lost to her
forever.

Lifting her face to the cold wind, she let the anger building in her burn red hot. Defiance flared and sent her

marching toward the downed fence. Without so much as checking her pace, she stepped over it. If Gable Rawlings and his brothers didn't like her trespassing, that was just too damn bad.

The storm that had been threatening all day was only hours away, the air that rushed through the open window of Cooper's pickup was sharp and biting. But it was free of perfume, and he dragged it in in relief. He could breathe again! And that trapped feeling that had made his skin itch was starting to ease as he left the house far behind and raced down one of the countless dirt roads that crisscrossed the ranch. Sudden laughter skimmed across the weathered lines of his lean face. Josey would probably be madder than a wet hen when she discovered he'd cut and run. He wouldn't put it past her to send Gable and Flynn after him.

Let 'em come, he thought, grinning. They'd have a fight on their hands if they thought for one minute they were going to drag him back to the house to those marriage-minded females!

The springs came into view then, the downed tree looking like a fallen soldier, its naked limbs poking into the air and standing out in stark relief against the darkening winter sky. Braking to a stop in a cloud of dust, he surveyed the damage with satisfaction. It was worse than he'd expected, easily a three-hour job. By the time he finished and made his way back to the house, even the most persistent females would have given up and gone home. It couldn't have worked out better if he'd planned it himself.

Grabbing his work gloves, he pushed open the cab door and moved around to the back of the truck to retrieve the chain saw. His mind already working on how he would dismantle the fallen tree, he was striding toward it when the flash of something red in the distance caught his eye. Surprised, he glanced toward the trees and nearly dropped his saw.

A woman! he thought incredulously, his gaze fixed on the slim figure in a red plaid jacket half hidden among the cottonwoods. What the devil was a woman doing out here in the middle of nowhere, strolling along the rocky bank of the springs like she was out for a walk in the park?

Unable to take his eyes from her, he watched her walk away from him without ever seeing him; and, if he hadn't known better, Cooper would have sworn she was something conjured up by the approaching storm. The wind swirled around her, cold and biting as it tossed dead leaves in her path and caught at her dark hair, but she didn't seem to notice its icy touch. She playfully kicked at the leaves and let her hair fly about her head, while her soft laughter danced on the wind.

He was entranced before he thought to note the danger, and just that quickly he knew who she was—one of the women Josey had invited to supper. He didn't remember having seen her at the house—he could never have forgotten that silky sable hair and slender figure—but considering the crowd there, he could easily have missed her.

Torn between exasperation and reluctant amusement, he had to give her credit for her perseverance. She'd obviously overheard him and Flynn talking about the fallen tree and decided to take the initiative and finagle her own introduction. If he'd been an active participant in Josey's scheme to find him a wife, he would have been flattered. But he wasn't. And when a man couldn't get away by himself on his own ranch, things had gone too far. His muttered curse torn away by the wind, he left the chain saw by the fallen tree and started toward her.

* * *

Caught up in her thoughts, Susannah didn't have a clue there was another human being within miles of her until a husky masculine voice suddenly drawled, "Sorry to disappoint you, sweetheart, but I'm really not looking for a woman... to bed or wed or anything else. So you've gone to a lot of trouble for nothing. I'm just not interested."

Startled, she whirled, so surprised by the sight of the unexpected man confronting her, she didn't even hear what he said. He was tall, six-one if he was an inch, and looked as hard and tough as an old fence post. Another time, another place, she might have noticed how attractive he was, how the deep dimples bracketing his sensuous mouth added laughter to his lean, angular face. But he stood before her in alligator boots that were well broken in, wearing jeans and a sheepskin coat as if he'd worn them all his life. A cowboy hat shaded his nearly black eyes, but she didn't need the hat or the clothes to tell her he was a cowboy. It was written all over him... in the way he stood, in the way he held himself, in the arrogant way he sized her up.

And she wanted nothing to do with cowboys.

His words of greeting abruptly registering, sudden amusement spilled into her smoky-gray eyes. Good Lord, what was he accusing her of? "I beg your pardon? What did you just say?"

"You heard me. I'm not interested."

Well, that was certainly blunt enough, she thought, struggling to hang on to her amusement. Determined not to misunderstand, she merely arched a delicate brow. "And you think I am? Interested in you, I mean?"

"Sweetheart, *you* followed *me* out here, not the other way around," he reminded her. "Nothing personal, but you're wasting your time, so I suggest you get in your car or your truck or whatever vehicle you used to get out here and go home. The party's over.''

Stiffening, Susannah tried to remind herself that she wasn't a woman who flew into a rage easily. Most of her friends had never even seen her lose her temper. She much preferred handling a difficult situation with humor, but this...*goat roper* was making that damn difficult. If he could be blunt, so could she.

Forcing a smile that was guaranteed to set his teeth on edge, she ran her eyes up and down him in a way that told him she wasn't the least impressed. ''One of us is confused here,'' she said sweetly, ''and it's not me. Maybe you have to beat women off with a stick—I don't know, and there's no accounting for taste—but believe me, you're safe. I wouldn't have you on a platter with an apple stuck in your mouth, *sweetheart*.''

Cooper knew he should have been relieved. Instead, he was perversely irritated. He wasn't as smooth with the ladies as his brothers, but he wasn't a total reject, either. ''Oh, really? And I suppose you're going to tell me why the hell not.''

''Oh, you better believe it,'' she purred. ''Aside from the fact that you've got an ego the size of Texas, you obviously work for the Rawlingses. And anyone low enough to work for that bunch leaves me cold. Now, if you'll excuse me, I'm going home.''

Her tone was as cool as the wind, her gray eyes positively icy as she started to brush past him. Whatever Cooper had been expecting, it wasn't a slam against his family and then a frosty dismissal. His gaze narrowed dangerously, he reached out and grabbed her arm, stopping her in her tracks. ''I don't work for the Rawlingses, woman, I *am* a Rawlings. Cooper Rawlings, if it's any of your business. And I'd

like to know what the hell you've got against my family. Do
I know you?''

Stunned, Susannah just stared at him. Know her? She'd
lived right down the road from him for the first twelve years
of her life. Because of her father's dislike of his neighbors,
her contact with them had been limited, but everyone in the
county had known how Mrs. Rawlings had named the kids
after her favorite movie stars from the forties and how close
they all were. She'd always envied them that closeness, not
only to one another, but to their parents. Oh, yes, she knew
Cooper Rawlings, but she wasn't surprised that she hadn't
recognized him any more than he'd known her. The last time
she saw him, he was a skinny fourteen-year-old who hadn't
known she existed.

He was still thin, but given his rough good looks, Susannah thought few women would object to that. Uncomfortable with the thought, she shied away from it and quickly
reminded herself why she wanted nothing to do with Cooper Rawlings or any other member of his family. Glancing
pointedly at where his fingers held her captive, she pulled
her arm free and met his gaze accusingly. ''You and your
family killed my father.''

The accusation came right out of left field and couldn't
have stunned Cooper more if she'd slapped him. ''Killed
your father!'' he repeated incredulously as she swept past
him and headed for the fence. Swearing, he started after her.
''Dammit, woman, where do you think you're going? You
can't throw that kind of accusation at a man, then walk
away without explaining yourself.''

But that was exactly what she did. Ignoring him, she
walked away without deigning to give him a second look.
Irritated, Cooper ordered himself not to be impressed, but
he was, dammit! Elegance. She projected it as easily as a
blue-blooded princess, in spite of the fact that the wind was

having a field day with her dark brown hair, she didn't have a smidgen of makeup on, and she was dressed in faded jeans, old tennis shoes and a plaid jacket that was designed more for comfort than sophistication.

"Dammit, who the hell are you?"

But even as he asked, he knew. Joe Patterson's daughter. God, what was her name? Sue...something. *Susannah.* Yeah, that was it. She'd been just a kid the last time he'd seen her, a dark-haired, big-eyed little girl full of sass and spunk, who had delighted in wiggling through the boundary fence when no one was looking to explore the springs. It must have been nearly twenty years since she'd left with her mother after her parents divorced, and, as far as he knew, this was her first time back.

Except, he'd heard, for her father's funeral two years ago.

A funeral he and his family hadn't attended, which hadn't surprised anyone since it was Joe Patterson who had shot Gable in the back—in the *back,* for God's sakes!—in an attempt to steal their ranch out from under them. And now Patterson's precious daughter had returned and was looking for someone to blame. Well, it sure as hell wasn't going to be him or his family!

"Hey, Susannah!"

The sound of her name on his tongue shocked her, startling her as she carefully picked her way through the bare limbs of the fallen tree tangled with the barbed wire of the fence. She hadn't thought he would recognize her. Freezing, she glanced over her shoulder at him. "Yes?"

"Your father died in prison. My family had nothing to do with that."

He threw the truth at her, daring her to deny it, which she did without blinking an eye. "He wouldn't have been there at all if your family hadn't been so vindictive," she retorted. "He was an old man with a weak heart. You might as well have put a bullet in his head. The result would have been the same."

Stubborn little witch, Cooper thought irritably, wanting to shake her. He should have known she'd be as stubborn as a mule. She was her father's daughter, wasn't she? And no one had been more bullheaded than Joe Patterson. Knowing that he couldn't change things, old Joe had clung to his hatred of the Rawlingses simply because the Double R had a never-ending source of water and the Pattersons didn't.

His jaw rigid, he glared at her in acute dislike. "Somehow I'm not surprised that a Patterson would find a way to twist the truth so completely. Like father, like daughter, right? Well, that's just fine with me, sweetheart. You think what you like, just do it from your side of the fence, okay? Or you're going to have more trouble than you can handle."

"Is that a threat?"

"You better believe it, baby. Consider yourself warned."

Outraged by his audacity, Susannah shot him a withering look that should have turned him to dust. Her father had claimed in his journal that one Rawlings was much like another—rude, overbearing, infuriatingly superior—and if that was true, she dreaded the day when she met the rest of them.

"Fine," she snapped. "Just remember that there's two sides to a fence. If I find you on my side, I'm calling the sheriff, no questions asked." Giving him one last look that told him exactly what she thought of him and his paltry threats, she made her way through the fallen branches of the tree onto her own land. Behind her, she heard his snort of contempt, but the effort was wasted on her. Without once looking in his direction, she started walking. She didn't once look back, but she didn't have to. With every step she took, she could feel his hawklike stare boring into her unprotected back.

Her anger carried her back to the house, but she had no intention of letting her encounter with Cooper Rawlings ruin the rest of the day. Putting him firmly out of her thoughts, she determinedly pulled out her laptop computer and settled down in her father's easy chair. With a sigh, she rested her fingers on the familiar keys and closed her eyes, willing herself to relax and let the words fill her ears, just as they always had whenever she sat down to write.

But it was the silence of her surroundings she heard, a thick, throbbing, unbroken quiet that threatened to go on forever. And in its echoing emptiness, the only words she heard were those of Cooper Rawlings as he'd coldly ordered her off his land.

Her fingers curled in frustration on the keyboard, and she opened her eyes in time to see a line of gibberish go streaking across the empty screen. With her teeth clenched on an oath she refused to utter, she stared at the nonsense in growing frustration, real fear starting to curl into her stomach. She knew she was rushing things trying to write after being home only a matter of days. But with every day that passed without her having anything to show for it, the fear grew that she would never write again. So she had to try, even if she got nowhere.

The sudden sharp ringing of the telephone cut through the quiet, and with a sigh of relief, she got up to answer it. Maybe it was her agent, she thought hopefully. Terry had promised to keep in touch, and right now, she could use a friendly ear.

But when she lifted the receiver, the only response she got to her hello was the click of a phone being hung up on the other end. Another wrong number, she thought, hanging up. She'd had three since she'd had the phone hooked up, and none of the callers had bothered to apologize before hanging up. Didn't anyone have any phone etiquette anymore?

Returning to her computer, she was tempted to chain herself to the darn thing until inspiration came, but she knew from experience she could stare at the screen for hours without coming up with a single intelligent sentence. Giving up, she turned off the machine and grabbed her jacket and her keys. She needed to talk to her father, and there was only one place she might find him.

The cemetery was a small one, an insignificant plot of land out in the middle of nowhere, and caught between four of the biggest ranches in the area. Surrounded by the encroaching desert, there was no carpet of green grass here, no trees or bushes of any kind to block the rush of the wind. Gravel covered most of the graves, and in the far corner, an ocotillo provided the only greenery in sight. What flowers there were were plastic, their once bright colors faded by the sun.

Susannah had never seen a lonelier sight in her life.

Slowly making her way to her father's simple grave, she hugged herself against the chill in the wind and stared down at the dates carved into the headstone that told so little about her father. The beginning and end, nothing more. Nothing of the type of man he'd been, nothing of the type of husband and father he'd been to his wife and only child.

Why? she silently cried. Why did you have to be so hard? So unforgiving? Why did you let us go without lifting a finger to stop us?

But her only answer was the moan of the wind as it swirled around the tombstones.

Shivering at the haunted sound, she hunched her shoulders inside her jacket, her heart as cold as stone. He wasn't there, she thought starkly. He never had been. He was lost in the memory of a twelve-year-old little girl, locked away with all the pain and hurt and confused love of her childhood that she couldn't bring herself to recall.

Defeated, she returned home and spent the rest of the day and evening attacking the disaster area that was the living room. She had hoped that the physical activity would take her mind off her past so that the dark, shadowed memories eluding her would surge, unforced, to the surface, but all she got for her effort was an aching back and three bags of trash to be burned. And she still had half the living room yet to clean. Annoyed with herself, she gave up in defeat and went to bed, only to toss and turn and struggle with half-formed images that teased her about a past that appeared determined to elude her.

The storm that had been building all afternoon and evening broke during the middle of the night. The temperature dropped like a rock, rain fell in torrents, and by morning the roads were starting to ice. The rain itself had stopped, but the sky was still weighed down with thick, heavy clouds, and the forecast was calling for sleet later in the afternoon.

It was the kind of dark, depressing day Susannah hated. The clouds seemed to press down on the house, against the windows, trapping her inside. Feeling claustrophobic, she took one look at the shadowy, half-cleaned living room and knew she had to get out of there. She needed people around her, noise. She needed to go shopping. Refusing to worry about the weather, she picked up her keys and jacket and headed for the front door.

The roads, thankfully, didn't appear to be as bad as she'd feared, but she didn't take any chances. Watching for ice, she slowly eased down her long drive to the highway and automatically turned into the small pullout where mailboxes for the nearby ranches were lined up like tin soldiers.

It wasn't until she braked to a stop that she realized she wasn't the only one out braving the weather. Another vehicle was already there, a dark green pickup with the distinctive logo of the Double R painted on the side of the door. And stepping from the cab was Cooper Rawlings.

Susannah groaned out loud at the sight of him and seriously considered going on into town and picking up the mail on the way back. It had taken her hours to finally get the man out of her head after her run-in with him yesterday, and the last thing she wanted or needed was another confrontation with him.

But it was too late. He'd seen her the minute she drove up, and judging by the thin white line of his flattened mouth, he wasn't any happier to see her than she was him. And for some crazy reason, that amused her no end.

After the way he had threatened her, however, she had no intention of even speaking to him. Pushing open her door, she headed for the mailbox with Patterson boldly painted across the side, barely sparing a glance for the man who watched her with sharp, narrowed brown eyes.

Little snot, Cooper thought, scowling. Leaning casually back against his pickup, he crossed his arms over his chest and observed her dispassionately. He had to give her credit, she was a damn fine-looking woman. Not beautiful—her mouth was a little too wide for that, her chin more than a little stubborn. But he'd seen her expression change like quicksilver, from surprise to disdain to anger and cold superiority, and with every change of emotion, she'd somehow managed to appear more captivating. It was her mouth, he decided, struggling to hang on to his acute dislike as unwanted heat spilled into his gut. Soft, sensuous, enticing. A woman with a mouth like hers had no business walking around free.

His teeth clamped on an oath, he watched her retrieve her mail and turn back toward her car as if she had no intention of lowering herself to speak to him. "Just for the record, how long are you staying?" he demanded harshly as she drew even with him. "A week? A month? What?"

He asked nothing more than she'd asked herself ever since she had arrived, but his belligerent tone grated on Susannah's nerves like sugar on a throbbing cavity. Giving him a saccharine smile, she shrugged. "Not that it's any of your business, but I haven't decided yet. Do you have a problem with that, Mr. Rawlings?"

"That depends on why you're here, *Ms.* Patterson," he tossed back in a tone that was as mocking as hers. "If you came back to pick up where your father left off, then you're damn right I have a problem with that. We don't need your kind of trouble here."

Her kind? she wanted to utter. He and his family had destroyed her father, and he was complaining about her? Her gray eyes snapping with outrage, she leveled him with nothing more than a glance. "Then I suggest you stay out of my way, cowboy, because I'm staying as long as I need to."

"I can't tell you how thrilled that makes me," he retorted scathingly. "Do me the same courtesy and we'll both get along fine. Okay?"

She couldn't have agreed more. The last thing she wanted to do was spend more time in this obnoxious man's company. "Fine." She jerked open the door to her car as he moved to climb into his truck. "If I see you coming, I'll be sure to go out of my way to avoid you."

Her last words nearly drowned out by the slamming of her car door, she turned the key in the ignition, revved the motor and hit the accelerator. Considering the state of the road, it was a stupid thing to do, but she made it onto the pavement without mishap. Within seconds, she was disappearing down the highway toward Lordsburg.

Staring after her, Cooper spit out a curse. Damn the woman, she wouldn't have to keep an eye out for him. If he had to go halfway to Mexico to avoid passing her on the street, he'd do it in a heartbeat!

Chapter 2

Suddenly realizing he was still staring after her long after she'd disappeared from view, Cooper yanked open the door to his truck and climbed into the cab, the set of his jaw rigid. He'd planned to take a ride over to Sonny Carpenter's place, a friend he'd gone to school with who now owned two hundred acres outside of Lordsburg, but there was no way in hell he was following *Ms. Patterson* down the highway. Damn the woman! He didn't think he had a particularly quick temper, but she could light his fuse faster than any female ever had.

Work, he told himself sourly as he started the motor and turned toward home. He needed work—hard, grinding, physical labor, the kind that wore him out and didn't give him time to think—so he could put Susannah Patterson out of his thoughts once and for all.

If it had been any other time of the year, he could have found his pick of chores, but there just wasn't that much to do during the winter. Fall roundup had long since passed and all the work that came with spring roundup and the annual selling of yearlings was still months away. The restlessness that had been plaguing him lately stirred to life, a discontentment he couldn't put a name to that seemed to come and go with the blowing of the wind. Fighting it, he turned to the shed that housed the old '55 Chevy that had been his first car. It hadn't run in years and needed a major overhaul, but he hadn't been able to part with it. Maybe it was time he took a look at it....

The shed was unheated and colder than the depths of hell, but he'd worked in worse conditions. Tugging on a pair of coveralls, he threw himself into the job as if his life depended on it. Unable to wear his gloves, he rubbed his hands together to warm them, then attacked bolts that hadn't been touched in probably a quarter of a century. Swearing, his muscles straining, he finally worked up a sweat that should have burned off the leftover irritation still humming in his gut. Instead, while his hands were busy, his mind was free to roam, and before he knew it, his thoughts were once again returning to *her*.

Lying flat on his back under the car on the frozen ground, his hands covered with grease, he wiped his brow with his forearm and wondered what the hell was wrong with him. The woman was a Patterson, a troublemaker right down to her sweet little toenails. Her father had always blamed everyone else for his problems, and she was just like him. She didn't know squat about what had gone on around here two years ago, but did that stop her from casting blame? Hell, no. She was determined to believe her old man was lily-white, and Cooper wasn't going to waste his time trying to change her mind. Let her live in a dreamworld. He wanted nothing to do with her.

Forget her!

But it wasn't that easy. By the time he went into the house for supper hours later, he was halfway through the major overhaul of the Chevy's motor. He was also tired, hungry and thoroughly disgusted with himself. In spite of the fact that he hadn't had an idle moment, *that woman,* as he'd come to think of her over the course of the afternoon, was as firmly lodged in his thoughts as ever. She hadn't granted him the slightest peace, and all he could think about was throttling her. Damn the girl, what did it take to get her out of his head?

"Hey, Coop," Flynn greeted him after he'd cleaned up and joined the rest of the family at the kitchen table for supper. "How'd your visit with Sonny Carpenter go? He bought those wild horses of his at a government auction, didn't he? Jake Henderson's thinking about buying some and letting them roam free on his spread. Maybe we should get some. I bet they're something to see when they're running wild, aren't they?"

Standing back so Alice, their housekeeper, could put a platter of fried chicken on the table, he waited until she joined the family before taking his seat across from Flynn. "I wouldn't know. I didn't go."

"What do you mean, you didn't go? You were headed there this morning when you left to get the mail. What happened?"

Not in the mood for needling, Cooper shot him a quelling look that silently warned him not to push. "I just decided not to go. I wasn't in the mood for socializing. So let's just drop it, okay?"

His tone was short and had No Trespassing stamped all over it. Silence fell like a brick into the usual supper conversation, and the rest of the family looked at him in surprise. Biting back a curse, Cooper wanted to kick himself for bringing his foul mood to the table. "Look, it's been a lousy day," he began in explanation.

"Anything we can help you with?" Josey asked. "Maybe if you talked about it—"

"No!" God, the last thing he wanted to do was discuss Susannah Patterson with Josey. He could just see it now. Thrilled that he was finally showing an interest in someone, she wouldn't care that his encounters with the woman were less than friendly. Her ears would perk up, those matchmaking wheels of hers would start turning, and he'd be in real trouble. "There's nothing to talk about," he assured her stiffly. "The day just didn't turn out the way I'd planned."

He saw the concern in her eyes, but from the moment Josey had married Gable and moved into a house already occupied by two brothers-in-law and a sister-in-law, she'd respected their privacy. Not pushing for a confidence he wasn't ready to give, she accepted his explanation with a small smile. He wasn't so lucky with the rest of the family. They were all staring at him speculatively, and he almost groaned aloud at the familiar glint in Flynn's eyes. He knew that look, and any minute now something was going to come out of his youngest brother's mouth that he didn't want to hear.

Cutting Flynn off before he could get started, Cooper ignored him and turned to Kat. "When do you go back to school for the spring semester? I want to do a tune-up on your Jeep before you go—"

"It's a woman, isn't it?" Flynn cut in, his blue eyes lit with knowing amusement. "That's why you're in such a foul mood. You met someone and she's got you tied up in knots."

Kat, just as nosy as Flynn and always quick to follow his lead, grinned widely, her dimples flashing impishly. "Who is she, Coop? Someone we know?" Just as quickly as her smile had appeared, it turned into a scowl. "I hope it's not someone like that old Mary Lou Henderson. She deserved to be scalped for what she did to you—"

"Kat," Gable warned softly, "that's enough."

Always quick to defend her family from hurt, Kat shut up, but only because she saw the tightening of Cooper's jaw. A glance around the table told her the others had, too. Alice, who had been with the family longer than any of them could remember and was as protective as a mother hen with her chicks, sniffed, stating her opinion of Mary Lou without saying a word. Josey, as usual, held her tongue, but Kat knew for a fact that every time she ran into Mary Lou in town, she was as frosty as a Canadian cold front.

Surprisingly, Flynn was silent, too, but his eyes, flashing with fire, told their own story. Deliberately changing the subject from Mary Lou, he brought the conversation back to the mystery woman who had somehow found a way to get under his brother's skin. "Come on," he teased, forcing a grin, "give us a name. Who is she?"

Caught in the trap of his brother's too observant gaze, Cooper gave him a look that should have nailed him to his chair. The fact that it didn't faze Flynn in the least had reluctant laughter itching to break out across Cooper's face. Dang fool, he'd pull the tail of the devil and laugh while he did it.

"Julia Roberts," he lied without cracking a smile. "She just happened to be driving through Lordsburg and we ran into each other at the Sagebrush Café. Seems she'd heard about the Rawlings men—*you* in particular—but hey, bro, what can I say? I saw her first, so I guess that makes her mine, doesn't it?"

"In your dreams," Flynn said, snorting, his grin broadening as the others laughed. "Julia Roberts wouldn't look twice at a skinny drink of water like you."

"And I suppose you think you'd knock her over with those dimples of yours?" he demanded good-naturedly. "Some women want a little something more than just cute, don't they, Josey?"

"Hey," she said with a laugh, her eyes dancing as she surveyed her two favorite brothers-in-law. "Don't drag me into this. I'm a married woman."

"You better believe she is," Gable said, his gaze possessive as he turned to where she sat at his right. Taking her hand, he gave it a squeeze, and glanced back down the table at his family. "If we could forget Julia Roberts for a moment—"

"You gotta be kidding," Kat said dryly. "These guys'll be old and gray and on the downhill side of eighty and still be dreaming about Julia Roberts."

Gable chuckled. "You're right. That was a stupid thing to say. But could we get serious here for a moment? Josey and I have something we need to tell you."

His serious tone, more than his words, got their attention. Suddenly alarmed, Cooper frowned. "What is it? What's wrong?"

"Is one of you sick?" Alice demanded.

"Josey's caught something at the clinic she's running out of her grandparents' place, hasn't she? I knew it! Dammit, Gable, I was afraid this would happen—"

"She's not sick—"

"I'm pregnant."

Josey's softly spoken announcement was nearly lost in the barrage of questions hurled at Gable, then suddenly her words registered. Stunned, Kat stared at her sister-in-law, delight dawning in her blue eyes. "You're pregnant? Really honest-to-God-going-to-have-a-real-live-baby pregnant?"

Josey laughed. "Yes, I'm really honest-to-God-going-to-have-a-real-live-baby pregnant. How do you feel about being an aunt?"

"How do I feel?" Sputtering over Josey's need to even ask, Kat let out a whoop, jumped up from her chair and ran around the table to give her a fierce hug. "A baby. Geez, we're going to have a baby!"

Alice was right behind her, her faded blue eyes glistening with tears as she wrapped her arms around Josey. "It's been a long time since we heard the patter of little feet around here. Congratulations, Mama."

Suddenly snapping out of the fog they'd been in, Cooper and Flynn surged to their feet as if propelled by springs. Laughing, they snatched Josey close, then turned to their older brother for slaps on the back and unabashedly affectionate hugs.

"This calls for a celebration, Dad. You know you're going to make a great one, don't you? You had all of us to practice on."

"He's going to be a pushover," Cooper predicted, grinning. "Especially if he has a girl. I can see it now. He'll take one look at her and won't know what hit him."

Supper forgotten, a bottle of champagne was opened, and it was a long time before the laughter and chatter turned to serious discussion. Reseating Josey at his right, Gable took his place at the end of the table and said, "This is going to change things."

"You better believe it," Cooper said ruefully. "It's been a long time since we had a new baby in the house."

"Nineteen," Flynn added, reaching across the table to tug teasingly on his sister's dark hair. "Ever since the brat here decided to put in an appearance. Nothing's been the same since."

Unperturbed, Kat only wrinkled her nose at him. "You're just jealous because I took over your spot as baby of the family."

"And played it to the hilt," he tossed back, grinning. "Talk about a spoiled brat—"

"Children, don't fight," Gable cut in dryly. "We've got business to discuss. Now that there's going to be a baby, I think we should seriously think about diversifying the ranching operations."

They'd been discussing the possibility for some time now, ever since they'd made the last loan payment two years ago, in fact. With the entire family fortune tied up in cattle, they'd all agreed they were too vulnerable to fluctuating market prices and the ever-decreasing demand for beef in today's cholesterol-conscious society. They needed to diversify, but the question was how. They'd tossed around the idea of farming cotton and peppers, but that would mean using some of their current grazing land for the new operation, and they didn't have any land to spare.

"I agree, the timing is right," Cooper said. "But that still brings us back to coming up with the land somewhere without taking away from the acreage we have to have for the cattle. Unless you plan to scale back on the number of head we're running."

Gable shook his head. "We may have to if there's no other alternative, but I'd rather not do that unless we're forced to. I was thinking instead that you might look around and see if you can find us the land we're going to need."

"Sure, I'll do it," he said with a shrug. "But do you think there's any available? As far as I know, none of our neighbors are selling off any of their holdings."

"They aren't. But I ran into the sheriff in town today and heard that Joe Patterson's daughter is back. Nobody seems to know how long she's staying, but she sold off all the cattle when Patterson died, so it's probably safe to say she's not going to run cattle on the place again."

"She hasn't been back in years, has she?" Flynn said, pushing his plate aside to lean his elbows on the table. "I thought Patterson disowned her."

"Evidently not. Anyway, the ranch is hers, and if she's looking to sell all or some of it, we want to be first in line." He glanced at Cooper, who sat at the opposite end of the table. "You've been looking for something else to do to keep you busy. This might be it. I'll warn you up front you're probably going to have your hands full. The lady may not have been on speaking terms with her father, but she's still a Patterson."

"Which means she'll probably tell you to take a flying leap," Kat retorted.

"Still, we won't know until we try," Gable argued. "Approach her and see what her plans are," he told Cooper. "If she's not interested in selling, she might be willing to lease us a hundred acres or so."

Cooper hesitated, torn. He didn't think they had a snow cone's chance in Egypt of getting their hands on even an acre of the Patterson ranch, but he could hardly say that without raising all sorts of questions. Like why he wanted nothing to do with Susannah, and why he hadn't mentioned until now that he had already run into her.

Swallowing a curse, he nodded. "I'll see what I can do."

He promised himself he'd approach her soon, but when he made no attempt to contact her, fate took care of the problem for him two days later when he almost ran into her at the Quick Stop. He was pulling open the door when she walked out, a bag of groceries in her arm, the thank-you that rose to her lips automatically dying at the sight of him holding the door for her.

Something stirred in him the second his eyes locked on her, something quick and hot and dangerous, something he wanted no part of. His mouth tightening with irritation, he almost strode past her with nothing more than a nod. But a niggling voice in his ear reminded him that as much as he disliked the woman, his family needed some of her land.

"Here," he said, taking her groceries from her before either of them could guess his intentions, "let me take that for you. Where's your car?"

Flustered, Susannah instinctively made a grab for the small paper bag that held nothing more than a loaf of bread and some sandwich meat. "Wait! I can carry it. It's not heavy."

"That's okay. I've got it. Which car's yours?"

"The white Volvo," she answered automatically, then could have kicked herself as he started toward her car. Frowning, she hurried after him. "This isn't necessary. Really, Mr. Rawlings—"

"Cooper," he corrected her easily. "We're not much on formality around here, and anyway, we're neighbors."

Neighbors who were bitter enemies. Coming to a stop at her car, Susannah stared up at him suspiciously, the words of her father's journal ringing in her ears. *A Rawlings is never nice unless he's after something.* Eyeing him warily, she snatched the bag of groceries out of his arms. "What do you want?"

"Want?" he echoed innocently. "Who said I wanted anything?"

"My father," she retorted flatly. "He didn't trust you or your family as far as he could throw you. Especially when you were being nice. What are you after, Mr. Rawlings?"

Her words punched him like a fist ... and struck all too close to home. Damn, he didn't like being in this position. All right, so he did want something from her—her land. But he was willing to pay her for it, which was a hell of a lot more than could be said about her father when he'd tried to steal the Double R right out from under them without paying them so much as a penny.

Annoyed, he warned, "If I were you, I wouldn't put a lot of stock in anything your father may have thought. You didn't know him. He was a criminal—"

"No!"

"Look, I know you don't like hearing this, but it's the truth, dammit! Your father was the organizer behind the conspiracy to steal the Double R from me and my family."

"Oh, *ple-ease,*" she groaned, "spare me!" Jerking open the door to her car, she tossed in her purse and groceries, too furious to care that she'd just smashed her bread. She turned on him angrily, her gray eyes as icy as an arctic front. "You Rawlingses are incredible, you know that? You twist the truth to suit your purposes, then expect everybody else to believe it. I know my father wasn't a saint, but he would never have done what you're accusing him of, so just save your lies, Mr. Rawlings. I'm not buying them."

"Lies?" he choked incredulously. "You think I'm lying?"

"You're a Rawlings. I think you would say anything, *do* anything, to make your family look good. Even if that meant destroying the reputation of a man who isn't here to defend himself."

"Sweetheart, I don't need to destroy your father's reputation. He did that all by himself."

"After your family got through slandering him!"

Unaware of the interested gazes they were drawing, they stood toe to toe in the middle of the parking lot, glaring at each other and breathing hard, both too stubborn to give an inch. Cooper, itching to shake some sense into her, just barely resisted the urge to reach for her. Infuriating, antagonistic, pigheaded—she was all those things, and damned irritating to boot.

And this close, she was too pretty for comfort.

The realization hit him like a ton of bricks and had him taking a quick step away from her. Where the hell had that come from? Scowling down at her, he said coldly, "Honey, if that's what you think, you're deluding yourself. But, hey, don't take my word for it. Ask around. Anybody else will tell you the same thing."

She snorted at that. "Of course they will. You own half of this corner of the world, and what you haven't got your name on isn't worth having. No one's going to bad-mouth you."

"Because there's nothing to say." Holding up his hand before she could dispute that, he growled, "If you don't like it here, lady, I don't see anybody chaining you to that ranch of yours. Why don't you just pack up your things and go back where you came from, wherever the hell that is. Believe me, nobody here will lift a finger to stop you."

With that parting shot, he turned his back on her and strode away. Anger carrying him across the parking lot to his truck, he drove off seconds later without bothering to glance her way once. It wasn't until he was miles down the road, the Quick Stop no longer visible in his rearview mirror, that he remembered he had approached Susannah Patterson for only one reason—to see if she was interested in selling some of her land.

"Damn!" he swore. He'd really blown it now.

* * *

Still fuming twenty minutes later, Susannah took one look at the sandwich she'd made herself and abruptly set it down, her appetite nonexistent.

Just pack up your things and go back where you came from.

Cooper's angry words rang in her ears as clearly as if he stood right there in her kitchen, hurting more than she wanted to admit. Oh, he was insufferable, she fumed. Imagine... telling her to get out of town like a sheriff right out of the Old West! Who the hell did he think he was? She was a landowner here, just as he was, and she wasn't going anywhere until she was good and ready.

Tossing out her lunch, she flatly refused to spend the rest of the day brooding about the man when she had better things to do. She'd finished cleaning the living room yesterday, and today she intended to reward herself with an afternoon of reading. She'd brought Tom Green's latest book with her from Dallas and had yet to even glance at it. After everything she'd had to deal with over the past few days, she was entitled to a break.

A smile spilled into her eyes at the thought of Tom. A retired combat pilot who was not only a good friend but her biggest competition in the genre, Tom wrote men's adventure novels that consistently made the *New York Times* bestseller list. His style was completely different from hers, but he had a way with words that often sparked her own creativity when she found herself struggling for just the right phrase. If she was lucky, her fingers would be itching to write after only a chapter or two.

But as the silence of the house drifted down around her and the well-written words tried to pull her into the story, it wasn't an image of the rugged, blond-haired hero Tom described that rose to mind, but the dark, lean good looks of

Cooper and the outraged fury in his eyes as he'd turned and crossed the Quick Stop parking lot to his truck.

With a soft exclamation of disgust, she slammed the book shut and tossed it onto the coffee table. What was the matter with her? It had been a long time since she'd let anyone get close enough to her to grab her attention, let alone irritate her, and if she hadn't known better, she'd have sworn she was becoming obsessed with that infuriating cowboy down the road. Which was ridiculous. She wasn't the type to moon over a man.

Oh, she'd had her share of dates, and once—when she was in college—she'd been so close to falling in love, she'd practically heard the wedding bells. But then she'd started writing her first book, and research took her halfway across the country. Absence had not made the heart grow fonder, and by the time she'd returned home, they'd drifted too far apart to find each other again.

The regrets she'd had hadn't lasted long. Her first Ace MacKenzie book came out and shot to the top of the bestseller list, and her life hadn't been the same since. Before she could catch her breath, another book idea had called to her, and she was once again off to parts unknown.

Since then, she'd moved around the country like a gypsy. In seven years, she'd written four books, each more successful than the last. The reason for that growing success was that she didn't just write her books, she lived them. In actuality, she *became* Ace MacKenzie. Where he lived, she lived. Whenever possible, she got involved with his latest cause or newest interest, and Ace had some pretty bizarre interests at times. She'd loved every minute of it.

She knew she sometimes went overboard in her research, but she really enjoyed moving about the country, getting to know different people and places. And it was her attention to detail that made her books so lifelike. After such extensive research, all she had to do was sit down at her computer, and the words just seemed to flow.

Until recently.

Which was why she couldn't become fixated on a man like Cooper Rawlings. She had enough problems in her life without adding another. And she didn't have to know the man better to know that that's just what he would be—a major problem. He was a man with rural roots that went deep, a man of the West, where chauvinism was inbred. It didn't take an Einstein to figure out that he was the type who would try to keep a woman close, within reach. Just as her father had tried to keep her mother close. And she wanted no part of that.

The ringing of the phone jarred her out of her musings, and she reached for it absently. "Hello?"

Silence answered her, a silence that skittered over her nerve endings. For reasons she couldn't begin to explain, she stiffened. "Hello?" she tried again, but again, there was only silence.

Disturbed, she hung up, a frown knitting her brow as she stared down at the now silent phone. Another wrong number. Over the past few days, she'd gotten more than her fair share of them, calls just like this one, which greeted her with nothing but silence. They weren't threatening, just annoying. If they kept up, she'd see about having the number restricted.

Realizing she needed something to occupy both her hands and her mind if she was going to get Cooper out of her head, she gave up on her reading and gravitated to the doorway of her father's study. Her hands on her hips as she surveyed the room's deplorable condition, she came to the reluctant conclusion that she could no longer put off cleaning it.

He was gone, she reminded herself. The house was hers, along with everything in it. But as she stood there, thinking about going through her father's private papers in the study, her stomach clenched. She felt like a child again, leery of bearding the lion in his den even though the lion was nowhere to be found.

What was she afraid of? she wondered. There was nothing here but old books and records and possibly more of her father's journals, certainly nothing that could hurt her. Still, she felt like a trespasser as she approached the desk. As far as she knew, not even her mother had dared go through her father's business papers. Shocked to realize that her fingers were shaking, she sank into the chair behind the desk and picked up a stack of receipts precariously balanced on top.

An hour later, her fingers were once again steady, and she chided herself for having been afraid in the first place. She'd found nothing more interesting than canceled checks, old bills, and outdated articles her father had clipped from newspapers and ranch magazines. Yellowed with age, they were worn thin from being folded and unfolded and read again and again.

By the time she'd gone through every scrap of paper and tossed it in the trash, the top of the desk was clean and she didn't know any more about her father and the past than she had before she started. Then she pulled open the center drawer and saw the small suede pouch lying there among her father's pencils.

Forgotten memories came rushing toward her like balloons just released from a closet. She couldn't have escaped them if she'd tried.

Jacks. There were jacks and a rubber ball in the pouch. Even before she picked up the small sack with fingers that were suddenly trembling again, she could feel the weight of the ball in her hand, the points of the metal jacks pressing into her palm, hear her mother's laughter. And her father's.

Squeezing her eyes tightly shut to capture the sweet moment more fully, she could see her parents playing jacks with her when she was around six years old. They were laughing and teasing each other, sprawled on the floor beside her as if they were kids themselves.

A hot lump of emotion lodged in her throat. How could she have forgotten the sound of her father's laughter? Had it been so rare that it was that difficult to recall? Or had she simply blocked it out because it was easier to deal with his absence from her life by remembering only the bad times? And why had he kept the jacks where he could see them every time he opened the desk drawer? He'd all but disowned her when she chose to live with her mother, and she'd assumed he'd hated her. Yet he'd left her his ranch.

Questions. She had so many questions. And no one to ask.

Her fingers tightened on the jacks, squeezing them as if she could force them to reveal more of her memories. But the ripple in time had closed as quickly as it had opened, and she was left with nothing. She wanted to scream out a protest; she *needed* to cry. But her eyes were hot and dry, the tears locked away as securely as her memories.

She half expected to dream of her father that night, but it was another man who came to her in the dark. Cooper, his brown eyes black with anger, glared at her, while images, fast and furious, flew at her. *Why don't you just pack up your things and go back where you came from? Nobody here will lift a finger to stop you.* The cold words lashed at her, cutting to the bone, echoing over and over again in her head, until all she could hear was the unmistakable vibration of hostility.

Moaning, she struggled against the viselike hold of the night, the pillow she managed to drag over her head doing nothing to block out the sound of Cooper's voice. Stop! she silently cried. Stop bothering me!

The ringing of the phone was sudden, sharp, innocently threatening. Susannah jumped, her hand already reaching for the bedside phone before she'd even clawed her way out of the depths of sleep. "Hullo..."

Silence mocked her greeting, the absolute absence of sound a thousand times more ominous in the dead of night than it had been in the brightness of the day. Her heart suddenly thundering in her ears, Susannah came awake with a start. "Who is this?" she cried. "I know you're there. Answer me!"

For a long moment, the cold, echoing silence throbbed in her ear and she expected the caller to hang up without saying a word, as usual. Then, from out of the darkness, a muffled voice rasped, "You're not wanted here. Do you hear me? Leave while you still can."

The menace in the husky masculine voice was fierce, ugly and so cold Susannah felt the chill of it through the phone. "Who are you?" she whispered hoarsely.

Her only answer was the soft click as the phone went dead.

Shaken, she slammed down the receiver, the pounding of her heart loud in the silence. Who was doing this to her? she wondered, her thoughts tumbling frantically. Why? She'd been here less than a week, knew practically no one—

Suddenly, the nightmare that had held her in its grip right before the phone rang flashed before her eyes, taunting her. *Why don't you leave?* She heard the words as clearly as if Cooper was standing in front of her with brown eyes blazing.

He wouldn't, she told herself. They obviously rubbed each other the wrong way, but not even Cooper Rawlings would stoop to calling her in the middle of the night to threaten her. Would he?

The whole damn Rawlings bunch is lower than dirt. I wouldn't trust the lot of them as far as I could throw them. When they want something, they'll do whatever it takes to get it.

She paled, suddenly remembering her father's appraisal of his neighbors and why he'd distrusted them so much. The Rawlingses wanted the ranch. And Cooper wanted her gone.

Just that quickly, she was furious. How dared he try to scare her into leaving! Who the hell did he think he was? Furiously throwing off the covers, she switched on the bedside lamp. He and his brothers might push the rest of their neighbors around, but she never had been and never would be anybody's pushover!

Grabbing the phone, she quickly punched out the number for information, requested the number for the Double R and within seconds was calling the ranch. So he thought he could scare her, did he? She'd show him—

"This damn well better be good!"

Susannah jumped at the angry growl that carried easily across the phone line, suddenly mortified as she realized that whoever had answered the phone wasn't Cooper, but one of his brothers, and he was livid. Mortified, she found herself starting to mutter a hasty apology and quickly stifled the impulse. She was the injured party here, and she'd be damned if she'd let a Rawlings intimidate her. "This is Susannah Patterson," she said icily. "I need to speak to Cooper."

"Now? Dammit, lady, it's two in the morning!"

Did he think she didn't know that? She'd also been awakened by a phone call! "I'm well aware of that, Mr.

Rawlings. I'm not any happier about it than you are, but the sooner you let me talk to him, the sooner we can all go back to bed."

"Oh, all right," he muttered. "But I'll warn you right now that he's a deadhead in the middle of the night. He won't thank you for waking him."

Susannah could have told him that she was pretty sure Cooper was awake—after all, he'd just called her a few minutes ago—but she never got the chance. With a terse, "Hold on," whichever Rawlings brother had answered the phone laid the receiver down with a clunk.

Cooper was on the line before she was ready for him, sounding sleepy and irritated and almost concerned. Susannah wasn't fooled. "Susannah? Is something wrong?"

"Wrong?" She laughed without a trace of humor. "You're damn right something's wrong. I don't like being threatened, especially by the likes of you. So lay off. You got that? You ever call me again and threaten me, and I'll have the sheriff on your tail so fast, you won't know what hit you."

"Threatened?" he repeated sharply. "What in blazes are you talking about?"

"Save it," she retorted. "I know it was you, so don't try to act innocent. You're not going to scare me into leaving. This is my ranch and I can stay as long as I want!"

She slammed down the phone before he could say another word. Biting out a curse, Cooper did the same. "Dammit to hell!"

Pulling out a chair from the kitchen table, Gable straddled it and crossed his arms across the top of the back. Disheveled from sleep, he surveyed Cooper with amusement. "Obviously the lady didn't call you in the middle of the night to whisper sweet nothings in your ear," he drawled. "She sounded more than a little ticked."

"You don't know the half of it," he grumbled, glaring at the phone. "She was steaming. For some crazy reason, she thinks I just called her and threatened her to try to scare her into leaving."

The humor in Gable's eyes fled. "She's being threatened? Did she call the sheriff?"

"I don't think so. She thought it was me, though why she'd think I'd do something like that, I don't know." He scowled. Damn the woman, what kind of nut did she think he was?

"I don't like the sound of this. Maybe you should go over there and check on her. She sold all the cattle and let all the hands go after Patterson died, and she's all alone. She could be in trouble."

Cooper had been thinking the same thing. As much as he disliked her, something twisted in his gut at the thought of her being scared and all alone in the middle of the night. "Maybe you're right. I think I'll take Sammy and run over there and check things out."

"Want me to go with you?"

"No. No sense both of us going out in the cold. Go on back to bed before Josey wakes up and we've got the whole household coming downstairs to see what's going on. I can handle this."

"Take your shotgun," Gable advised. "And if you need any help, call, for God's sake. Though I don't think you will. It was probably just a prank call."

Cooper agreed, but as he headed for the Patterson ranch a few minutes later, his shotgun hanging on the rack across the back windshield and Sammy, his German shepherd, in the back of his truck, he knew he wouldn't sleep until he saw with his own eyes that she was safe. And it wasn't because he was the least bit interested in the woman, he told himself irritably. It was just that damn knight-in-shining-armor complex of his.

His father had raised him and his brothers never to walk away from anyone in trouble—especially a woman or a child—and he never had. On more than one occasion, the instinctive urge to help had blown up in his face...like when he met Mary Lou. She was hurting bad after her breakup with the man she'd dated since high school, and he'd simply wanted to take that sad look from her beautiful eyes. Instead, he'd fallen in love with her, only to lose her back to that same high school sweetheart when they made up.

Like Mary Lou, Susannah was obviously a woman with problems. That didn't mean he could ignore her when she was in trouble. He'd make sure she was okay. Then he was getting the hell out of there.

Chapter 3

Too agitated to sleep, Susannah was in the kitchen making coffee when there was a knock at the front door. Startled, she jumped, her heart in her throat, and scattered coffee grounds across the counter top. Grumbling at her clumsiness, she grabbed a dishrag to wipe up the mess, but her fingers were shaking so badly, the task took her twice as long as it should have. Finishing up, she deposited the rest of the spilled grounds in the trash just as another heavy knock reverberated through the house.

Cooper.

Even before she heard him call her name, she knew it was him. For some reason, she seemed to have a sixth sense where he was concerned, and part of her had known when she hung up on him that he wouldn't let her get away with that. Well, if he was looking for a fight, he'd come to the right place!

Tightening the sash on the pink flannel robe she'd pulled on over her gown, she crossed the living room and jerked open the door, her chin set at a belligerent angle. "You don't have to keep pounding on the door as if I'm deaf," she greeted him hostilely. "I heard you the first time. What do you want?"

Want? Cooper almost laughed, his throat going dry at the sight of her. He wanted to go home and forget he'd ever heard her name, let alone seen her in her nightclothes. Dressed for bed in soft flannel, her usually sleek pageboy mussed from sleep, she stood stiffly before him, her arms crossed protectively across her breasts, her eyes spitting fire at him. A blind man couldn't have missed the warning signs posted all over her, and Cooper saw them. But he also saw for the first time how small she was, how vulnerable... how touchable.

His body stirred in response, heat spilling into his loins, and he almost turned then and there and walked away from her. He didn't want this, didn't want to want her, and the less he had to do with her, the better. But the hot color flaring in her cheeks couldn't hide the paleness of her skin, and behind the anger sparking in her eyes were shadows that he knew were traces of fear. Surely she wasn't scared of him?

Stunned by the thought, he glanced down at his black-and-tan shepherd, who sat at his side, waiting patiently. "Stay," he ordered softly, then pulled open the screen door and stepped inside before Susannah could think to block his way. "An explanation about your call to the house, for starters," he told her. "And then maybe you could tell me why you're looking at me like I'm Jack the Ripper. I've never hurt a woman in my life."

Her throat as dry as day-old toast, Susannah fought against the surprisingly strong urge to fall for his injured-innocent act. He actually looked hurt, as if he couldn't for the life of him understand what he had done to make her afraid of him. And God help her, she wanted to believe him.

But he was a Rawlings and not to be trusted. Why was she finding it so hard to remember that?

Confused, angry—what was it about this man that threw her so every time she thought she had figured him out?—she squared her shoulders and looked him right in the eye. "Nice try, Cooper, but I'm not buying it. I heard you on the phone. I know it was you."

"Then I was sleepwalking when I made the call because I was sound asleep when Gable woke me up to tell me you were on the phone. If you don't believe me, call Gable and ask him."

He sounded so logical, so honest. *Don't listen,* a voice in her head whispered. *You know what you heard.* "He's your brother," she reminded him. "He'll back up anything you say."

His eyes glinted at that slap in the face, but he only said, "Then think, woman! Why would I do something like this? What possible motive could I have?"

"You made it clear from the moment we met that you'd like nothing better than if I disappeared off the face of the earth. You were counting on the anger between our two families driving me away, and when it didn't, you started making those damn calls—"

"You mean there's been others?" he cut in sharply. "When? How many? Have you called the sheriff?"

His eyes were almost black with concern, his dark brows knit with what appeared to be genuine worry, and suddenly it was too much. "No," she retorted. "I haven't called anyone but you because *you're* the one harassing me. I thought if I told you I was on to you, you'd at least have the decency to admit the truth. Guess I was wrong, huh? So why don't you just leave? It's late, I'm tired, and I haven't got time for any more of your lies."

She started to step around him, intending to show him the door, but the second she took a step, he cursed and stepped in front of her, grabbing her by the arms. "Dammit, woman, what do I have to say to get through to you? I don't know anything about any phone calls. I don't even know your damn number."

Startled, Susannah gasped. "Let go of me!"

She tried to wrench free, but he held her fast, his grip as fierce as the scowl he directed down at her. Giving her a shake, he drew her up on her toes. "I know you think all Rawlingses are lower than pond scum, but we're not sneaks. We don't plot behind people's backs. And we don't terrorize women! Have I made myself clear?"

Caught in the sure grip of his strong hands, her eyes wide and heart slamming against her ribs, she stared up at him searchingly. She'd thought she'd seen him angry before, but evidently that had been nothing but the rumble of thunder before a storm. Cooper Rawlings in a true temper was something to see. A muscle twitched along his dark, unshaved jaw, and his mouth was pressed flat into a thin white line. But it was his eyes that stole her breath. Black and intense with fury, they condemned her for suspecting that he was even capable of such a thing. Yet at the same time, they demanded that she believe him.

He was serious, she realized, stunned, her gaze locked with his. Struggling against the sudden doubts weakening her own anger, she tried to tell herself she was a fool to cut him any slack. He was a Rawlings, and according to her father, that was more than enough incentive to convict him of just about anything. But unless he was a hell of a fine actor, the emotion roiling in his narrowed eyes was real. Her accusations infuriated him, not because he had been found out, but because she even suspected him. Dear God, had she misjudged him?

Confused, she frowned. "But if you didn't do it, who did? I haven't even been here a week. I don't know anyone else."

She believed him. The relief that coursed through him nearly rocked him back on his heels. He wasn't so arrogant that he didn't care what people thought of him, but when had this little spitfire's opinion of him become so important to him? What was going on here?

"Tell me about the calls," he said tightly. "All of them."

He released her as quickly as he'd grabbed her, and without quite knowing how it happened, Susannah found herself standing with half the room between them. She knew she should have been glad. She could breathe again without dragging in the clean, manly scent of him with every breath she took—which would have been fine if she hadn't been able to still feel his hands on her. Suddenly cold, she hugged herself, her fingers unconsciously closing over the same spots where he'd touched her. "There's not really much to tell. Come on into the kitchen and I'll pour us some coffee. I don't know about you, but I'm running out of gas fast and need a shot of caffeine."

Without a word, he followed her into the kitchen, and within minutes they were both seated at the old pine table that had sat in the same spot as long as Susannah could remember, their hands wrapped around steaming cups of coffee. Staring down at the black liquid, Susannah began with the first call, which had come through the day she'd had the phone hooked up. "I figured it was a wrong number. The caller never said anything, just waited a moment or two after I answered, then hung up. I didn't think anything about it and just shrugged it off."

"How often did he call? Was there a pattern?"

She added a spoonful of sugar to her cup and stirred it absently. "Not that I noticed. I'd get one or two calls a day, at odd times. Only a few were in the evening. And until to-night, they were all the same. The minute I answered, who-ever was calling hung up."

"Is this the first time you've gotten a call in the middle of the night?" At her nod, he frowned. "Tell me again what he said."

If she lived to be a hundred, she knew she would never forget those cold, raspy words. Swallowing to ease her sud-denly tight throat, she repeated huskily, " 'You're not wanted here. Do you hear me? Leave while you still can.' "

Cooper's eyes turned as hard as ebony. "Then what? Did he say what would happen if you stayed?"

"No. He hung up."

Wrapping her hands tighter around her mug to offset the sudden chill that numbed her all the way to the bone, she heard again the menace that had thickened the caller's voice. The silky, wicked hatefulness. She'd met so few people in the short time she'd been here—the clerk at the Quick Stop, the rural postal carrier, a handful of kind faces at church. She couldn't remember half their names, yet she'd obvi-ously infuriated someone so badly he wanted to run her out of town. How? she wondered in growing panic. How could she have made someone that mad without even knowing it? Was she really that insensitive?

Unable to sit still another moment, she pushed away from the table and rose to pace in growing agitation. "Who could hate me that much? I don't know anyone well enough to stir up that kind of emotion in them. Except you, of course," she added ruefully.

Cooper let that pass with nothing more than a twitch of his lips. "There's nothing that says you've done anything. If this guy's a nut case, there's no telling what's going on inside his head. I'm going to call the sheriff."

Alarmed, Susannah stopped abruptly. "Do you really think that's necessary? What if this turns out to be just a bunch of innocent crank calls? The sheriff would probably think I'm some kind of nut case myself."

"And if they're not?" he demanded. "What if this guy's dead serious. What then?"

She could be in real danger.

Cooper saw the knowledge in her face, the fear, and moved to the wall phone near the kitchen cabinets. Within seconds, he was talking to Jacob Pierce, the deputy sheriff who usually worked the graveyard shift, giving him the whole story.

Susannah listened to him give the deputy a detailed accounting of the calls and wanted to cringe. It sounded like something out of a Hollywood psychological thriller, or worse yet, the overactive imaginings of a paranoid woman who heard a bump in the night and immediately assumed it had been made by an ax murderer. Was she overreacting? She wasn't normally skittish—her work had taken her to some pretty odd places and she'd never had any reason to fear anyone. But something in the caller's voice had raised the fine hairs on the back of her neck.

Pacing again, she turned to face Cooper as he ended his conversation with the deputy and hung up. From the grim set of his mouth, the call obviously hadn't gone the way he had hoped. She arched a brow at him. "Well?"

"That was Jacob Pierce I was talking to, the deputy. He was sympathetic, but there's nothing he can do right now. Since you've actually only received one threatening call, the authorities have no choice but to consider it a prank."

Not surprised, Susannah said, "I figured as much. It's not like somebody approached me with a gun or anything." Unconsciously, her gaze drifted to the blackness of the night that stared back at her through the parted curtains at the kitchen windows. If she let herself, it would be all too easy to imagine hostile eyes out there in the all-consuming darkness, watching her every move.

A chill skated over her skin, sending goose bumps chasing after it. "I'm perfectly safe here," she said confidently, but even she could hear the doubts in her voice. "There's nothing to be worried about."

As long as the caller restricted his threats to the phone.

Not liking the tone of the unwanted thought that wormed its way into his head, Cooper scowled. "Jacob's going to leave a report for Sheriff Whitaker in the morning, so he'll probably give you a call some time tomorrow. And, of course, if you have any more problems, they want to hear about it."

"Of course."

There didn't seem to be much more to say after that. The authorities had been notified and there wasn't anything anyone could do now except wait to see if the caller tried something bolder. Reminding himself that he didn't intend to get any more involved than he had to, Cooper knew it was time to walk away. Yet the thought of her being on the thousand-acre ranch all by herself held his boots glued to the old parquet floor.

"Would you like me to stay the rest of the night? I could stretch out on the couch if you'd rather not be alone."

The offer came out of the blue, stunning them both. "Oh, no!" Susannah exclaimed quickly. "That's not necessary. Really."

He had to be out of his mind, but Cooper couldn't let it go. "Are you sure? You don't have to prove anything to anyone, you know. Even my sister, Kat, wouldn't stay home alone if she'd gotten the type of call you just got, and she's lived here all her life."

Her heart thundering, Susannah couldn't seem to drag her gaze away from his. Why did he have to choose now to be nice to her? she wondered wildly. And why did she have to choose now to notice how wickedly good-looking the man was in the middle of the night? With his chiseled jaw unshaved and dark with a night's growth of beard, his brown eyes still slightly shadowed with the sleep she'd dragged him from, he had the look of a phantom lover, a walking dream in cowboy boots and a worn sheepskin jacket that she could all too easily picture herself snuggling up to.

Oh, God, what was she doing?

"I appreciate the offer," she said huskily, "but it's not necessary. I'll just unplug the phone and I'll be fine."

His eyes still locked with hers, Cooper reminded himself that his mama hadn't raised any idiots. It was time to get out of there. Pronto. Wrapped in that damn soft flannel gown that exactly matched the sudden color spilling into her cheeks, the woman only had to stand there looking good enough to eat to burn a man to cinders. Damn, he needed to go home!

"Have it your way," he said curtly, and headed for the front door as fast as he could before he could dredge up another reason to stay. "But I'm still not leaving you alone. Sammy'll stay to keep you company."

She trailed behind him. "Sammy?"

"My dog. He's a damn fine watchdog and won't let anyone within a thousand feet of you."

"But—"

Already at the door, he whirled so fast, she almost ran into him. "I'm not asking your permission, Susannah. Sammy's staying."

He sounded like her father had, laying down the law to her mother, and she had no intention of taking that from anyone. Especially Cooper Rawlings. "You're pushing it, Rawlings. This isn't the Double R."

"Don't mess with me, Patterson," he warned. "I'm not in the mood."

For two cents, she would not only have messed with him, she would have told him exactly what she thought of him! She didn't want him here, didn't want him to leave his dog so he would have to come back to get him. But one look at the suddenly hot glint in his eyes reminded her that she was standing there in her gown and robe and was far more aware of him than she would have liked.

Abruptly, she gave in, though she was less than gracious about it. "Oh, all right, he can stay. But I still don't think it's necessary. I'll bring him home in the morning."

"There's no hurry. I've got to go to El Paso on ranch business for a couple of days, so he might as well stay here while I'm gone. One of the hands'll bring over some dog food for him tomorrow, and I'll pick him up when I get back."

Opening the door and stepping out onto the front porch, he reached down to affectionately pet the shepherd. "Keep an eye on the lady, Sam, and I'll see you when I get back. Stay." He turned back to Susannah for one last word of advice, his eyes meeting hers through the screen door. "If you get scared, don't try to tough it out with just you and Sammy. Call one of my brothers and then the sheriff...even if it's the middle of the night again. It doesn't hurt to be too cautious."

Susannah almost choked at the irony of that suggestion. Somehow she didn't think dragging any more of the Rawlingses' men into her life qualified as a cautious move, though she had no intention of telling *him* that. "I'm sure I won't have any more trouble. Cowards who hide behind phone lines don't usually have the nerve to confront their own shadows, let alone anyone else. But I'll be sure to call if Sammy so much as barks at the moon," she assured him quickly when he started to scowl again. "I'll be fine."

He looked as if he wanted to say something more, but with a muttered curse, he only growled, "Good. Then I'll see you when I get back."

Turning on his heel, he disappeared into the darkness where his truck waited. Still standing at the front door, she heard the motor roar to life, saw the pickup headlights spring on. Seconds later, he was driving down the mile-long gravel drive that led to the highway.

Plopped down on his rump on the other side of the screen door, Sammy whined in protest at being left behind. And suddenly Susannah knew just how the dog felt. As she stared at the truck's taillights as they grew smaller and smaller in the distance, a crazy loneliness hit her, a hollow emptiness that lodged somewhere in the region of her heart. Horrified, she reached for the door and quickly shut it, only to discover that out of sight didn't mean out of mind.

Finally reaching the highway, Cooper called himself seven kinds of a fool as he turned toward home. What had happened to his vow to get in and out as quickly as possible? Talk about blowing it! He'd taken one look at her pale face and haunted eyes and completely lost his head. He hadn't cared that she was a woman who was more than capable of taking care of herself or that she hadn't wanted anything to do with him or his dog. Just like a knight tripping over his feet when he finally encountered his first damsel in distress, he'd forced her to accept his help whether she wanted to or not. Damn!

What did it take for him to learn? he thought in disgust. Mary Lou had taught him just how painful saving damsels in distress could be, and the hell of it was, she hadn't even known it. She'd considered him a friend, nothing more, and all the time, he'd been falling in love with her. When she'd innocently confided that she was still crazy about her ex-boyfriend, she'd stabbed him right in the heart and she hadn't even known it.

That day, he'd known what it was like to step through the gates of Hell. He'd wanted to rage at her to open her eyes; instead he'd talked her into working things out with the man she loved. Later, she was so grateful for his help, she'd invited him to the wedding, and like a fool with too much pride, he'd gone. And while the newly wedded couple had honeymooned in Hawaii, he'd gone on a two-week drunk.

When he'd sobered up, he was a changed man. He didn't have to get burned twice to know to avoid the fire. For nearly two years, he'd managed to adroitly sidestep any female who looked the slightest bit helpless. Not that Susannah fit that description—far from it. But she was old man Patterson's daughter, for Pete's sake! She'd put her father up on some type of pedestal, and it was only a matter of time before the truth came crashing down on her head and she realized he wasn't the saint she evidently thought he was. And now, on top of everything else, she was being harassed by a weirdo with a phone fetish.

Trouble. She was trouble, he told himself, the kind that could tie him in knots if he gave her half a chance. He didn't intend to give her that chance. Once he got back from the auction sale in El Paso, he'd collect Sammy and get out of her life for good.

When one of the Double R ranch hands brought a sack of food for Sammy, Susannah almost instructed him to take the dog back home. But Sammy had been good company, and it wasn't the animal's fault that every time she looked at him, she thought of his master and why she wanted nothing to do with him. She knew men of his stamp too well. The West was full of them . . . chauvinistic, domineering, take-charge men who kept their women at home and controlled every facet of their lives.

From the soles of his boots to the top of his Stetson, her father had been just like that. He'd kept her mother under his thumb, refusing to let her out of the house without knowing where she was going, refusing to let her go to college as she'd longed to do or develop any outside interests.

The arguments they'd had! She'd only been a child, but she could still remember the anger that had often filled the house. Her mother had tried to reason with him, to convince him that she loved him and that he wasn't going to lose her by letting her pursue her own interests. But nothing she could say had made a dent in his stubborn stand, and, in the end, he himself had caused what he was trying to prevent— he had destroyed her mother's love.

And once the love was gone, there was nothing left to keep her mother in virtual captivity. She had divorced him and taken Susannah with her to Dallas, where she not only attended college, but eventually became a tenured English professor at Southern Methodist University.

Her mother had died happy, but she'd had to walk through the fires of Hades to get where she'd wanted to be in life, and Susannah would never forget the pain she had suffered. As they all had. Her father had never understood why being his wife and the mother of his daughter hadn't been enough for her mother. He'd had even more trouble accepting what he saw as Susannah's desertion of him.

Staring down at the old family album she'd found hidden away in her father's study, she studied a black-and-white snapshot of her and her father taken on her tenth birthday, her throat tight with pain. She hadn't wanted to desert him, but as he had with her mother, he'd all but forced her to.

She'd returned to New Mexico a month after the divorce for a visit, but he'd been so possessive, so determined to hang on to her now that he'd lost her mother, that she'd felt as if she were suffocating. When she'd rebelled, he'd forced her to choose between him and her mother, and she'd left, never to return—not because she hadn't wanted to return, but because he'd made it clear he wanted nothing more to do with her.

Even now, she still had a hard time forgiving him for that.

And Cooper Rawlings was too much like him. In the short time she'd known him, it hadn't taken her long to recognize that he was a man to contend with. He was as unyielding as steel, with the kind of strength she naturally rebelled against. Because if she didn't, she knew she'd be swept up in his power and carried helplessly away. And that was something she was determined not to let happen.

Lost in the unbreakable silence of her musings, she nearly jumped out of her skin when Sammy suddenly growled from his position on the porch, where he'd curled up on the welcome mat just as the sun started to set. Alarmed, she stumbled to her feet, the blood draining from her face as Sammy growled again, the tone a definite warning, before he barked angrily and went tearing off the porch into the night.

Her heart in her throat, Susannah rushed to the front door and switched on the floodlights, but when she glanced out the window, Sammy was nowhere in sight and everything looked perfectly normal. In the distance, she heard Sammy snarling and barking, a cry of pain, and then nothing...just a silence that seemed to go on forever.

Horrified, Susannah gasped. "Oh, no!"

Fumbling with the dead bolt, she started to throw it clear and jerk open the door when she froze. Oh, God, what if whoever was out there was waiting for her to do just that? The minute she rushed outside, she would be at his mercy.

She couldn't do it. But if something happened to Sammy, Cooper would never forgive her. She couldn't just stand there....

Torn, her hand resting on the dead bolt, she suddenly heard a muffled bark and Sammy trotted up on the porch. Laughing in relief, she didn't wait another second to throw open the door and step outside. "You crazy dog, you scared me to death! What'd you do, see a rabbit or what?"

But it wasn't a rabbit he held in his teeth. Tail wagging and black eyes dancing, he stopped before her and dropped a bloody rag at her feet as if it were a trophy.

Staring transfixed at the stained and tattered piece of material, it was a long moment before she could move. Her blood as cold as ice, she reached down and gingerly picked up the rag and recognized it for what it was. A piece of a man's shirt.

"Oh, God, oh, God!" she whispered hoarsely. Sitting at her feet, Sammy whined, his dark eyes confused as he stared up at her. "You did good, boy," she praised him, patting him on the head. "Real good. Keep up the good work while I call the sheriff."

By the time Riley Whitaker arrived nearly an hour later, Susannah was a nervous wreck. Sammy hadn't barked again, and she'd checked to make sure all the doors and windows were locked, but she still jumped at every little sound. When she saw the headlights of the county patrol car as it turned down her drive, she almost wilted in relief. For the first time since Sammy had growled and raced off into the darkness, her heart slowed its frantic beating.

Half-expecting the sheriff to be a good ol' boy with thinning hair, a belly that stuck out over his belt and an easygoing manner and quick smile that would help him garner votes on election day, Susannah took one look at Riley

Whitaker and blinked. A good twenty-five years younger than she'd expected, there was nothing of the good ol' boy about him. Dressed in a khaki uniform, a black leather jacket stretched across his broad shoulders and a black cowboy hat on his dark head, he was tall, lean, and intimidating as hell. If he ever smiled, it wasn't often, and his blue eyes were sharp as a hawk's and far too discerning for comfort. He recognized Sammy immediately and spoke quietly to him. By the time he'd introduced himself and stepped into the living room, he'd sized up his surroundings in a single, all-encompassing glance.

Watching him, noting how his eyes held the glint of knowledge of a much older man, Susannah wondered what his story was. Everyone had one, and his was right there in those shuttered eyes, waiting to be tapped. But he wasn't there to talk about himself.

"Thank you for coming all the way out here so quickly," she told him. "I'm sure whoever was here is long gone by now, but I appreciate you checking it out yourself. After the phone calls I've been getting, I've been as jumpy as a scalded cat."

"No problem," he said, removing his hat. "That's what I'm here for. Tell me again about the calls." He'd read the report Jacob had written up, and he'd talked to Susannah himself that very morning, but it never hurt to be too careful. Especially when you were dealing with a nut case. "He didn't make an actual threat until last night?"

Gripping her suddenly cold hands, she nodded. "That's right." Word for word, she gave him the same details she'd given him that morning. "When the phone didn't ring once today, I thought he was finally going to leave me alone. Then this evening, right before I called you, Sammy heard something and went charging off into the darkness. He came back with this."

She lifted the bloody scrap of cloth with two fingers and held it out to him. He took it, careful to touch as little of the material as possible, and placed it in a small plastic evidence bag. "Did you hear a car? See any headlights?"

"No, nothing."

Brows knit, he studied the bloodstained material. Dark blue cotton, it was too small to give a clue as to the size of the shirt it had been torn from. "When Sammy raced off the porch, which way did he go?"

"North," she said. "And I heard someone cry out. At first I was afraid it was Sammy, but then he came back with the shirt. He hasn't barked since."

"Let me get my flashlight from the car and check it out," he said, turning toward the front door. "I'll be right back."

Standing at the window, hugging herself, Susannah watched him retrieve a large flashlight from his patrol car and turn it into the darkness past the reach of the floodlights, which still burned brightly. With Sammy at his side, he slowly, methodically worked his way north of the house with broad, searching strokes of the light, missing nothing.

He was nearly a thousand feet from the house when she saw him stop suddenly and kneel, examining something at his feet. For a long moment he didn't move, and when he did it was to look off into the distance, as if with his eyes alone he could pierce the darkness of the night and find the prowler whose menace still lingered in the air.

Susannah shivered. Who was doing this to her? And why?

She was still racking her brain for the answers when the sheriff came back thirty minutes later. Opening the front door for him, she asked expectantly, "Well? Did you find anything?"

He nodded, his jaw rigid. "He had a horse. I found the tracks about a hundred yards from where he ran into Sammy. He rode out to the north. Of course, he could have changed direction as soon as he got safely away. I won't know more for sure until tomorrow morning, and even then, the chances of tracking him farther are slim. He could come back any time between now and then and cover his tracks."

Susannah paled. She hadn't considered that he might come back. "Do you think he will?"

"Don't know," he replied, shrugging. "If he was just trying to scare you, I'm sure he's already done that. If he wants something else, however, there's no telling."

His narrowed gaze traveled over her, the frown lines gouging his brow deepening as his eyes moved from her to the house still filled with her father's things, then to the windows where the night peeked in through the half-closed curtains. "I know this isn't any of my business, but what the hell are you doing living out here in the boonies all by yourself?"

Taken aback by his fierceness, she blinked. "My father left the place to me. Is there any reason why I shouldn't live here?"

"Right offhand, I can think of at least three or four," he retorted. Holding up a broad hand, he counted them off on his fingers. "You're a woman alone. You even have to borrow a dog from one of your neighbors to protect yourself. You're miles from the closest help in case of an emergency, and Mexico is too damn close. And," he continued before she could so much as open her mouth, "crime is up in the county. There's been a rash of burglaries in the past few months, and I haven't been able to catch the culprit yet. I will," he promised, "but in the meantime, you're out here alone and unprotected. I don't like it."

Unmoved, Susannah eyed him suspiciously. "Cooper talked to you before he left for El Paso, didn't he?"

He merely arched a dark brow at her. "I beg your pardon?"

"He told you to talk to me, to try to convince me to leave." Suddenly furious, she began to pace. "He just doesn't know when to quit, does he? When he got nowhere with me, he decided to bring in the big guns. Well, it's not going to work and you can tell him I said so!"

Unperturbed, Riley watched her steam and had to fight a grin. "I haven't talked to Coop."

"Just wait till he gets back! He's going to get an earful—what did you say?"

He grinned then, unable to stop himself. "Last time I talked to Coop was a couple of weeks ago. I haven't seen him since."

Mortified, Susannah felt hot color spill into her cheeks. "Well," she said finally with a sigh, "nothing like making a fool of yourself in front of a total stranger. It seems I owe you an apology, Sheriff." She forced a rueful smile. "Believe it or not, I don't usually fly off the handle like that. It's just that Cooper has been saying virtually the same thing you have, and every time we run into each other, we argue."

"No problem," he said easily. "With these calls you've been getting, no one would blame you for being stressed out. Or for being scared. I wish I could assure you that I'll have this guy in custody soon, but he's not going to be easy to catch. Unless he pulls another stupid stunt like he did tonight and makes a major mistake, it could take a while."

Susannah had suspected as much, but hearing it only confirmed her fears. "I see. Well, I appreciate your honesty."

"Look, even though Cooper's been hassling you about staying here all by yourself, he's obviously concerned about your safety if he left Sammy with you. Why don't you spend the rest of the night at the Double R? The Rawlingses would be happy to have you, and you'd get more sleep there than you'll probably get here."

He held the suggestion out to her like a carrot, and she only had to replay last night's threatening phone call to be oh, so tempted to jump at it. But the Rawlingses had hated her father as much as he'd hated them, and she just couldn't put herself in their debt more than she already had for the loan of Sammy.

"No, I don't think so," she said firmly. "Sammy's still on guard, so I'm sure I'll be fine."

It was obvious from the tone of her voice and the stubborn set of her jaw that she didn't intend to change her mind. Accepting her decision, the sheriff suggested she call the phone company and have her number restricted until the caller was caught. Soon after that, he left, promising to be in touch as soon as he had any news. Watching him leave, Susannah knew she'd never be able to sleep.

She was right. She stayed up the rest of the night.

Chapter 4

The gas gauge pushing empty, Cooper drove into the Shamrock station in Lordsburg, pulling wide to allow for the stock trailer hitched to his truck. Forty more miles, he thought tiredly, as he got out to pump the gas, and he'd be home. It had been a grinding two days at the auction sales in El Paso, and he had no one to blame but himself. He'd run into some friends he hadn't seen in years, and they'd sat up half the night catching up on the latest news and buying rounds of beers. He was beat. As soon as he got home and unloaded the cutting horses he'd bought at the auction, he was hitting the sack. With a little peace and quiet, he could probably sleep around the clock.

His eyes focused unseeingly on the clicking numbers of the gas pump, he didn't notice the county patrol car that pulled up right next to him until Riley Whitaker rolled down his window and drawled, "Well, I see you're back. From the looks of you, it must have been a wild trip."

Jerking back to awareness, Cooper looked over in time to see the amused, knowing glint in the sheriff's eyes. "It was strictly business," he lied, his mouth twitching. "I swear it."

Riley snorted, a rare grin stealing across his mouth. "Monkey business, you mean. I know how you Rawlings boys are when you're in the partying mood. Is El Paso still standing?"

"Just barely," Cooper laughed. "How've things been around here? Slow as usual?"

Riley hiked a brow. "Slow? Where you been? It hasn't been slow around here in months. This week alone we had three more burglaries, a fight at the Crossroads and a prowler out at Susannah Patterson's place."

"Son of a bitch!" Cooper cursed. "What happened? Is she okay? Dammit, I knew she had no business staying out there all by herself!"

If Riley noticed that Cooper's feelings were a little too intense for a woman who was nothing but a stranger to him, he kept the thought to himself. "She's fine," he assured him, "thanks to Sammy." He told him of the dog's confrontation with the prowler and the piece of material Sammy had been able to tear from the man's shirt before he got away. "I found his tracks—evidently he rode out on horseback and was sneaking up on the house on foot when he ran into Sammy. He managed to get away and make it back to his horse, so he was long gone before I was able to get out there. When I came back the next morning, I lost the tracks in the rocks in that old dry creekbed a mile west of the house."

"Any idea who he is?"

He shook his head, his mouth pressed flat in disgust. "He's got a horse, knows the terrain and was wearing a blue cotton shirt when Sammy got hold of him. That's not a hell of a lot to go on."

That description could have fit just about any one of dozens of men within a fifty-mile radius. Cooper swore. So they were still at square one. "Susannah didn't stay there alone after that, did she? I told her to call Gable or Flynn if she had any trouble...."

Something in his friend's expression had his eyes sharpening. "She did go to the Double R, didn't she? Tell me she didn't stay at her place alone with that nut on the loose. She wouldn't be that stupid."

Riley hesitated. "I don't know if I'd call it stupid. She did have Sammy."

The string of curses that rolled from Cooper's tongue told his friend exactly what he thought of that rationalization. "You let her stay? Dammit, Riley, what were you thinking of?"

"Let her stay?" Riley choked. "Man, you obviously don't know the lady very well. Stubborn takes on a whole new meaning when it's applied to her. I tried to get her to go to the Double R, but she insisted she'd be fine. And I couldn't very well force her," he added, defending himself. "She dug in her heels, and nothing short of a bulldozer was going to get her off her old man's ranch."

Cooper's jaw clenched. He knew better than anyone just how difficult it was to budge the woman when she didn't want to be budged. "God forbid she should go running to the Double R when she's in trouble," he muttered to himself. "Her old man would probably turn over in his grave."

"The hard feelings between your family and hers have been building for a long time," Riley reminded him. "You can't expect the lady to forget that overnight."

"I can when she lets it jeopardize her safety," Cooper retorted grimly. "And that's exactly what I intend to tell her as soon as I see her."

Riley knew that look and almost warned Cooper that when it came to stubbornness, Cooper could teach Susannah a few things himself. But a good sheriff—and friend—only butted in so far. "You know the lady better than I do, man. If you have any more trouble, just give me a call."

Cooper would have gone to the Patterson place immediately, but he had the horses to settle and he needed some time to cool off before he faced her. But an hour later, when he turned down the long pitted road to Susannah's house, his blood was still hot with temper.

Pulling up in a cloud of dust before her front porch, he heard Sammy give a sharp, excited bark of greeting and stepped from the truck just as the dog came hurtling toward him, his tail wagging wildly and a sappy grin on his face.

Laughing, Cooper caught the shepherd as he launched himself at him. "Hey, you old bag of bones, don't tell me you missed me," he teased, ruffling his fur. "I heard you almost caught yourself a big rat the other night. You got a piece of him, didn't you?"

Playing with the dog, he didn't realize Susannah had overheard the entire conversation until she pushed open the screen door and stepped out onto the porch. "I take it you've been talking with the sheriff," she said quietly.

He glanced up. The affectionate smile he'd given Sammy slowly died at the sight of her standing there before him in green cords and a lavender sweater. Desire, swift and hot and not totally unexpected, slammed into him. He'd thought of nothing but her for three days, and he'd finally come to the reluctant conclusion that, like it or not, he was never going to be indifferent to her. Somehow, some way, he was going to have to deal with that.

"Are you all right?"

"I'm fine," she said in that cool tone that made him want to do something to heat her up. "Thanks to Sammy. He was pretty impressive." Giving the devil his due, she forced out words of gratitude that obviously wanted to stick in her throat. "I don't know how I'll ever thank you for leaving him with me. I would have been in real trouble without him. I didn't suspect anyone was around until he growled."

Another time, Cooper would probably have gloated over the admission—finally she was admitting she was wrong about something! But he was so ticked off, he needed all his self-control not to take the porch steps in two long strides and give her the good, hard shaking she deserved. "Do you know how damn lucky you were?" he growled, glaring up at her from the bottom of the steps. "What would you have done if the bastard had come back after the sheriff had left?"

"Sammy was here—"

"Sammy's not invincible. He could have been taken out of the picture with one shot from a rifle. And you could have, too. Or didn't you think of that?"

She paled, her gray eyes widening. "There was no indication that he wanted to physically harm me," she began. "He's just trying to scare me—"

"You should have been scared," he snapped, his anger spiking again at her naïveté. It had never entered her head that the man harassing her might be so determined to get rid of her that he would resort to killing her! "You don't know a damn thing about this weirdo. He could be a mass murderer, a rapist, God only knows what else. But did you leave? Did you go to the Double R so you'd be safe? Did you even call over there to let Flynn or Gable know what had happened?

Throwing the questions at her like accusations, Cooper half expected her to snap back at him any second. But, dammit, when she'd allowed him to leave Sammy with her, she'd given him the right to protect her, and he was entitled to a few answers.

Bracing himself for a sharp retort, she surprised him by saying quietly "I didn't think it was necessary to leave. Sammy wasn't going to let anyone sneak up on me."

He might have bought that if he hadn't known how she felt about his family. "Come off it, Susannah. That's not why you stayed and you know it. Admit it. You'd rather face the devil himself than be beholden to my family."

"That's not true!"

He merely lifted a brow. "Isn't it?"

The hot, guilty color flushing her cheeks gave him the only answer he needed, but she still stubbornly refused to admit the truth. "It wasn't like that," she said stiffly. "My decision to stay here was no reflection on your family. How could it be? I don't even know them."

"You would if you didn't insist on clinging to a feud you know nothing about."

She ignored that, the only sign that she had heard him the sudden stiffening of her spine. "I stayed because I can take care of myself," she continued doggedly. "I have for years. It had nothing to do with your family."

His narrowed eyes studied her shrewdly. "Oh, so you've dealt with perverts before, have you? How many? One? Two? A half dozen? You must have led an interesting life. Just what exactly do you do?"

"I'm a writer," she retorted, stung. "And no, I haven't had to deal with this kind of situation before. But that doesn't mean I can't handle it."

"It does as far as I'm concerned," he said tightly, advancing up the steps. "Go pack your bags. You're staying at the Double R until this nut's caught."

Susannah blinked. She couldn't have heard him correctly. "I beg your pardon?"

"You heard me. It's too dangerous for you to stay here alone. Go pack your things. You're coming home with me."

For a long, timeless moment, she could only stare at him while a forgotten conversation from the past echoed hauntingly in her ears. Her father, his tone sounding much like Cooper's, laying down the law and telling her mother where she could and couldn't go, what she could and couldn't do. As if she were a child being told to pick up her clothes or come in out of the rain, Susannah thought, her heart constricting painfully. Even now, years...a lifetime later, she could hear her mother pleading with her father, trying to reason with him, until she'd finally, inevitably, come to the conclusion that all the talking in the world wasn't going to change anything.

But she wasn't her mother, she reminded herself. And Cooper, thank God, wasn't her father. Propping one hip against the porch railing, she crossed her arms on her chest and surveyed him with a calm that didn't come easily. Fighting the need to tell him to take a hike, she cocked her head and asked curiously, "Do the women in your life really let you get away with ordering them around or is it just me you feel you have to boss? In case you haven't noticed, I don't take orders well...from anyone. It's this crazy quirk I have," she explained with a sweet, needling smile. "I don't like being treated like a simpleton."

His brows snapped together at that. "I never said—"

She arched a delicate brow, the flash of her dimples irritatingly smug. "No?"

She waited patiently as every word he'd just said replayed through his head. Watching her watch him, Cooper winced, unable to remember the last time he'd felt like such a jerk. He wasn't normally a jackass where women were concerned, but this one just seemed to have a knack for bringing out the worst in him.

A crooked, self-deprecating grin lifted up one corner of his mouth. "I just love the taste of crow, don't you? Would it help if I said I'm sorry?"

Susannah tried not to be charmed, but he made that nearly impossible. "It wouldn't hurt," she said, biting back a smile. "A woman always likes to hear she's right."

"I'm sorry," he said gruffly, simply. "I've got no excuses. Riley told me what happened here the other night, and all I could think about was that you could have been seriously hurt."

"But I wasn't."

"Not this time," he agreed. "But who knows about next time? You're in trouble, and regardless of what you think of me and my family, we don't stand around with our hands in our pockets when someone needs help. Which is why I want you to come home with me."

His eyes held hers captive, silently urging her to say yes. God, how she wanted to! But alarm bells were already ringing in her ears, refusing to be ignored. Cooper Rawlings, when he was giving her a piece of his mind, was far too attractive for words. But when he was being nice, when his smile came easily and his eyes glinted with humor, he was downright dangerous.

She shook her head. "I'm sorry. I can't."

"Why?"

Because he made her blood pump. Because he made her dream of things she hadn't dreamed in years. Because he and his brothers were partly responsible for her father's death, yet he had only to smile at her to make her forget why she wanted nothing to do with him.

But she couldn't say those things, couldn't even think them. "Because of the reasons you just gave," she said, grasping at straws. "I've got a nut case bothering me and you're a neighbor. If I go home with you, he may start to hassle your family, as well."

"Not if he knows anything about my family, he won't," Cooper retorted. "Anyway, that's a risk we're willing to take."

"But I'm not."

Her jaw was set, her mind made up. With any other woman, he would have respected her decision and let it go, figuring he'd done everything he could to talk some sense into her. But from that first day, when he'd caught her trespassing at the springs, nothing had been that simple. And the hell of it was, he didn't know why. He just knew he'd never be able to sleep nights now that he knew the bastard harassing her had actually tried to get to her.

"All right," he said, trying another angle. "If you don't want to stay at the Double R, fine. That doesn't mean you have to stick around here and wait for that jackass to get his hands on you. Why don't you leave? Go somewhere else where you'll be safe."

"The ranch—"

"We'll buy it from you," he promised rashly. "We're expanding into growing crops, so we could use your land. Just name your price, and if it's anywhere close to reasonable, it's yours. You can be out of here by tonight and never have to worry again about threatening phone calls or prowlers sneaking up on you."

The Rawlingses want my land. They always have.

Understanding hit Susannah right between the eyes, nearly sending her to her knees. The ranch, she thought dully. He wanted the ranch. Why hadn't she seen it coming? She'd known. Dear God, she'd known what the Rawlingses were like. Her father had left her written warnings!

"That's what you've been after from the very beginning, isn't it? The land. That's why you pretended to be so concerned about me. You want my ranch."

Taken aback, Cooper wouldn't have been more surprised if she'd hauled off and slapped him. "What? Don't be ridiculous. You're in danger, dammit! Or have you forgotten that?"

"Have *you* forgotten you just made an offer for this place only minutes after you came rushing over here pretending to be worried about me?" she tossed right back at him furiously. "No, I can see you haven't."

She shook her head at her own stupidity. "I can't believe I read about you in my father's diary and still didn't see this coming. He said the Rawlingses wouldn't be happy until they owned everything for as far as the eye could see. I guess he was right."

Cooper told himself not to be insulted. She'd jumped to the wrong conclusions, and with a few simple words, he could clear everything up. But it was too late. He was already furious. "You know, that's really rich, coming from your old man," he said contemptuously. "Talk about the pot calling the kettle black. He was the one who lied and plotted—"

"Stop right there!" she said angrily. "You're standing on my father's porch, trying to convince me to sell his land to you after you've just pretended to be concerned about me—"

"For God's sakes, woman, I *am* concerned about you!" he roared. "Do you think I left Sammy with you just for the fun of it? Someone was out here the other night. Someone who wants you gone from this place."

"And you're here to help him, aren't you," she goaded, too angry to realize what she was accusing him of. "Run,

Susannah. Just make sure you sell us your land first, right?
Forget it. I'll never sell to a Rawlings."

His mouth compressed into a thin white line. "Fine,
sweetheart, you keep your land. But when you've got more
trouble than you can handle, don't say I didn't warn you."

With that parting shot, he strode across the porch and
down the steps to his truck. Sammy, trotting at his side,
waited expectantly for him to let down the tailgate so he
could jump into the back, but Cooper only shook his head
and gave him a reassuring rub behind the ears. "Sorry, boy,
you're staying here as long as the lady needs you. Take good
care of her."

Shooting Susannah a hard look where she still stood on
the porch, he asked coldly, "Do you have enough dog food
for him to last a while or do I need to have one of the hands
bring some more over later?"

"There's plenty," she began stiffly, "but—"

He didn't wait to hear more. Without another word, he
started to walk around to the driver's side of the pickup.
"Cooper..."

She hadn't meant to call after him, hadn't meant to try to
make peace with him when he had just proved beyond a
shadow of a doubt that the Rawlingses were just as land
hungry as her father had claimed. But something that painfully resembled hurt clutched her heart, and she knew she
couldn't let him leave like this. Across the hood of his truck,
his hard, piercing eyes met hers. Swallowing, she said huskily, "You don't have to leave Sammy."

His rugged face carved in stern lines, he met her gaze unblinkingly. Silence stretched into an eternity. Just when she
thought he intended to slide behind the wheel and drive off
without a word, some emotion she couldn't read flared in
his eyes as they swept over her from head to toe and back

again. She knew she should move, say something, but she couldn't. Trapped, she felt her heart begin to thud.

''Yes, I do,'' he said thickly.

Within seconds, he was gone. Gazing after the pickup as it dragged a trail of dust after it, Susannah felt as if she'd just escaped a close call with an electrical storm. And he hadn't even touched her, she thought dazedly. God help her if he ever did.

After that, she knew pushing him from her thoughts was going to be next to impossible. She didn't even try. But she didn't sit around and brood over the man either. Restlessness drove her inside and upstairs. The second floor was still in desperate need of cleaning, but she didn't spare it a glance as she continued on up to the attic.

An hour later, dusty and tired, her arms aching from moving old furniture, most of which needed one type of repair or another, she found the trunks. Six of them. Old camelback trunks that looked as if they hadn't been moved in centuries. Dropping to her knees beside the biggest one, she pushed at the lid, which refused to budge. Frowning, she looked for a lock, but found none and gave the lid another shove. With a deep groan of protest, it grudgingly opened.

Receipts, she thought, stunned, staring at the papers that filled the trunk almost to overflowing. Bills of sale. Old newspapers. Had her father kept every scrap of paper that ever came into his possession? she wondered, shuffling through the top layer. But then a yellowed clipping from a newspaper caught her attention, and she reached for it, her eyes narrowing at the date. 1912! Twenty-five years before her father was even born!

Which meant that the trunk and its contents must have belonged to her grandparents, she thought. She didn't know much about them except that they had owned a small grocery store in Santa Fe back in the twenties. When they'd died, her father had taken the money from the sale of the store to buy the ranch.

Turning the paper toward the single bare bulb that hung from the ceiling, she lifted a brow at the headline. Rancher Retrieves Stolen Cattle. Fascinated, she began to read.

The idea, when it hit her, caught her completely off guard. One minute she was casually reading the clipping and the next she was thinking about the rancher who had defied the odds and gone after the ruthless band of rustlers who'd stolen his entire herd. Images flickering before her eyes, she saw the story unfold like a movie on a screen, stunning her with its completeness.

"Yes!" Her excited cry echoing off the rafters, she jumped to her feet, laughing. A book! She finally had a book idea! Her writer's block was broken! The yellowed newspaper clipping clutched in her hand, she ran for the stairs.

Within minutes, she was downstairs at her computer, her fingers flying over the keys as she quickly typed out as much of the story as she could remember before it slipped away and was lost forever. There were still holes, of course, places to fill in, details to work out later, but those never bothered her. It was the starting she loved, the blinding flash of insight that gave her the bare skeleton of the story and always came as such a surprise. Then there was the creating of the characters, the hero in particular. He moved into her thoughts as if he owned them, teasing her until she knew his personality as well as she knew her own. Which was why she'd ended up writing four Ace MacKenzie books, she reminded herself, grinning as her fingers danced on the keys. Ace was such a delight to write, she hadn't been able to stop with just one book. But it wasn't Ace she found herself writing about now. Closing her eyes, hardly aware of where her creativity was taking her, she let the words and images form, uncensored.

His name came to her as easily as her own—Diego Kelly. Tall and dark, as rugged as the West itself, with a slow wicked smile he'd inherited from his Irish father and nearly black eyes that were his gift from his Mexican mother, he was a handsome devil who had only to step into a room to draw the attention of every woman in sight. A rogue in cowboy boots and a Stetson, he was also a hard man who fought for what was his.

Lost in the scenes that played out before her closed eyes, Susannah had no idea how long she pounded away at her computer, capturing the images that drove her. The story flowed like a flooded river rushing out of its banks, gushing swiftly along, almost too fast to keep up with. But the madcap pace couldn't continue, and finally it slowed to a trickle, then stopped altogether. Feeling as if she'd just been caught in the floodwaters herself, Susannah all but collapsed in her chair.

It was good, she thought in delight, almost laughing out loud with excitement as she read what she'd written. She'd always avoided Westerns in the past, afraid that the genre would remind her too much of her father and the jumbled tangle of emotions that always stirred in her whenever she thought of him. But now she was surrounded by the past, the West, and she wanted to remember. Everything. All she had to do was give herself time and not try to push memories that weren't ready to come.

And this story just might help her, she decided, her gaze quickly skimming the words she'd used to describe Diego Kelly. Tall and dark, rugged, a hard man with nearly black eyes and a slow, wicked smile. Cooper, she thought, dazed. He sounded just like Cooper. She had created a fascinating, intriguing rogue of a character...who happened to look just like Cooper Rawlings.

"No!"

The soft, horrified explanation bounced off the walls of her father's study, where she'd set up her laptop. Her eyes fixed on the computer screen, her face pale, she shook her head in denial. The man had already pushed his way into her life, into her thoughts, more than she wanted. She couldn't, *wouldn't*, let him push his way into her writing!

Impulsively, she hit the delete button and eliminated Diego Kelly with a flick of her finger. Forget him, she told herself firmly. She was a professional writer; she had dozens of heroes in her head, just waiting to be brought to life. She'd just pull another out and start over.

Later, she told herself that she'd tried. She really had. But Diego quickly proved he wasn't a character who could be erased from her thoughts with a delete button. No other name but Diego Kelly came to mind. And he might have been a character right out of the Old West, but his personality, his features, were those of only one man—Cooper. Every time she tried to come up with something different, she hit a blank wall.

Because she was becoming fascinated with Cooper Rawlings. And there didn't seem to be a damn thing she could do about it.

Cooper arrived home in a foul mood, fit for no one's company but his own. He would have liked nothing better than to haul a couple of six-packs out to a back pasture and get rip-roaring drunk. But when he pulled up in front of the house and saw the family over at the corral where he'd unloaded the cutting horses he'd bought at the auction, he knew he couldn't just walk away from them without a word.

Reining in his seething emotions and wishing his siblings couldn't read him like a book, he forced an easy smile and strolled over to the corral. "Well, I see you've already checked them out," he said, nodding toward the horses, who were munching on the apples Gable had brought them. "What do you think?"

"You must have paid a fortune for them," Kat said. "I wish I had time to try out the little black mare before I head back to school in the morning. I'll bet she's quick as a cat."

Cooper grinned. "I saw her in action before the auction, and she's nearly as good as Zeus."

Gable merely lifted a brow over twinkling eyes. Zeus was his, and the best cutting horse in the county. "I doubt that, but we'll see. We didn't even know you were home until Josey saw the horses in the corral. When'd you get back?"

"About an hour ago."

"An hour ago!" Flynn exclaimed. "Then where've you been?"

That Flynn was the one to push his nose into his business didn't surprise Cooper in the least. Shooting him a discouraging look he knew was wasted, he said, "Over at the Patterson place."

"Oh, really?" Dawning understanding gleamed like mischief in Flynn's eyes. "Well, now, ain't that interesting? The minute you get back from El Paso, you go running over to Susannah Patterson's. I wonder why."

In no mood for his teasing, Cooper didn't crack a smile. "It was nothing personal. I ran into Riley Whitaker in town and he told me she had a problem the other night." He'd already told them about the bastard badgering her and now gave them a quick accounting of Sammy's run-in with the man. "I went over there to see why she didn't call over here when it happened. I'm sure Josey would have insisted she spend the night."

"Of course," Josey said quickly, concern darkening her eyes as she moved to his side. "Is she okay?"

"She'd be a hell of a lot better if she wasn't so damn bullheaded," he retorted, his hold on his frustration slipping a notch. "There's just no reasoning with the woman!"

Surprised by his heated tone, Josey exchanged a meaningful glance with her husband, speculation dancing in her eyes. "Maybe I should call her and invite her to supper," she said softly. "In fact, I should have done it already. After all, I know what it's like to be alone here and not know anyone. If we can convince her that we don't hold her father's sins against her, then she might realize she can call on us when she's in trouble."

"No!" Seeing eyebrows climb at his vehement denial, Cooper just barely bit back a curse. The last thing he wanted was to sit down to supper and find himself across the table from the woman who was driving him crazy! "She won't come, Josey," he said stiffly. "I made an offer to buy her ranch and she blew up. She thinks we're just as land hungry as her father claimed we were, and she wants nothing to do with us."

"Land hungry?" Flynn choked, his blue eyes flashing at the insult. "Us? You gotta be kidding! Her old man's the one who—"

"I know, I know," Cooper said tiredly. "Believe me, I've tried to talk some sense into her, but there's no reasoning with her where her father's concerned."

Gable, who had more reason than anyone to hate the Pattersons after Joe had shot him in the back, said, "That's understandable, Coop. He was her father. You'd feel the same way if she was running down Dad."

"Dad never shot anyone," he pointed out hotly. "And he sure as hell never plotted to steal anyone's ranch out from under them."

"No, he didn't. But if he had, we'd still have found a way to defend him." Grinning at the irritation still gleaming in his brother's eyes, he laughed. "Lighten up, little brother. The lady'll come around. I'm really not surprised that she refused to sell—that ranch has been in her family for a long time. That doesn't mean you can't talk her into letting us use the land, though. Why don't you see if she'll lease it? At least then she could make some money off it."

It was a logical suggestion, but Cooper was anything but thrilled with it. He'd rather face a riled rattlesnake than come anywhere near Susannah Patterson again. He'd never worried over a woman so much in his life, and he didn't like it. The entire time he was in El Paso, all he could think of was the way she'd looked when he'd rushed over to her house in the middle of the night—flushed from sleep, scared, defiant and sexy as hell. He couldn't get her out of his head . . . or his dreams. And the more he saw her, the worse it got.

He wanted her out of his life. Now! Which meant he had to find a way to convince her to lease not only her land, but the house as well, to the family she hated more than any other in the world. He'd find a way to do it if he had to get down on his knees.

He nodded. "All right. I'll see what I can do."

He let four days pass before he approached her, telling himself he was giving her plenty of time to cool off. But as he pulled up before her house and approached her front door with Sammy wiggling excitedly at his side, he knew he'd postponed the meeting because he was the one who needed time. This time, when he faced the infuriating woman, he would not let her goad him into losing his temper . . . or let her get under his skin. This time he was ready for her.

Or so he thought. Until she opened the front door. Then every sane thought he had dried up and blew away at the sight of her.

She had been playing in the dirt or digging in a dusty closet, he thought, his eyes fixed on the cobwebs caught in her dark hair and smudges of dirt dotting her chin, forehead and nose. Without taking his gaze from her face, he somehow noted that the jeans and long-sleeved shirt she wore were old and tattered, but it didn't matter. She was beautiful.

And obviously surprised to see him, he noted, watching her eyes widen at the sight of him. After the way he'd stormed off last time, he couldn't blame her for not expecting to see him again. Or for not welcoming him with open arms.

Her hand went to the screen door's handle, but she made no move to unlock it. "Yes?"

Squelching his irritation, he reminded himself to be patient and forced his jaw to unclench. "Can we talk?"

"About what?"

"Your land."

For a second, he could have sworn something that very nearly resembled disappointment flashed in her eyes, but then shutters dropped into place, concealing her thoughts. "We've already had this discussion," she said flatly, and stepped back to close the wooden door.

"Wait!" He reached for the screen door, but it was locked and he swore. "Dammit, Susannah, will you just listen to me for a second? I'm not making another offer to buy your land. We just want to lease it."

Her first instinct was to say no and shut the door in his face. But she hesitated, unable to stop herself. Try as she might, she hadn't been able to put Diego Kelly—and the man he reminded her of—out of her head. For the past four days, she'd found herself writing about Diego Kelly every time she sat down at her computer, and now she had no choice but to accept the fact that she was going to write a Western whether she wanted to or not.

Which meant she had a problem. She knew writers who hummed a few bars and faked it when it came to research, but she'd never been able to do that. In order to have plenty of authentic stories for her Ace MacKenzie books, she'd taken temporary jobs as everything from a gofer on an archaeological dig in Egypt—thanks to her mother's connections at SMU—to a grape picker in Napa Valley. And she would need that same type of experience to write a bestselling Western.

For the daughter of a rancher, that should have been a piece of cake. But her father hadn't believed in women getting involved in the workings of the ranch, so she knew next to nothing about cowboys or horses or anything else that had to do with ranching. Granted, Diego Kelly's story would take place a hundred years ago, but the life of a cowboy hadn't changed all that much in a century. The tools of his trade were still a good horse, a saddle and a rope, his workplace the endless miles of grazing land that stretched from Texas to Montana. To write with any degree of authority, she had to know how to saddle and ride a horse, how to rope, what it felt like to sit in the saddle in all kinds of weather. And she couldn't think of a better man to teach her than the man standing in front of her.

Making a snap decision she prayed she wouldn't regret, she reached over and unlocked the screen door. "Come on in, Cooper. I just might be willing to make you a deal."

Chapter 5

"**Y**ou want me to do *what?*"

Standing halfway across the room from where she sat on the lumpy couch in the living room, Cooper stared at her as if she had lost her mind. From the minute she'd abruptly changed her mind and asked him inside, he'd been as wary as a cat caught on a high wire in a strong wind. Now he knew why.

"You don't have to sound so shocked," she said, amusement softening her eyes to dove gray. "It's not like I'm asking you to rob a bank or anything. I told you I was a writer. I've decided to write a Western, so I need to know everything there is to know about cowboys. How they dress, work, play, think. And I figured you could teach me . . . if you want to lease my land."

He shot her a hard look. "That's blackmail."

She was in the driver's seat for the first time and apparently liked it. Grinning, she only shrugged. "I prefer to think of it as bribery. I have something you want and you have knowledge that I need. I'm willing to trade. What's wrong with that? We'll both be getting what we want."

What he wanted, he realized with a sudden fierce frown, was to jerk her into his arms and kiss that smug little grin off her tantalizing mouth. Digging his hands into the back pockets of his jeans, he clenched his teeth on an oath and stayed right where he was. "I thought writers did their research in libraries. Why can't you just get yourself some good books?"

"Because even the best books don't tell me everything I need to know," she explained patiently. "Like what it's like out on the range in all sorts of weather, and how a cowboy feels about his horse, how he takes care of it. You can teach me all that. And in return, I'll lease you some of my land."

Some of her land? he thought, glowering at her. She was dangling the offer before him like a Hershey's Kiss in front of a chocoholic who hadn't had a fix in a week, and he had to admit it was damn tempting. If they were going to grow crops in the spring, they needed more land, and they needed it soon.

But not this way, a voice in his head argued. He wanted all of her land, including the house, so she would have to leave. So he could finally sleep nights without dreaming of her. And he'd hardly accomplish that by accepting her deal. She wanted information, but it wasn't the kind he could just sit down and tell her off the top of his head over a couple of cups of coffee. Oh, no. If he was stupid enough to agree to this crazy deal, she would expect him to take her around the ranch, personally teach her about horses and cattle, bring her into the bunkhouse, onto the range so she could see how the hands worked together. Days, he thought with a scowl. She was talking days, possibly weeks.

"No."

He hadn't realized he'd spoken aloud until she straightened in surprise, obviously unable to believe she'd heard him correctly. "Don't get me wrong," he said. "I still want to lease your land, and I'll pay you a fair price for it. But I can't help you with your research."

He'd given her no excuses, just a flat no. "Well," she said, her breath escaping in a huff. "If you can't do it, you can't do it. I guess we've got nothing more to talk about." Rising to her feet, she started for the door. "I guess I'll just have to find someone else. There's bound to be a cowboy or rancher around here somewhere I can find to help me. After all, it's winter, and things are kind of slow right now from what I've seen. Maybe I'll talk to the mailman. I'm sure he can recommend someone since he probably knows just about everyone." Her hand on the doorhandle, she lifted an inquiring brow. "Unless you can," she said as he crossed the rug toward her. "You've lived here all your life. Do you know anyone who might be willing to help me? Maybe one of your brothers—"

His eyes sharpened to obsidian at that. With Josey's pregnancy and his regular duties as manager of the Double R, Gable wouldn't have time to mess with her. And Flynn...

An image of his younger brother's wickedly teasing smile flashed before Cooper's eyes, taunting him. Flynn was the biggest flirt in the world, and the ladies loved him for it. He'd take one look at Susannah and think he'd died and gone to heaven. He'd bend over backward to help her, and, in the process, charm the socks off her.

And for some reason, the very idea of his good-looking brother even smiling at her made him want to throw something. He wasn't jealous, he vowed, irritated at the mere suggestion. But she was here all alone, with no family or friends, and obviously vulnerable whether she wanted to admit it or not. Someone had to look out for her.

Why it had to be him, he couldn't for the life of him figure out.

Ignoring the door she held open for him, he frowned down at her. "Gable and Flynn have other things to do," he said without elaborating.

Undaunted, she persisted. "Then how about one of the Double R hands? Or a cowboy from another ranch? If you could just give me a name..."

Cooper thought of the cowboys he knew, good men who were as tough as the unforgiving land they called home, men who worked hard and played even harder. He could think of any number of them who would be only too happy to teach Susannah anything she wanted to learn. Over his dead body. "Sorry," he said with a shrug. "I can't think of a soul."

It was an out-and-out lie, and they both knew it. But Susannah only said lightly, "Then I guess I'll have to find someone of my own. While I'm doing that, would you like me to ask around and see if anyone is interested in leasing some of their land to you and your brothers? Since we couldn't come to terms, I imagine you'll have to look elsewhere. Unless, of course, you've decided to give up on diversifying altogether," she added, her sparkling eyes boldly meeting his. "It would be a shame to put your plans on hold just because you can't find any available land, but I guess these things happen. I'm sure you'll work something out."

His eyes caught on the mischievous curve of her mouth, and suddenly the craving that had been eating at him for far too long was a hot flame in his gut. Without a thought, he gave into it and reached for her.

The kiss was quick and hard and had been coming from the moment they'd met. He should have gotten her out of his system, then put the lady out of his arms. But she felt so right against him, and the taste of her—

He didn't want to let her go. Suddenly realizing his arms had tightened around her until she was molded to him from chest to hips, he jerked back, shaken. One look at her dazed expression and it was all he could do not to kiss her again.

Right then and there, he should have told her it wouldn't make or break the Double R if he and his brothers didn't get to plant this year. But just the thought of her approaching any randy cowboy she happened to come across and asking him for help made his blood boil. She'd do it, he thought grimly, and have no idea what kind of trouble she was inviting.

His eyes hard with promise, he reached out to cup her cheek in his palm, his thumb gently rubbing her lower lip. "If anyone is going to teach you, it's going to be me. Just remember—you asked for it."

The first thing Cooper decided she needed was a horse... one she could get to know, take care of and learn to trust. A cowboy's relationship with his horse could be as complicated as that with a woman, and the only way she would really understand it well enough to write about it was to buy one of her own. And Max Rafferty, the owner of the High Canyon Ranch, fifty miles to the east, had just what she needed. His grandchildren were all teenagers now and too experienced for the cow pony they'd all learned to ride on. Cooper thought it would be just perfect for Susannah. The only trouble was after the kiss they'd shared, he was feeling damn possessive, and he didn't want her anywhere near Max.

When he introduced the two, it was all he could do to remember Max was a friend. His skin tough and weathered, laugh lines at the corners of his eyes and mouth, Max was a big man—with broad shoulders and beefy arms—and looked more like a lumberjack than a rancher. He took one look at Susannah and grinned in delight.

"Well, hello, darlin'," he drawled, swallowing her offered hand whole in his and shooting Cooper a reproachful look. "When Cooper called last night to tell me he was bringing someone over to look at that old cow pony of mine, he didn't tell me it was a woman. Is there a man in your life, sweetheart?" he asked boldly, his green eyes twinkling. An out-and-out flirt, he didn't believe in wasting time. "If not, I'll tell you right up front I'm available."

Susannah laughed. Flashing her dimples at him, she carefully withdrew her hand. "Sorry. I'm not in the market for a man, just a horse."

"Hell," he swore good-naturedly. "And here I thought I was damn near irresistible."

Cooper snorted. "Shows how much you know," he said dryly, fighting the urge to step between Susannah and the other man. "I've been trying to tell you the truth for years, but you always were hardheaded. Face it, Rafferty, you just ain't got what it takes."

They'd been friends for years and had a habit of no holds barred kidding, but Max hadn't missed the jealousy that had flashed in Cooper's eyes the moment he'd taken Susannah's hand in his. Amused, he slapped him on the shoulder and immediately backed off. "You tall drink of water, you're just jealous because you're not as pretty as I am. C'mon, let's take a look at the pony."

He led them to the barn a hundred yards from the house. "I don't know if Cooper told you anything about her," he told Susannah as he stopped at a stall where a large black pony dozed in a corner. "But she's a good pony. Real gentle. My grandchildren loved her, but they all want something with a little more get-up-and-go." His eyes danced as he added, "Old Tiny's get-up-and-go got up and went a long time ago. Which is why she's so good for a beginner."

"How long since she's been ridden?" Cooper asked, his knowing eyes going expertly over the animal.

Max rubbed his square jaw, trying to remember. "Probably a couple of years. Like I said, the kids sorta lost interest in her, so she's gotten pretty fat and lazy. I probably ought to warn you she could be barn spoiled." His grin was unapologetic. "She's like the rest of us when we reach a certain age. She likes her creature comforts."

"Barn spoiled?" Susannah echoed. "What's that?"

"She comes back to the barn the first chance she gets," Cooper answered her, frowning. It wasn't a trait he wanted in Susannah's first mount. "I don't know, Max—"

A sudden whinny from the other barn cut through the air, and he turned to see a black and white horse stick his head over the top rail. Cooper's eyes lit up with interest. "Who's this?" he asked, heading for the other stall.

"Oh, no," Max said, hurrying after him. "You can't have Paintbrush, Cooper. He's one in a million, and he's not for sale."

Ignoring him, Cooper scratched the black and white paint between the eyes and studied him shrewdly. Fourteen and a half hands tall, dark eyes, wide front end and rear, black hooves, a gelding. Just what he was looking for. "Is he off the ranch?" he asked his friend without taking his gaze from the horse. "Do you work him?"

"Yes, but—"

"Is he gentle?"

"As a lamb," Max retorted in exasperation. "But he's not for sale."

Cooper shot him a narrow-eyed look as Susannah joined them. He watched her hesitantly greet the animal, who didn't shy away from her touch but only let out a huff of breath as he sniffed her hand. She smiled at the tickling sensation, and over her head, Cooper's gaze locked with Max's. "How much?" he demanded.

"Dammit to hell, Cooper, haven't you heard a word I've said? He's not for sale!"

"If you're afraid I won't take good care of him," Susannah said quietly, "you don't need to. Cooper has agreed to teach me everything I need to know."

"No, it isn't that—"

"Then let's make a deal," Cooper cut in quickly. "Name your price."

Max swore, a reluctant grin tugging at his mouth. "You Rawlingses are damn hardheaded," he grumbled. "I should have known better than to try to do business with you. You don't know how to take no for an answer." Glancing down at Susannah, he sighed in defeat. "If you've really got your heart set on having him, he's yours. But it's going to cost you."

The last in a long line of horse traders, there was nothing Max loved more than haggling with a prospective buyer. He drove a hard bargain, but when Susannah and Cooper left nearly an hour later, Paintbrush was in the horse trailer attached to the back of Cooper's pickup and Susannah was considerably lighter in the pocketbook. But Cooper could see from the look on her face that she didn't regret the deal. The moment the horse had blown a friendly greeting on her hand, he'd stolen her heart.

Sensing her smile as they raced down the highway toward her ranch, he gave her an inquisitive look. "I was just thinking about Max," she explained. "I liked him."

The announcement hardly surprised Cooper. He hadn't missed the way she and Max had taken to each other like long lost buddies. He should have been pleased—if Max hadn't liked her, there was no way he would have parted with Paintbrush—but every time she'd smiled at his friend in a way she'd never smiled at him, he'd had this urge to plant a fist right in Max's face. Jealous, he thought in amazement. Good God, he was jealous.

The realization shook him, more than he cared to admit, and suddenly keeping his tone light wasn't as easy as it should have been. "You knocked him out of his boots the minute he laid eyes on you. Though I guess you already know that. He made it pretty obvious he'd like to get to know you better."

His eyes back on the road, he spoke in an offhand manner, but Susannah heard the accusation he tried to hide. Suddenly the memory of a kiss they should never have shared was back between them, stronger than ever.

Her heart starting to pound, she clamped her teeth on the urge to explain that she hadn't taken Max seriously. She didn't owe him an explanation. "I haven't got time for a man in my life right now," she retorted easily. "Especially a cowboy."

That was the wrong thing to say to a man who sat beside her in jeans, boots and a cowboy hat that said as much about who he was as his signature. "What have you got against cowboys?" he demanded, scowling.

"They're chauvinistic, autocratic and domineering," she retorted without missing a beat. "Any woman with a streak of independence in her blood is a threat to them. I guess they're intimidated," she concluded, amusement curling up one corner of her mouth. "Which is why they treat most females like they don't have the sense to add two plus two correctly, let alone come in out of the rain."

Not the least intimidated by her, Cooper gave her a hard, suspicious look. "Are you talking about me?"

Her gray eyes, alight with the hidden laughter she rarely showed him, danced impishly. "I don't know, Coop. You tell me. Does the boot fit?"

He had to grin. The little witch made him take a good hard look at himself whether he wanted to or not. "I never treated you like you didn't have a brain in your head. Anyone that can manage to make a living as a writer is no idiot."

"Okay, so you do credit me with some sense," she conceded. "That still leaves chauvinistic, autocratic and domineering."

If she expected him to squirm, she was doomed to disappointment. Wickedness twinkling in the depths of his dark eyes, he shrugged, unperturbed. "I prefer to think of myself as strong, protective, masterful. You just have to look at it from the right point of view."

"Yours, I presume," she said dryly, the smile she couldn't hide contagious.

He grinned. "Exactly."

She laughed, she couldn't help herself. The man was a rogue. Just like Diego Kelly. The thought was a sobering one, and for just a moment, she wondered wildly what had ever possessed her to strike a bargain with him. She'd made a pact with the devil, a heart-stealing, good-looking devil who hopefully didn't have a clue that it took nothing more than a long look from those dark eyes of his to set her heart thumping crazily in her chest. God help her if he ever found out.

She told herself she could handle him, but later that afternoon, she wasn't so sure. He was showing her how to saddle Paintbrush, and before she knew it, they were both in the horse's stall in the barn, standing so close that she couldn't take a breath without dragging in the fresh, intoxicating scent of Cooper's after-shave. Cursing herself for letting him scramble her thoughts so easily, she forced herself to concentrate all her attention on his quiet instructions.

"Whenever you're going to saddle him, get his halter on him first—like this—" he showed her "—then tie him so he can't get away from you. Not that he's going to try anything," he assured her. "He's used to being ridden, and Max wouldn't have sold him to you if he hadn't thought you could handle him. And I certainly wouldn't have let you buy him if I'd had any doubts about him."

She gave him a speaking glance. "You wouldn't have let me buy him? Do I file that under masterfulness or protectiveness?" she taunted sweetly, reminding him of their conversation during the ride back from Max's. "From where I'm standing, it sounds an awful lot like arrogance."

The quick flash of his grin told her she'd scored a direct hit, but he had no intention of admitting it. "Brush him down before you put the saddle blanket on him," he continued smoothly as he suited his actions to his words. "Then the saddle. You flank up the front girth first," he told her, tightening the strap under the horse's belly, "so the saddle just moves a little. See?"

Before he had time to think about it, he automatically moved her in front of him and placed her hand at the back of the saddle, under his, to show her how the saddle would only give a little. Too close. She was too close. The thought slammed into him like a sledgehammer at the precise moment he felt her stiffen, her fingers curling under his. The fresh, tantalizing scent of her teased his senses and sent an all-too-familiar heat coiling into his gut. The lesson forgotten, all he could think of was getting her out of that stall and carrying her up to the loft, where the hay was clean and soft and inviting. He wanted to see her there, in the muted light that seeped through the cracks of the barn, her hair dark against the hay, her eyes smoky with desire, her body bare—

Suddenly realizing where his thoughts had wandered, he jerked himself up sharply. What the hell was he doing? He wanted her—he could hardly deny it when his blood was already hot for her. But if he touched her now, he didn't think he'd ever be able to let go. And that scared the hell out of him. He was thinking long-term about a woman who had no use for cowboys.

Swallowing, he tightened his fingers over hers and barely moved the saddle. "See?" he said in a voice that was hoarse, thick, revealing.

Susannah nodded, unable to manage a word. Caught between him and Paintbrush, his heat surrounded her as his breath caressed the nape of her neck in moist, hot puffs that drove every ounce of air from her lungs. Suddenly her heart was slamming in an uneven rhythm against her ribs, her palms were damp, and the starch in her knees felt as if it was going to give out at any moment. She'd never wanted to turn to a man so badly in her life.

But she didn't. Staring blindly at the horse, she choked, "Y-yes. Now what?"

He didn't answer, and for one long, heart-stopping second, she found herself holding her breath, half-expecting him to tell her that what came next had nothing to do with lessons on saddling a horse. His chest just brushing her back, his fingers covering hers in a grip that suddenly tightened, she could almost feel the struggle going on in him, a tense battle that sent her pulse leaping. The thunder of her racing pulse echoing in her ears, she waited, but then he moved away from her abruptly, releasing her to finish adjusting the saddle.

"You hook up the back girth," he said tightly. "Then the chest harness."

All his attention focused on Paintbrush, he continued with the lesson in a carefully controlled voice, having her repeat his instructions, then saddle the horse herself. He hovered close enough to help her if she needed him to, but he didn't once look her in the eye. And he made sure he didn't touch her again.

He didn't hang around after the lesson. With a promise to come back the following afternoon for her first riding lesson, he drove away like a man who was running for his life. Susannah knew she should have been relieved. But as she watched his truck barreling down her graveled drive to the highway, she was forced to admit that she'd wanted him to continue touching her so badly she still ached from the disappointment that had flooded her when he'd turned away.

Panic skittered through her at the thought. She had to find someone else to help her with her research, she decided, hugging herself. She had no other choice. Because she had a horrible feeling that if she didn't do something soon, she was going to make a complete fool of herself over Cooper Rawlings, and that was something she was determined not to do.

The only problem was she didn't know anyone else who might be willing to teach a greenhorn the things she needed to know for her book. Hours later, she was still racking her brains for a likely name from the few people she'd met since she'd returned to the ranch when she heard a car pull up in front of the house. Frowning, she opened the front door and watched a young woman who wasn't much older than herself step out of an old yellow Jeep. Catching sight of Susannah watching her from behind the screen door, she smiled easily and hurried up the steps.

"Hi, you must be Susannah. I'm Josey Rawlings... Gable's wife," she added, her smile stretching into a grin when Susannah's eyes widened in surprise. "I know I should have called first, but I was on my way home from town and thought it was about time I stopped by and welcomed you to the neighborhood. When I moved here from Boston, there were times I felt like I'd stepped off the edge of the earth, and days I didn't see anyone but the mailman. I know what it's like to need someone to talk to."

"You're from Boston?" Susannah asked, surprised. "I just assumed—"

"That all the Rawlingses had been here since the beginning of time?" she finished for her, her green eyes twinkling. "The rest of them have. I'm the lone Yankee in the family. May I come in?"

Susannah blushed. "Oh . . . of course!" She pushed open the screen door. "Please, sit down. Can I get you some tea? A soda?"

"Not this time," Josey said, settling on the couch. "I can't stay long. I've been at the clinic all day and Gable's probably worried sick by now...." She could see the questions hovering on Susannah's tongue and explained, "I'm pregnant, and Gable's as protective as a mother hen. He's got this crazy idea that a pregnant woman can't work."

"You work?"

"I'm a doctor." She chuckled. "The only one for forty miles."

Susannah couldn't hide her amazement. She'd just assumed from Cooper's penchant to take over that his brothers would be just as dictatorial. Yet Gable's wife was a professional woman! Fascinated, she sank down into the chair opposite Josey. "And your husband doesn't mind?"

Josey's lips twitched. "Obviously Cooper's been throwing his weight around. All the Rawlings men do," she confided. "Gable was worse than Cooper and Flynn combined."

"But he's not now?"

"Of course he is," she replied, laughing. "But now he's got me to keep him in line. From the moment he laid eyes on me, the poor guy didn't know what hit him."

Grinning, Susannah said shrewdly, "And you're crazy about him."

"Absolutely nuts," Josey agreed without hesitation. "He's the best thing that ever happened to me. Why don't you come to supper tomorrow night and meet him for yourself? And the rest of the family, too, of course. Kat's gone back to college in Santa Fe, but Flynn will be there. And Cooper, of course."

The invitation came from out of the blue and caught Susannah with her mouth open. "Oh, I don't know—"

"I know it's last-minute notice," Josey said quickly. "I should have called sooner, but this is a sort of spur-of-the-moment thing...a small dinner with just a few neighbors and friends. Nothing fancy. I hope you'll come."

Susannah hesitated. She couldn't, she warned herself. In spite of all her best efforts, Cooper was becoming too important to her. Socializing with him and his family could be nothing but a mistake. "I appreciate you asking me," she began.

Sensing a "but" coming, Josey had no intention of accepting it. "Cooper told me you're a writer, and there'll be several people there who'll bend your ear with stories," she wheedled. "It's going to be fun."

Susannah's lips twitched. "That's dirty pool. How am I supposed to turn you down when you make it sound so tempting?"

"That's the whole point," Josey said, chuckling. "You're not!"

Knowing when she was beaten, Susannah graciously gave in. "Then I guess I can't. What time should I be there?"

* * *

The following evening, Cooper sat at the opposite end of the table from where Susannah sat next to Flynn. He still couldn't believe that Josey had not only organized another dinner party, but had invited Susannah. When she'd come home yesterday and told him what she'd done, he'd hotly denied he was interested in the woman and told his sister-in-law if she'd arranged the dinner for his benefit, she could just cancel the whole damn thing. Instead, Josey had taken him at his word that he wanted nothing to do with Susannah and had invited a slew of other females that she hoped might catch his interest. She might as well have saved herself the trouble. He couldn't take his eyes off Susannah and Flynn.

"I was just thrilled when Josey invited me tonight," the woman seated to his right murmured, leaning toward him with a slow, suggestive smile. "I've been wanting to meet you for ages."

Cooper dragged his eyes from Susannah to the blonde who had been flirting with him ever since she found herself seated next to him at the table. What was her name? he thought with a frown. Jennifer Something-or-Other. She was pretty, petite and not the least bit shy. Five minutes after she'd sat down, she'd rubbed her foot against his and smiled invitingly into his eyes.

And all he'd felt was irritation...with her boldness, with her damn agreeableness—she was so pleasant it set his teeth on edge!—and with the fact that his attention kept wandering to the other end of the table...to Susannah. Unlike Jennifer Whatever-Her-Name-Was, she could never be accused of pandering to his ego. If anything, she delighted in confronting him.

And that was what he wanted in a woman.

The thought staggered him. Dazed, he mumbled what he hoped was an appropriate reply to the woman at his side and tried to convince himself that he was mistaken. He was just getting caught up in Josey's matchmaking schemes—it was the only logical explanation. He wasn't looking for a relationship with anyone...especially with a woman like Susannah.

So why, then, did he feel like throwing something every time she smiled at Flynn as if his baby brother was the greatest thing since sliced bread?

Disturbed by his thoughts, he escaped to the study just as soon as the meal was over and joined the neighboring ranchers who were discussing the latest decline in beef prices with Gable. The discussion was hot and heavy, but it couldn't hold his interest. From the living room, he heard Susannah laugh, and without being aware of what he was doing, he stepped to the doorway. The room was crowded, but he found her immediately, standing in the far corner, grinning up at Flynn. Jealousy, like a double-edged knife, stabbed him in the gut.

"You've been giving poor Flynn dirty looks ever since we sat down to supper," Gable murmured teasingly as he joined him and noted the direction of his gaze. "He's just being nice to the lady." At Cooper's snort, the laughter dancing in Gable's eyes tugged his mouth into a slow grin. "I wish you could see yourself. Better watch it, little brother. You've got it bad."

"The hell I do. I just hate to see Flynn making a fool of himself over Patterson's daughter."

Gable only chuckled. "Oh, really? And here I thought you might be interested in the lady. Guess I was wrong."

With an effort that cost him more than he liked, he turned his back on the couple in the living room and met Gable's amused gaze head on. "I couldn't care less what Susannah

Patterson does . . . or who she does it with. If she and Flynn hit it off, more power to them. We didn't.''

Gable only nodded, but Cooper wasn't fooled. From the glint in his brother's eyes, it was obvious he knew he was lying through his teeth.

Chapter 6

He was looking for a wife.

Still reeling from that interesting bit of information, Susannah stood off to the side and watched a blonde named Jennifer Something-or-Other glide up to Cooper and take his arm possessively. The figure-hugging dress she wore should have carried a warning label, Susannah thought cattily. The woman was obviously a barracuda on the prowl, and Cooper didn't have the sense to see that he was her next meal.

Of course, the short-skirted blonde might be just what he was looking for, Susannah thought sourly. Over dinner, Flynn had filled her ears with stories of Cooper's restlessness and how Josey had figured out that he needed a wife. Supposedly, he'd disagreed with her, but that hadn't stopped his sister-in-law from arranging a series of parties and dinners to introduce him to every eligible female within a hundred-mile radius.

And for a man who claimed not to be interested, he certainly seemed to be enjoying himself. He had a half dozen women tripping over themselves to get his attention, and the hot little Jennifer was plastered to his side like wet newspaper. He should have been trying to untangle himself from her clinging touch; instead he gave her a slow smile that only encouraged her. Susannah huffed irritably. If that wasn't just like a man!

Annoyed that she'd even noticed, she told herself she didn't care what he did as long as he didn't get any ideas about her. She wasn't looking for a cowboy husband, especially one with the Rawlings name. God, she had to get out of here!

Weaving her way through the crowd, she reached Josey's side and thanked her for inviting her. "Oh, surely you don't have to leave so early," the other woman objected. "We've hardly had time to talk, and Cooper—"

"Won't even notice that I've gone," Susannah finished for her dryly, smiling. "He's already got every female here drooling over him. He certainly doesn't need me."

Studying her shrewdly, Josey didn't miss the flare of jealousy that smoked in Susannah's eyes before it was ruthlessly suppressed—or the pride that kept her smile steady. She wanted to tell her she was wrong—she was exactly what Cooper needed—but that was something Susannah would have to discover for herself.

Keeping that thought to herself, she gracefully accepted her excuses for leaving early. "I'll call you tomorrow. Maybe we can have lunch together."

Susannah agreed, but as she slipped outside and made her way to her car, she knew she wouldn't be having lunch with Josey. She liked her and the rest of the family too much already, but she couldn't be friends with them. She'd seen the way they watched her and Cooper, the speculation they hadn't been able to hide, and it wouldn't do to let them get any matchmaking ideas. She and Cooper might strike sparks off each other every time their eyes clashed, but she was only here for a short time before the demands of her career dragged her away. And he was a cowboy who would want the woman in his life close at hand. There could be no future for them.

Her hands tight on the steering wheel, she turned onto the highway, leaving the Double R—and Cooper—far behind her. It was for the best, she told herself, determinedly ignoring the creeping loneliness that left a hollow feeling in her stomach. Far in the distance, she saw the porch light she'd left on burning like a beacon in the night, guiding her home. Her throat tight, she raced toward it.

Within minutes, she was pulling up in her yard, her mind already jumping ahead to the attic and the trunks she had yet to go through. She would check them out tonight, lose herself in them and forget all about Cooper and the need that sometimes hit her in the dark of the night, the need just to be held. . . .

Hastily pushing the traitorous longing aside, she hurried inside, only to stop abruptly in the dark. The house was quiet as a tomb, the silence humming in her ears. She'd left the porch light on, but the rest of the house was bathed in the blackness of the night. Hugging herself, she told herself that everything was perfectly normal. But a sudden chill brushed over her skin, dragging goose bumps behind it. Her eyes wide, she frantically searched the shadowed corners of the living room. Nothing moved.

Someone had been here. She could almost feel their intrusion into her space.

The thought slipped out of the blackness engulfing her and grabbed her by the throat. No! she wanted to scream. Her imagination was playing tricks on her, that was all. The front door had been locked, and even if it hadn't been, no one could have gotten near the house without Sammy taking a chunk out of them—

She froze at the thought, her blood suddenly running cold. From the day Cooper had left the shepherd with her, he'd always been there to greet her whenever she came home. Until tonight.

"Oh, God!" The hoarse whisper escaped before she could stop it and sounded like a shout in the darkness. Her heart slamming against her ribs, she caught her breath, listening. But the house was as still as an abandoned church. Only her ragged breathing disturbed the quiet of the night.

She never knew how long she stood there, the pounding of her heart echoing in her ears, before she blindly stumbled in the dark to the fireplace. With unerring accuracy, her fingers closed around a poker. Only then did she turn on a light.

Blinking, she saw in an instant that the living room was boringly normal. The windows were all closed, the drapes shut, the furniture in its usual place. Everything was just as it had been earlier, right down to the old newspaper clippings she'd brought down from the attic that afternoon and left on top of the coffee table.

If a prowler had been there, he'd found nothing to interest him in the living room...which left the rest of the house to check. Her heart almost stopped at the thought. She was not Ace MacKenzie, she reminded herself. She didn't go brashly chasing off into the night after bad guys. But she wasn't a scared rabbit who jumped at shadows, either. If she went running for help, only to discover the only intruder was her overactive imagination, she'd die of mortification.

The decision made, her fingers gripped the poker until the metal bit into her palms. Holding it like a baseball bat, she silently tiptoed to the open kitchen door and the darkness that waited just over the threshold for her.

Later, she didn't remember turning on the light. One minute she was staring at the opaque shadows beyond the doorway and the next she was staring in horror at what had only hours before been her neat kitchen. Her eyes huge in her suddenly bloodless face, she dropped the poker and didn't even blink.

The room looked as if it had been hit by a tornado. Pots and pans had been pulled from the cabinets, glasses and dishes thrown so that they'd shattered where they fell. The contents of the refrigerator were dumped on the floor, and there was broken glass everywhere. To top off the mess, there was a fine dusting of flour and sugar from the canisters over everything. But it was the message left in the middle of the floor that chilled her to the bone and left her standing in the doorway like a frozen statue.

LEAVE.

Written in ketchup that looked horrifyingly like blood, the single word was as threatening as a knife held to her throat. As she blindly reached for the wall phone just inside the kitchen door, her eyes never left the warning on the floor.

Cooper was cutting through the kitchen to the back porch and giving serious consideration to escaping to the barn when the phone rang. For a split second, he ignored it, rationalizing that someone else would get it. He had to get out of there before the women who had been circling him like buzzards figured out where he had slipped off to. Talk about aggressive! They were the worst bunch yet, and if Gable didn't have a serious talk with his wife about her matchmaking, he would! A man could only take so much—

The phone rang again, and from the chatter of female voices coming from the living room, it was obvious no one was going to hear anything. Grinding out a curse between his clenched teeth, he cast a quick glance over his shoulder to make sure no one had followed him and snatched up the phone. "Double R," he growled.

"C-Cooper?"

His dark brows snapped together at the shaky greeting that was hardly more than a whisper. "Susannah? Is that you?"

"Y-yes. I know y-you've probably still got company... but c-could you come over?"

Behind him, Flynn came into the kitchen, teasing him about the women who were looking for him, but all he heard was Susannah's hastily swallowed sob. Alarmed, he curtly motioned for his brother to be quiet and pressed the phone closer to his ear. "I can hardly hear you, honey. What's wrong?"

"The kitchen...someone's been in the k-kitchen."

Cooper's heart stopped in midbeat. "Is he still there?" he demanded, clutching at the phone. "Are you okay? Dammit, Susannah, answer me!"

"I'm okay, just scared. Whoever was here is g-gone...I think...but so is Sammy—"

"What do you mean he's gone? He wasn't there when you got home?"

"No. And I don't know what h-happened to him."

Cooper didn't need to hear more. "I'll be right there."

Slamming down the phone, he turned and almost plowed into Flynn, who had been listening to the one-sided conversation with a darkening frown. "What's wrong?"

"Someone was in Susannah's kitchen while she was over here for supper," he said, already heading for the door.

"Call the sheriff, will you? I'm getting my gun and going over there."

"I'll call him from her place," Flynn said, following Cooper to the gun cabinet in the study. "I'm going with you."

Sitting in her father's study, his unloaded revolver clutched in her sweaty palms and every light in the house blazing, Susannah heard Cooper the moment he braked his truck to a skidding stop in the drive. She jumped up, the gun forgotten in her hand, and hurried to the front door. Before she could reach it, he was pounding on it and yelling her name.

Her heart hammering, she fumbled with the dead bolt and finally managed to get it open. She stepped back and the door went flying.

Until then, she'd been so sure she was fine... scared, naturally, but in control. Then he was there, his eyes, dark with worry, meeting hers, his hands reaching for her, and suddenly she was shaking.

"Cooper." It was all she could manage, just his name. In the next instant, she was in his arms.

"You're shaking," he murmured huskily, dragging her closer. And so was he. He'd burned up the road getting to her, terrified that she was wrong, that the bastard terrorizing her was still there, waiting for her in the darkness. He could have lost her, he thought numbly, tightening his arms around her.

"It's okay, honey," he rasped against the soft cloud of her dark hair. "You're safe. No one's going to hurt you."

Her face buried against the soft sheepskin of his jacket, she nodded. "I know." But still, she couldn't quite control her trembling. "I w-was just so scared. The minute I stepped into the house, I—I knew he'd been here. I knew it! The kitchen—"

Over her head, Cooper's eyes met his brother's. Nodding at the unspoken message that passed between them, Flynn moved past them and headed for the kitchen. Five seconds later, his curse cut through the tense silence. "You'd better take a look at this, Coop," he called grimly. "Whoever did this wasn't playing around."

Susannah told herself she wasn't a coward. In her travels, she'd rushed in where angels feared to tread, but she wasn't ready to go back into the kitchen and face the destruction there. Pushing free of Cooper's arms, she stepped away. "Go on," she said tightly. "I don't need to see it again."

Swearing under his breath, Cooper wanted to snatch her back against him, then told himself not to be a fool. It was terror that had sent her rushing into his arms, nothing more. She wasn't a weak woman. Only seconds ago, she had been shaking with fear, but already she was coming to grips with it, fighting her lapse of control, drawing on that inner strength of hers that at times both infuriated and fascinated him and made him want to drag her close. She didn't need him.

Without a word, he stepped into the kitchen, only to stop short, the savage curse that rose to his tongue, short crude and furious. It was a disaster; there was no other way to describe it. The cabinet doors hung open drunkenly, and the contents from the shelves had been swept furiously to the floor. Rage. He could almost feel the anger of the man who had done this, smell the stench of it on the air, see it in the stark, uncompromising message spelled out in ketchup on the floor. No wonder Susannah had been scared out of her wits. This kind of destruction was the result of a fury that struck out blindly, destroying everything in its path. And for some reason it was directed squarely at Susannah.

And that, more than anything, was what worried him. She'd left here as a little girl and hadn't been back in almost twenty years. She'd only been home a couple of weeks and hadn't had time to make many friends, let alone an enemy. So who the hell was doing this to her? And why?

"C'mon," he told his brother tersely, turning back into the living room. "Let's check the rest of the house and the outbuildings. The bastard's probably long gone, but I don't want to take any chances."

"I'll take the upstairs," Flynn said, heading for the stairs. "Holler if you find anything."

Cooper moved to a door that opened off the living room, but before he could step into the next room, Susannah was behind him. "I'm going with you."

"That's not necessary—"

"Oh, yes it is," she argued. "This is my house, my things. If there are any more nasty little messages for me, I want to see them with my own two eyes."

Scowling, Cooper whirled, intending to tell her that was just exactly what he wanted to avoid. The memory of her clinging to him, pale, shaken and terrified, was one he wouldn't soon push from his thoughts, and he intended to do whatever it took to see that she didn't have to suffer that kind of fear again. Even if that meant protecting her from her own stubbornness.

But he took one look at her set face and had to reconsider. She was still too pale, but there were twin flags of hot color in her cheeks, and in her gray eyes there was a storm brewing that threatened to be a doozy. She glared at him, but Cooper knew it wasn't him she was angry with. No, her growing fury was solely directed at the man who had dared to violate her space and leave his mark on it. The bastard's biggest mistake, however, was daring to order her to leave. Orders were something she took from no man.

Unable to hold back a grin, he could only shake his head at her in reluctant admiration. "You're something else, you know that? You've just had your house trashed by a weirdo who'll evidently go to any lengths to scare you into leaving. Any other woman would be in tears, but not you. You're ready to fight."

"I don't like bullies," she said simply. "And any man who would sneak around in the dark to try and scare a woman isn't much of a man, is he?" Stepping around him, she pushed open the door to what had once been her mother's sewing room and motioned for him to precede her. "Be my guest."

Between the three of them, they searched the house from top to bottom, but as they'd expected, the intruder hadn't waited around to be caught. He was gone, and with him, any sign of how he had gotten into the house in the first place. Despite a thorough examination of every outside door and all the windows on the ground floor, there was no sign of a forced entry. And Sammy was still missing.

Standing outside in the cold night air, the floodlights illuminating every inch of the yard, Cooper stared out at the night that waited beyond the reach of the lights and knew in his gut the dog was in trouble. Otherwise he would have found a way to come running the minute he heard the pickup, just as he usually did.

Taking a flashlight from his truck, he told his brother, "Call Riley and tell him what's happened. While you're doing that, I'm going to look for Sammy. Susannah—"

"I'm going with you," she cut in, the stubborn set of her jaw telling him it was pointless to argue with her. "Let's go."

Armed with a flashlight, she walked boldly toward the darkness that surrounded the house and yard, but worry twisted her stomach in knots. She'd seen with her own eyes the viciousness of the man who had destroyed her kitchen. Someone with that kind of ugliness gripping his soul wouldn't have let a mere dog get in his way. Which meant Sammy was probably hurt... or worse. Cringing from the thought, she quickened her pace.

Twenty minutes later, they found him. At first, Susannah was sure she was mistaken. Sending the beam of her flashlight far out in front of her, she saw nothing but the desert at night, the stark outline of cactus, the eery, swaying limbs of scrub mesquite, sagebrush. Then, just when she was about to send the light in a different direction, she caught a glimpse of tan-and-black fur in what she'd mistaken for a mound of buffalo grass. Her heart froze in midbeat. In the next instant she was running.

"Oh, God, no! Please..."

Half-turned away from her, searching the area to his right, Cooper whirled to see her stumbling over the uneven ground to the dark pile of fur in the distance. Sammy. And he wasn't moving.

Before Susannah could drop to her knees in the dirt next to the still dog, Cooper was at her side. "Easy, honey, don't try to move him just yet. Hold the flashlight and let me check him over and see what's wrong."

Her eyes burning with tears that wouldn't fall, she struggled to hold the light steady. "Is he—"

No! Cooper wanted to thunder. But he couldn't be sure until he touched him. The pain of denial clutching his heart, he reached out and carefully laid his hand against Sammy's rib cage. At the feel of the dog's slow, shallow breathing, his breath rushed out in relief. "He's alive!"

"Oh, thank God!" She leaned over to brush trembling fingers over Sammy's soft fur. "What's wrong with him? He's so still."

"I think he's been drugged," Cooper replied, running his hands expertly over the dog but finding no sign of an injury. "But I can't be sure. We've got to get him to the vet." Handing her his flashlight, he hefted Sammy as easily as if he weighed no more than a feather and quickly headed back for the house.

Flynn came running the minute they stepped back into the yard and immediately hurried forward to help Cooper with the ninety-pound dog. "He's been drugged," Cooper huffed. "Let's get him in the truck so we can take him to the vet. Riley—"

"Was out of the office," Flynn said in disgust. "There's been another string of burglaries, and he's been hopscotching across the county all evening checking them out. Jacob said nobody can ever remember a crime spree like this around here. He can't leave the jail, and he doesn't know when Riley'll be able to get out here. Probably sometime tomorrow."

"Great. That's just great," Cooper ground out between clenched teeth, glancing over his shoulder to judge the distance to his truck. He would have said more, but there wasn't time. "Susannah, there's a blanket behind the cab seat on the driver's side. Get it, will you? Then spread it out in the back and let the tailgate down. Okay, Flynn, let's see if we can get him up there. Damn, he weighs a ton."

Panting and cursing, each cautioning the other to be careful, they finally managed to lay the comatose dog onto the hastily folded blanket Susannah had spread out on the bottom of the pickup's bed. Cooper took time only to make sure the dog was still breathing before he closed the tailgate and tossed his brother the keys. "Get him to Doc Taylor's place as fast as you can without jostling him too much."

Flynn automatically caught the keys one-handed. "What about Susannah? She can't stay here by herself and wait for the guy to come back and finish trashing her house. And there's no way Sammy's going to be in any shape to watch over her tonight. She needs to come home with us."

Startled, Susannah's heart skipped a beat. "Oh, I don't think so—"

Cooper turned on her before she could say another word. In the harsh glare of the floodlights, the frown furrowing his brow looked as if it had been carved by a hammer and chisel. "Flynn's right. You can't stay here alone. So you can either come home with us or I'm spending the night. The choice is yours."

Choice? She almost choked. What choice? If he was going to appoint himself her personal bodyguard, she'd never be able to sleep knowing he was within calling distance. Which meant she could either lie awake most of the night in her own house or his. What kind of choice was that?

Her mind made up, she shook her head. "I appreciate your help, but I couldn't impose on your family and I'm too old for a baby-sitter. I'll be fine."

"Impose!" Flynn echoed, his frown a carbon copy of his brother's. "What the hell are you talking about...impose?" He snorted. "Do you honestly think any of us could sleep tonight knowing you were here all by yourself and terrified? C'mon, Susannah, what kind of monsters do you think we are?"

"I'm not sure you want her to answer that," Cooper said dryly, his dark eyes locked with hers. "Well, what's it gonna be, sweetheart? My house or yours?"

She wanted to tell him not to call her sweetheart. She should have demanded that he quit giving her ultimatums. But when he looked at her like that, as if he could see into her very soul, her knees had an alarming tendency to weaken and she couldn't seem to catch her breath, let alone think straight. And that was just from a single probing look. If he stayed the night, and it was just the two of them in her house, in the darkness . . . alone together—

"Your house," she said abruptly in a voice she hardly recognized.

Thankfully, he didn't gloat, but he didn't have to. The mocking light in his eyes spoke louder than words. He knew she hadn't chosen to stay at the Double R because she was ready to bury the hatchet and make friends with his family. She just didn't want him in her house overnight, sleeping right down the hall from her bedroom.

Turning to his brother, he said, "Go ahead and take Sammy to Doc Taylor. We'll take Susannah's car back to the Double R as soon as she packs an overnight bag and locks up here."

Attending a dinner party at the Double R was one thing; spending the night there was another, Susannah discovered as Cooper showed her inside. She tried to distance herself from him both emotionally and physically, but that was nearly impossible when he held her overnight bag in one hand and rested the other at the back of her waist, his innocent touch branding her until she burned. Her heart thrumming, she quickly dredged up memories of her father and what Cooper and his brothers had done to him, but the resentment she hoped to shield her heart with simply wasn't there. Alarmed, she knew she was in trouble, but she was trapped by circumstances and there didn't seem to be anything she could do about it.

Bed, she thought desperately. If she could just escape to bed, put some space between them, *get some rest,* she'd be able to think more clearly.

Even though the dinner guests had all left, Josey and Gable were still awake and downstairs, ready to tease Cooper for sneaking away from his own dinner party without saying a word. But then they saw Susannah, pale and drawn, her overnight bag in Cooper's hand, and the party was forgotten. They rushed forward, their concern genuine, throwing questions at her.

By the time she and Cooper finished telling them about the trashing of her house, Flynn had returned with the news that Sammy was going to be all right, but Doc Taylor was keeping him overnight for observation. Consequently, it was nearly midnight before Cooper showed Susannah to the guest room upstairs.

He flipped on a bedside light, illuminating a room that might have looked the same at the turn of the century. Pink rosebud wallpaper covered the walls, and ivory lace sheers hung at the long Victorian windows, complementing the black-and-pink oval rag rug on the parquet floor. A carved oak dresser stood against one wall and a matching rocker took up a corner, but it was the bed that was the focal point of the room. Made of old polished brass, it was huge, beautiful and inviting, its predominantly pink patchwork quilt obviously handmade and well treasured.

"The private bath's through here," he said, setting her overnight bag on the bed and moving to a closed door that she'd assumed was a closet. Switching on the light in there as well, he checked to make sure there were plenty of towels, then turned to face her. "I think you'll find everything you need, but if not, just ask. My room's next door, and Flynn's is down from that. Gable and Josey are at the other end of the hall."

Still standing just inside the open hall door, the bed strategically placed between them, she digested the news that he would be right next door. She wouldn't be able to turn over without him hearing her. And neither would he.

Without any prompting at all, she was suddenly hit with images of him stretched out on a bed just on the other side of the wall, his dark hair tousled, his broad shoulders naked and tempting in the dark, his lean, hard body vulnerable in sleep in a way it never was in waking. A woman would only have to touch him—

"Susannah? Are you sure you're going to be okay in here by yourself?"

She blinked, jerking back to awareness in time to find him stepping toward her in concern, his brown eyes narrowed on her face. Hot color flooded her cheeks. "I'm fine," she said huskily. "Really. Just a little tired. After everything that's happened, I'm sure I'll drop off the minute my head touches the pillow."

Common sense told Cooper to take her at her word and get the hell out of there before he did something stupid . . . like take her into his arms and drag her down to the bed that was too damn close, too tempting. But something in her eyes held him where he was, something that set his blood heating and scrambled his brain and made him itch to reach for her.

"Susannah?"

Her name was barely a whisper on his lips, but it was loud enough, rough enough, to make her forget that they were standing in front of an open bedroom door and that a member of his family could walk by at any moment. Transfixed, her heart thumping, she couldn't have said which one of them moved, but suddenly he was so close that if she so much as swayed, she'd find herself in his arms. Like a deer caught in the beam of headlights, she held herself perfectly still. Even when his mouth slowly lowered to hers, she couldn't take the single step that would free her from the heat in his eyes.

Cooper wanted to believe he would have stopped if she'd given the slightest indication that she didn't want a kiss or anything else from him. But a heartbeat before his lips touched hers, she lifted her mouth to his, and he was lost. Murmuring her name, he gently took her sweetly parted lips.

Her mouth was hot, damp, enticing, and it was all he could do not to sink into her and sate himself on the taste of her. But somehow he managed to hang onto some remnant of his common sense. If he pulled her close and felt her softness molding to the contours of his hardness, he wouldn't let her go again tonight.

So he kept it short and light, his tongue softly coaxing, teasing, seducing. With another woman, it might have been enough. But not with Susannah. God, she made him ache!

When he finally lifted his head, Susannah felt like someone had tossed her in the middle of a whirlpool. Head spinning, her heart slamming against her ribs, she stared up at him with only one thought in her head. If he'd have drawn her against him then, he could have made her forget her own name.

But he didn't. Disappointment streaking through her, she found the strength to take a step back. "It's been a long day. I guess I'll turn in now."

As far as hints went, it wasn't very subtle. Something deep inside him ripped at the thought of leaving her just yet, but through the open door, he could hear his brother and sister-in-law coming up the stairs. Aching to haul her close and just hold her, he knew that was out of the question. Murmuring a quiet good night, he stepped into the hall and shut the door behind him.

Susannah didn't sleep very well, but then she didn't expect to. When she wasn't reliving the nightmare she'd walked into in her kitchen, she was dreaming about Cooper and a kiss that had been so incredibly sweet and tender that just the memory of it had her reaching for him in the night.

By the time the sun finally crept over the horizon at dawn, she knew accepting Cooper's hospitality was one of the biggest mistakes she'd ever made. Before, when she'd been on her own turf, she'd had a hard enough time fighting her attraction to him, but now she'd seen him in the home he'd grown up in, she'd watched him with his family, and she'd found out for herself how easy it was to lean on him. And that, more than anything, terrified her. Because she had always made it a point not to lean on any man. She'd seen how a man could mistake vulnerability for weakness, how easy it was for him to assume that his naturally superior strength gave him the right to dominate. And no man was going to dominate her the way her father had dominated her mother until she'd finally worked up the courage to walk away.

Throwing off the covers, she hurried to dress. She had to get out of here...away from the Double R, away from the Rawlingses, away from *him*...while she still could, while she still wanted to.

She would be safe at her place now that the sun was up, she reasoned as she pulled on jeans and a fuzzy red sweater, then soundlessly started down the stairs in her socks. Nothing ever happened during the day. Dropping down on the bottom step, she tugged on her Nikes, half-expecting to be discovered any moment. But the house was quiet as a tomb.

Relieved, she was almost to the front door when guilt slowed her steps. She couldn't just slip out without a word, not after the Rawlingses had opened their home to her and bent over backward to make her feel welcome. Not only was it rude, it was cowardly, and that was something she'd never allowed herself to be. Quietly pulling pencil and paper from her purse, she scribbled a hasty thank-you note. Seconds later, the note propped against a vase on the entrance table, she silently let herself out the front door.

She should have known, however, that she couldn't give Cooper the slip that easily. Within thirty minutes, he was stalking through her front door without knocking, the note she'd left clutched in his balled fist. Spying her at the kitchen door, he headed right for her, a scowl deepening the lines in his face until he fairly glowered at her.

Shaking the crushed note at her, he growled, "You want to tell me what the hell this is about? *Thank you for your hospitality,*" he mimicked. "What hospitality? You didn't even wait around for breakfast! And what are you doing with that broom?" he demanded, suddenly noting it and the dustpan she held. "Don't touch the kitchen until Riley has a chance to look at it. He needs all the clues he can get."

"Clues?" she echoed incredulously. "What clues? There's not a fingerprint or footprint anywhere."

"Maybe not, but you're going to leave it until Riley gets here."

It was the wrong thing to say. He knew it the minute he saw her eyes narrow, but spoiling for a fight himself, he didn't care. She couldn't be half as mad as he'd been when he'd discovered that infuriating little note of hers.

"You heard me," he growled, crossing to take the broom from her. From two feet away, his eyes bored into hers. "Why did you run away the minute the sun was up?"

"I didn't—"

"You did." His voice was soft and flat, accusing. With a single step, he eliminated half the distance between them and set the air humming. "You bolted like a skittish mare. I want to know why."

She stiffened, her heart starting to pound crazily. "There was no reason to stay."

"Not the day, no," he agreed, surprising her. "But you could have at least stuck around long enough for a cup of coffee. But you ran and I can't help wondering why." Unable to stop himself, he reached up to smooth the sleep tousled curls she hadn't even stopped to run a comb through. "If I didn't know you weren't afraid of just about anything, I would almost think you skipped out because of me," he murmured, his eyes trapping hers. "Is that it? Are you afraid of me? Of this...heat that sparks between us every time we get within touching distance?"

Held motionless by nothing more than the feel of his hand in her hair, she stared up at him, looking for the answer in his eyes. Oh, yes, she was afraid, she thought shakily. Afraid of what he could make her feel if she gave him the chance, what he could make her forget. And what he could make her want—the impossible.

But before she could decide if she was ready to make such an admission, let alone find the words, the sound of a car pulling up in front of the house drew their attention. They both glanced toward the still-open front door in time to see Riley Whitaker step out of his patrol car.

Feeling as if she'd just been granted a reprieve, Susannah almost wilted in relief. But the feeling didn't last long. When Cooper's eyes returned to hers, they were hard with promise. "Later," he said, and went to greet his friend.

Riley went over the kitchen with a fine-tooth comb, then moved outside to check the exterior of the house and the outbuildings. When he finished and returned to the porch, where Susannah and Cooper waited for him, his expression was a mixture of disgust and grimness.

"Nothing," he said flatly. "I couldn't find a damn thing. And that's what worries me. There were six burglaries in the county last night, and every one of them was just like this one...no forced entry, no fingerprints, no nothing."

"You think they're connected?" Cooper asked, surprised. "But nothing was taken here."

"I know," Riley said, exasperation lining his face. "It makes no sense, but there's just something about the whole setup that smells the same. And I don't like it. Whoever is doing this is one cool customer who knows how to cover his tracks."

Pushing his cowboy hat to the back of his head, he sighed in disgust and turned regretful to Susannah. "I hate like hell to tell you this, but my chances of catching this creep are slim to none unless I can catch him in the act. And that's not going to be easy to do when I'm understaffed and running all over the county after a damn burglar."

Susannah paled. "Are you saying I'm basically on my own?"

He grimaced, not liking the sound of that. "Not exactly. But I don't have the manpower to stick someone out here to watch your place until this nut shows himself. So for your own protection, you might consider getting a gun." He saw the objection forming on her tongue and held up a hand, stopping her. "I know. That's not what you want to hear. But if you don't want to do that, the only other suggestion I can make is that you take the message on your kitchen floor to heart."

She stiffened, outraged. Leave. He was telling her to leave. "No."

"That's what I thought you'd say," he said. "And I don't blame you. I wouldn't let someone drive me away from my home either." Shooting Cooper a glance that seemed to say "I tried," he went on, "I'll try to get out here as often as I can to check on you, and I'll leave word with Jacob to do the same thing when he's on duty, but for now, that's all I can do."

It wasn't much, but Susannah knew she couldn't blame Riley for a budget that didn't allow for around-the-clock protection just for her. "Thank you, Sheriff, for your help. I'll let you know if I have any more trouble."

In the silence that followed his leave-taking, the tension was back, stronger than ever. "You're not staying here alone," Cooper said flatly, "so don't even think about it. It's too dangerous."

Susannah couldn't have agreed more, but no man, especially a Rawlings, was going to come on her ranch and lay down the law like her father had. "You heard Riley. It could be weeks before he makes an arrest. There's no way I'm going to impose on your family that long."

She threw up that stubborn chin of hers, just daring him to argue with her, but he'd be damned if he'd give her the satisfaction. "You're not staying here alone," he repeated. The matter settled as far as he was concerned, he ignored the protest sputtering on her lips and stalked off to his truck before she could say another word.

Chapter 7

Susannah threw herself into the unenviable job of cleaning the kitchen, all the while muttering dire curses about stubborn, bossy men in general, and one in particular. He was some piece of work, she fumed, dragging the broom through the broken glass on the floor. Ordering her around as if he had every right in the world, telling her what she could and couldn't do, cavalierly assuming that she was going to fall right into line like some sort of raw recruit tripping all over herself to please a drill sergeant. Like hell!

Spurred on by the thought, she attacked the floor with renewed vigor, a contemplative light gleaming in her eyes. Just let him try to make her leave here, she steamed. Talk about having a fight on his hands. He wouldn't know what hit him!

By the time she finished setting the kitchen to rights, her temper had had hours to simmer, and she was ready to take on Cooper and whatever he could dish out. But when he appeared at her front door later that afternoon comfortably dressed in a plaid flannel shirt and old jeans that had been softened by countless washings, he was maddeningly calm and all business. "It looks like it's going to rain," he said by way of greeting the moment she opened the door. "Since I don't know how Paintbrush handles changes in the weather, the riding lesson's going to have to be postponed for some other day. We can start with roping instead. If you're ready, let's get started."

Without waiting for so much as a nod of agreement from her, he turned away and started down the porch steps. Standing in the doorway, Susannah didn't budge. This was never going to work. She'd known it after the first lesson, when he'd taught her how to groom and saddle Paintbrush and all she'd been able to think about was turning into his arms. Berating herself for not finding someone else to help her with her research, she knew there was no way she could go through another lesson. Especially since the heat he'd so boldly dared her to deny this morning had flared back to life, hotter than ever, the minute her eyes had just now met his through the screen.

"Problems?"

Glancing up from her thoughts, she found him watching her from the bottom step, that challenging half smile of his just daring her to run as she had run from him that morning. Irritated, she snapped her spine straight as a poker. She knew he was pushing her buttons, but like a trout going after a fly, she was helpless to do anything but rise to the bait.

"No, of course not," she replied smoothly, her expression as unruffled as his as she stepped out onto the porch. "I wasn't doing anything that can't be put off till later, so let's get started. What do I do?"

Until that moment, Cooper would have bet good money she was going to tell him to go to the devil, then slam the door in his face. Sassy woman, he thought, turning away as the grin he'd been trying to hold back broke free. When was he ever going to figure her out?

"Come down here and watch what I do," he told her as he strode to the middle of the front yard. "Then you can give it a try. And don't worry about trying to rope anything yet. Right now you're just trying to get used to the feel of the rope in your hands and get the basic moves down."

Taking up a position halfway between the porch and the barbed wire fence that formed the pasture boundary on the other side of the drive, he uncoiled the lariat and set the loop at the end of it spinning with the practiced rotation of his wrist. Then, with a grace and ease that stole Susannah's breath, he sent the loop circling over his head several turns before sending it flying. In the next instant, the loop dropped over a fence post as lightly as a bird landing in the top of a willow.

Glancing back over his shoulder at her, he sent her a devilish grin. "See? Nothing to it."

Caught in the trap of his wicked smile, Susannah felt her insides tilt precariously and hastily tore her gaze away from his. "Maybe not for you," she agreed, her eyes drifting past him to where the rope was looped over the cedar fence post and caught on the top row of barbed wire. "But you're talking to someone who can't hit the side of a barn with a Sherman tank, let alone a single fence post with a measly piece of rope. That *was* the fence post you were aiming for, wasn't it?"

"Yes," he said with a chuckle, flicking the loop free. Dragging it toward him, he expertly gathered the rope and held it out to her. "I told you not to worry about roping anything just yet. Here. Give it a try."

She looked at the lariat as if he held out a snake to her, sure she was about to make an utter fool of herself. But she was the one who had pushed for these lessons, and if she was going to write Diego Kelly's story with any degree of realism, she had to master the skills Cooper could teach her.

She took the rope gingerly and almost dropped it. "It's stiff," she said in surprise, her eyes flying to his.

"It has to be so the loop won't collapse on you when you throw it," he said. Moving to her side, he took her hand and moved it to the open knot, which the remainder of the rope was fed through to make a loop. "This is the honda. The loop can be made bigger or smaller by adjusting the main line through it. When you want to rope something, you hold the loop and mainline in your right hand—you are right-handed, aren't you?" At her nod, he continued, "The slack is coiled in your left hand and you let it out as you need it by letting rope slide through your thumb and index finger. Got it?"

Susannah stared at the simple rope loop in her right hand, the excess in her left, and had a feeling this wasn't going to be nearly as simple as Cooper made it sound. Glancing up at him, a whimsical smile playing about her mouth, she shrugged. "I guess we'll find out soon enough, won't we? Stand back and I'll give it a shot."

"Make sure you keep the honda about a fourth of the way down the loop for balance," he said, giving her room. "And don't worry if the loop collapses on you at first. Roping takes a lot of practice."

Taking him at his word, she didn't get discouraged when the loop dropped like a deflated balloon about her head and shoulders the first couple of times. She just made the adjustments he suggested and tried again. And again. Without success.

"This isn't working," she finally said in defeat, letting her tired right arm drop to her side. "Maybe this rope is too long for me. Or I'm too short. Or I'm just not cut out to be Annie Oakley."

"You just need to practice—"

"How?" she groaned. "My arm feels like it's turned to Jell-O. Face it, Cooper. All the practice in the world isn't going to do any good. I'm a wimp."

What she was was adorable. And he wanted her with a need that bordered on pain.

He wasn't a man who let his passions rule his head. During the long hours of the night, while he'd lain awake aching for her, he hadn't had to remind himself why, out of all the women in the world he could be attracted to, he couldn't have Susannah Patterson. Proud, prickly, stubborn as an old boot, she was her father's daughter. He knew all the reasons by heart; they just no longer seemed to matter. Like an alcoholic who couldn't resist the lure of a bar, there was no way he could continue to keep his distance.

Rising from the porch step where he'd retreated to watch her, he approached her with a suggestion that he'd had to bite back a half dozen times in the past hour. "You just haven't got the hang of it yet," he said. "Here, let me show you."

Instead of taking the lariat as she so obviously expected, he stepped around behind her so that he could guide her every movement. His touch angel-soft, he let his hands glide down her arms until they were covering hers. "Like this," he said quietly in her ear, and let his fingers speak wordlessly to hers as he showed her how to hold the rope.

The movement brought him close, and in the sudden stillness, he felt her soundless start of surprise, felt it ripple through her, through him. Touching her, wanting her, should have been as simple as giving in to a craving. But suddenly, without warning, the desire he'd been so sure he could control was a fire under the skin, burning hotly, and nothing was simple at all.

Any man with an iota of sense would have known he was in over his head and got the hell out of there. But his feet wouldn't obey the dictates of his mind, and instead of running, his fingers tightened around hers as his eyes swept over the sleek pageboy he suddenly itched to muss, the delicate skin of her nape he suddenly longed to kiss.

At the first touch of his lips on her neck, the ground seemed to shift beneath Susannah's feet. She gasped, and the rope she clutched like a lifeline slid out of fingers that were suddenly nerveless. Her senses reeling, she tried to remember the last man who had turned her boneless with nothing more than a brush of his lips, but she couldn't come up with a single name. Only Cooper.

It wasn't that she hadn't known desire before—her career and the hopping around that she'd done working odd jobs to gather material for her books hadn't left her much time for a social life, but she hadn't been a complete recluse, either. She'd had her share of hot and heavy dates. But this...this was something out of the realm of her experience, an ache that wouldn't go away, that dogged her footsteps every day and climbed into bed with her every night.

And he was going to make her acknowledge that, she thought, panicking as he turned her to face him. Her heart lurched at the intensity she saw in his eyes. He was going to kiss her, and he would know—they *both* would know—that she found it impossible to resist him.

"No!" she cried, her hands jerking up to his chest, holding him at a distance. "If you're looking for a wife, you can just look somewhere else. I'm not interested."

His gaze had been focused on her mouth, but at her words, his eyes snapped up to hers. "A wife?" he repeated, shocked. "Who the hell said I was looking for a wife?"

"Flynn. That's what last night's little dinner party was all about, wasn't it? A cattle call for all the available females in the area?"

Impatience flickered across his brow. "Flynn talks too much, and anyway, that was Josey's idea, not mine. She and Gable are head over heels about each other, and she wants the rest of the world to be as happy as she is."

She gave him a look that clearly said she knew malarkey when she heard it and she wasn't buying it. "And I suppose you just suffered through it like the good sport that you are?" She laughed without humor at her own blindness. "No wonder there were so many women there last night. And I never suspected a thing. But then, why would I? I'm not looking for a husband, and even if I was, it wouldn't be you."

She threw the words at him like a gauntlet, just daring him to pick them up, and for a minute, he was damn tempted. His ego stung, he merely lifted a brow at her, his lips twitching with amusement. "Why? Because I'm a Rawlings?"

She shrugged. "That's one reason. But mainly because I'm not attracted to you."

She saw something flare in his eyes, but he didn't stalk off as she'd expected. Instead, his eyes narrowed dangerously and his smile, just a teasing curl of his lips, turned wicked. Leaning closer, he lifted a hand to the flush burning in her hot cheeks. "Liar," he rasped softly.

She gave him a withering look. "The truth hurts, but you asked for it. Don't blame me because it isn't what you want to hear."

"Want me to prove it to you?"

"And bruise your ego even more?" she asked, arching a brow at him. "I don't think so."

"What's the matter?" he taunted, his breath a warm caress against her skin as he turned her face up to his. "You afraid we both might discover just who's telling the truth here?"

"No, of course not—"

"Good, because my ego can take anything you can dish out, sweetheart. Come here."

"No—"

But it was too late. His hands moved into her hair, holding her captive before him, and in the next instant his mouth covered hers. Slowly. Completely. Inexorably.

Hunger, longing, need. The emotions came at her from all sides, fast and furious, even as she told herself she couldn't, wouldn't, want this, want *him*. But she did. Dear God, had she ever known such need before? It swirled through her like lightning captured in a bottle, delighting her, terrifying her. Her head spinning, she almost cried out in protest. No! She couldn't let him get to her this easily.

As if he sensed the struggle going on in her, his hands gentled, his mouth softened. With the patience of a man who knew he had all the time in the world, he wooed and cajoled her, brushing his lips over hers, once, twice and then a third time. Molding her against his hard length, he wrapped her close, murmuring her name in a way no man had ever called to her before. Whisper-soft and hoarse, hungry, thick with a longing that seemed to stun him as much as it did her. Her heart, traitor that it was, slammed against her ribs in response.

Dazed, she melted against him even as she tried to remind herself that she'd wounded his ego and he had something to prove. But she couldn't think about that when his need was weakening her knees and starting a slow, hot burning in the very core of her. He needed her. This big, strong, tough cowboy actually *needed* her. The thought staggered her, and without a care to her own vulnerability, she hugged him close and blindly yielded, her mouth open and seeking beneath his.

It was a mistake. She knew it the minute his tongue tasted her in a lazy, thorough way that stole her breath, the second he groaned and dragged her hips against his. Desires she hadn't even known she had rushed through her like hot steam escaping from a break in a pipe, setting her aflame, swamping her with a hunger that threatened to consume her, making her ache so badly it scared her.

She was out of her league.

The thought came to her slowly, swimming up out of the thick, murky depths of passion, hammering at her reeling senses until it finally registered. Awareness returned with heart-jarring swiftness. Suddenly realizing that she was plastered to Cooper like a second skin, her mouth as hot and eager as his, she stiffened, her blood abruptly running cold. Dear God, what was she doing?

"No." Muffled against his lips, her first protest was embarrassingly weak before she finally managed the strength of will to jerk out of his arms. "No!" she cried again, shying away from him when he automatically reached for her. "You stay away from me! I don't want this."

As stunned as she, his breath sawing through his lungs, desire a burning knot in his gut, Cooper stared down at her as if he'd never seen her before. With just a kiss, she'd knocked him for a loop in a way no woman ever had, and his heart was still banging painfully from the experience . . . while she stood six feet away, defying him, daring him to touch her again.

A smart man would have taken the warning to heart and chalked up the experience as a mistake that wouldn't happen again. But he'd been on the other end of that kiss and he knew for a fact that, for a moment there, she'd been as lost to reason as he had. She'd wanted him, and he was half tempted to prove it to her again. But he had a feeling if he touched her now, she just might scratch his eyes out.

Pushing his cowboy hat to the back of his head, he gave her a long, steady look that saw right through her, all the way to her soul. "If you think I'm going to stand here and let you pretend that I was the only one who felt something just now, you can think again. You were just as caught up in the moment as I was."

Denying it would have been senseless—the most obtuse man couldn't have missed her response. Heat singeing her cheeks, her eyes met his defiantly. "So? It was just physical. It meant nothing."

If her eyes hadn't been smoky with the leftover residue of passion, he might have believed her, she was that convincing. But he'd felt the heat in her when he'd held her, tasted the fire in her when he'd kissed her, and she wasn't nearly as unaffected as she wanted him to believe. Unable to hold back a grin, he took a step toward her. "Just physical, huh? I wonder if you can say that and mean it when I'm touching you."

Alarmed, she gave him a look that just dared him to try. "Don't even think it."

"Then you'd better stay out of reach, sweetheart. Or you just might find yourself being kissed again."

"You wouldn't!"

He only grinned, enjoying her temper. "Watch me," he growled, his voice a husky taunt full of promise. "You just watch me."

It was a threat, pure and simple, tied with silken threads. And she wanted oh, so badly, to throw it back in his face and just dare him to try to kiss her when she didn't want to be kissed. But deep down inside, she knew he not only would dare to try, he would make her like it, too.

Heat blooming in her cheeks, she whirled, mortified, and headed for her front porch. "I've got better things to do with my time," she tossed back over her shoulder. "Go find yourself another woman to kiss. I'm busy."

She stormed inside and slammed the door behind her. But long after he'd driven away, she could still hear his chuckle ringing in her ears.

Concentrating on anything after that was impossible. His scent clung to her, his flavor lingered tantalizingly. Frustrated, she tried to lose herself in her writing, but Diego Kelly was trapped and waiting inside her computer, only too eager to remind her of his maddening alter ego. Muttering a curse, she reached for some of the research material she'd retrieved from one of the attic trunks and brought downstairs to study more thoroughly. But every time she started to read, the words began to blur and run together and she found her thoughts making a beeline straight for Cooper.

By the time the gray day faded into an even grayer evening, she was standing at the front windows, more disturbed than she wanted to admit. The rain that had threatened for hours was now a steady, quiet drizzle that had the eaves dripping and the night crying. She'd always found the sound of rain comforting, but now its soft murmur only reminded her that she was alone and, in spite of her best efforts to the contrary, still thinking of Cooper.

As if her thoughts had finally conjured him up, a green pickup splashed up her drive, the Double R logo clearly stamped on the passenger door. She didn't have to see the driver to know that it was Cooper. Her heart had started to pound the minute she'd spied the truck.

So he was back, she thought, her eyes narrowing. And no doubt expecting to just waltz back onto her property and take up where they had broken off earlier. Just let him try!

But instead of pulling up in front of the house as she expected, he passed right by the house and parked in front of the small cottage that had once been used by her father's ranch foreman. Surprised, she headed for the front door. What was he doing? The house was empty but for a few pieces of abandoned furniture, and hadn't been used in years. What possible reason could he have for going in there?

Frowning, she grabbed a jacket and umbrella and stepped out into the wet night. The yard was full of puddles, but she dodged them easily and reached the cottage only minutes after Cooper. The front door was still open, the early-evening air rushing uninvited over the threshold. Poking her head around the doorjamb, she stopped in her tracks at the sight of Cooper sweeping the small living room. "What are you doing?"

The broom looking impossibly small in his hands, he glanced up, not that surprised to see her. After the way she'd stormed into her house earlier, he'd known she'd still be spoiling for a fight the minute she saw him again. Which was fine with him, because he'd thought of nothing but her since he'd left her.

"Cleaning this place up," he retorted, returning his attention to his sweeping. "I'm going to be staying here for a while."

Susannah couldn't have been more shocked if he'd told her he was going to lasso the cottage, hook it up to his truck and pull it down. "You're going to do *what?*"

Over the top of the broom handle, his eyes locked with hers. "I told you this morning that you weren't staying here alone as long as the bastard who has been harassing you was on the loose. I meant it."

Shocked, Susannah could only stare at him. She'd been so busy trying to forget his kiss that she'd completely forgotten his high-handedness that morning after the sheriff left. And now he was back, prepared to take up residence less than a stone's throw from her house.

An outraged voice in her head screamed that the man couldn't move onto her ranch without so much as a by-your-leave. His arrogance was really too much, and it was high time that someone put him in his place.

But, her eyes locked on the uncompromising set of his jaw, she knew it wasn't going to be her. She would have never given him the satisfaction of admitting it, but she was glad he was there. Thanks to him, she'd managed to forget the man who was terrorizing her, but now that darkness had fallen, it would only be a matter of time before she found herself jumping at the slightest sound and looking for bogeymen in the dark. Knowing that Cooper was close enough to hear her if she yelled for help would go a long way toward easing her fears.

"Then I'll leave you to get settled in," she said quietly. "Good night."

Her easy compliance clearly caught him off guard, and he glanced up in surprise, his eyes searching hers and questioning what kind of game she was playing. But something in her expression must have reassured him because he only said, "Holler if you get scared. I'm a light sleeper—I'll hear you."

An image of him rushing to her rescue in the dead of night flashed before her, setting her pulse pounding. Her throat suddenly tight, she nodded, then whirled away and quickly walked back to her house, determined to forget him and his presence on her ranch. But all through the evening, she was very aware that she only had to call out for him to hear her, and at odd times she found herself wondering what he was doing to pass the time. When she finally went to bed, she didn't know how long she stood in the dark at her rain-splattered bedroom window, hugging herself and staring across the way at the blurred lights of the cottage.

All through the long night, there was never any question in Cooper's mind that he'd done the right thing by moving into the foreman's cottage. The coward who was bent on trying to drive Susannah away wouldn't be nearly so quick to make a move against her now that there was a man on her place to protect her. No, he'd done the right thing, he assured himself. She was safe, and that was all that mattered.

But knowing that didn't make it any easier to sleep.

After climbing out of bed for what seemed like the hundredth time to walk to the window and scowl at her dark, silent house, he could no longer avoid the truth. Her safety had been only one of the reasons he'd moved into the cottage. The other—the *main* reason—was because he couldn't stay away from her.

The knowledge vibrated through him like an earthquake, shaking him. Wanting her so badly he ached for her was one thing. Not being able to stay away was something else entirely. He was getting dangerously close to needing her, and a man didn't just blindly rush into that without any thought of his own self-preservation.

Too fast. He was getting involved too fast, starting to care too much, and moving onto her ranch wasn't going to help matters. But leaving was out of the question as long as she was in danger. Which meant he had to find a way to handle being so close to her night and day without completely losing his head, he decided, turning away from the window. Time. He needed some time to think.

By dawn, he'd come up with a plan. The land she had leased him and his brothers had sat empty and unworked for two years, and there were fences to check, windmills to repair, wells to be inspected for possible irrigation use, pastures to be prepared for spring planting. With so much to do, he could easily steer clear of Susannah for hours at a time. He didn't, however, plan to leave her there all day unprotected. So at first light, he drove back to the Double R for his shotgun and Sammy, who had completely recovered from the drugging he'd suffered.

When he returned an hour later, after having breakfast with the family and telling them of the work he planned to do on the newly leased land, the sun was shining, the sky was clear and Susannah was hanging a load of freshly washed laundry on the lines behind the house. At the sight of Sammy running to greet her, his busy tail wagging in excitement, she dropped her clothespins and bent to her knees to give him a tight hug, laughing as he squirmed and licked her cheek.

"Silly dog! What are you doing here? Are you okay? I was afraid I'd seen the last of you."

"He's pretty tough," Cooper said quietly. "The vet said he's good as new. So he's going to stay and keep you company while I'm working around the ranch."

At the sound of his voice, her traitorous heart leapt and her arms automatically tightened around Sammy before she forced herself to let him go and glanced up at the man who had spent the night tramping through her dreams. He stood twenty feet away, watching her with shuttered eyes, his face drawn in stern lines, a rifle comfortably held in his hand, the barrel pointed at the ground. Her eyes searched his for a flicker of the heat that had sizzled between them yesterday when he'd kissed her, but if it was there, it was safely hidden.

Pushing slowly to her feet, she faced him, her mouth as unsmiling as his. "Are you sure you want to leave him? If something happened to him a second time, I'd never forgive myself."

"All the attacks have come at night, and I'll be back long before dark," he assured her. "But there's no use taking any chances. I'm leaving you my shotgun, too. Have you ever used one before?"

"No."

Cooper almost laughed at the irony of the situation. Great. Just what he needed . . . something else to teach her. The memory of the last lesson he'd given her suddenly throbbing between them, heating the air until it seemed to singe his lungs, he said tersely, "It's not difficult. Once you know how to load it, you just point it and pull the trigger. You don't need to be a good shot. With buckshot in it, you'll hit anything in front of you."

Keeping his distance, he told her everything she needed to know without once touching her. Only then did he hold out the weapon to her, making sure it was safely pointed away from them both. "That's it," he said in obvious relief. "Keep it by the front door and don't hesitate to use it if you need to. If you need me, just fire it into the air. I should be close enough to hear you. Okay?"

Her throat dry, Susannah nodded. She'd really have to be terrified in order to deliberately shoot someone, but she had no intention of telling Cooper that. Carefully taking the rifle, she forced a smile. "I'm sure I'll be fine. There's no reason for you to worry."

It was an obvious dismissal, but now that he had a clear conscience about leaving her alone for a while, Cooper hesitated, torn. She was armed with a loaded shotgun and a German shepherd who wouldn't hesitate to take off the leg of anyone who tried to harm her. There was no reason to worry about her.

But he couldn't shake the image of her ashen face when she'd run into his arms after coming home alone to her vandalized kitchen.

Before he could make himself walk away, he found himself moving toward her. With a will of its own, his hand rose to her cheek, and in her eyes, he saw the memory of the promise he'd made to kiss her again if she got within reach. So she had not forgotten. Neither had he. "I'll be back in a little while," he said gruffly, and headed for his truck.

For two days, they managed to coexist without saying a word to each other. Over the course of each day, Cooper came back to the foreman's cottage several times—probably to make sure she was okay—and in the evenings he was always back well before dark. Each time she heard his truck and Sammy's familiar bark of greeting, Susannah went to the door and waved to him across the yard just as if they were the best of friends. They weren't.

Watching him from a distance, seeing him but having no contact with him, Susannah knew things couldn't continue as they had. She was too vulnerable where he was concerned, too susceptible. Days had passed since he'd kissed her, but the memory, instead of fading as it should have, was stronger than ever.

There could be no more lessons, she decided. Of any kind. She'd find someone else to help her with the rest of her research, someone who wouldn't keep her awake nights longing for something she couldn't have.

So on the third night after Cooper had moved into the cottage, she called Flynn and explained what she needed. "Do you think you could arrange for me to visit the bunkhouse at the Double R?"

"Well, sure," he said, surprised. "But I thought Cooper was helping you with your research."

Not surprised that Flynn knew of her and Cooper's agreement, she replied, "He was, but he's been working so hard getting ready for spring planting that I hate to ask for any more of his help. When do you think we could do this?''

"How about tomorrow night?" he suggested. "The boys have a hot poker game lined up, and I was thinking about joining them. I'll pick you up. Oh, and bring your pennies and they'll deal you in, too. The more, the better."

For the first time in days, Susannah laughed. "It sounds like fun. I'll be ready."

Chapter 8

"I hate to do this to you, boys, but I do believe four of a kind beats a straight, doesn't it? Which means I win... again."

Red, who hadn't been a boy since long before Susannah was born, threw down his cards in disgust, a mock frown deepening the road map of lines carving his grizzled face. "Damn," he began, only to swear under his breath and change the good-natured curse to, "Dadblame it, if you ain't got the devil's own luck, girl, then I don't know who does. Where'd you learn to play poker like a cardsharp?"

"A cargo ship headed for Africa." Susannah chuckled, grinning into his twinkling blue eyes. "Only we didn't play for pennies."

"That figures," drawled Shag. A big lumberjack of a man with a head of fuzzy blond hair in desperate need of a trim, he tossed down his cards and leaned back precariously in his chair with total disregard for his balance, a slow smile cracking his usually deadpan features. "Don't surprise me at all that any man crazy enough to get that far from dry land would lose everything but his shorts to you. Did you end up owning the ship by the time you docked?''

"Not quite." Her own eyes dancing, she gathered in the pile of pennies in the middle of the scarred wooden table. "Just cargo."

"You ought to go to Vegas," Mike, the youngest of the Double R cowboys, told her, collecting the cards for his shuffle. "You'd clean up."

"Vegas, hell," one of the others spit out good-naturedly. "She's cleaning up here!"

Laughter echoed off the bare walls of the bunkhouse, the cowboys' teasing gibes flying back and forth across the table. Standing unnoticed in the doorway, his mouth compressed, Cooper narrowed his eyes as he surveyed the scene before him. When he'd seen Susannah leave her place with Flynn, jealousy, like an arrow shot out of the darkness, had nailed him right between the eyes, infuriating him. She wouldn't have accepted a date with his brother, he'd told himself fiercely. And dammit, Flynn wouldn't have asked her out—not after the way he'd teased Cooper about being infatuated with the woman. He might be a flirt, but he didn't horn in on another man's territory, especially his own brother's.

Not even asking himself when he'd come to think of Susannah as his, he'd jumped in his truck and followed them at a safe distance, reasoning that he was just going to see where they were going. He'd had every intention of returning to the Patterson place just as soon as he'd satisfied his curiosity, but then Flynn had returned to the Double R and pulled up before the bunkhouse, and he'd known exactly what was going on. She had finagled Flynn into helping her with the rest of her research.

Long after they'd gone inside, he'd sat in his truck arguing with himself. For the past two days, he'd worked his fingers to the bone avoiding her, telling himself that it was for the best. He needed time for his head to clear and his blood to settle, and he ought to be thanking his lucky stars that Flynn had taken her off his hands. Instead, all he could think of was that they'd made a deal, and that deal didn't include Flynn. Anger pulled at him. Any thought of leaving without Susannah had died a swift death.

Now, standing in the doorway, watching her joke and cut up with his brother and the ranch hands, he was forced to face the truth. It didn't matter that once again he was playing knight to a woman who needed someone, anyone, to come charging to her rescue. It didn't matter who her daddy was. She was as relaxed with the Double R ranch hands as Kat was and they liked her in spite of the fact that she was fleecing them but good. And dammit, so did he. Liking, in fact, didn't even come close to what he felt for her.

He'd always prided himself on being a reasonable, civilized man, but right now every instinct he possessed was urging him to storm over to her like a caveman, throw her over his shoulder and drag her out of there while he still had the element of surprise on his side. Crazy, he thought, unable to take his eyes away from her teasing grin. The woman was making him crazy.

Drawn to her like an addict to a fix, he stepped farther into the bunkhouse. "Is this a private game or can anyone join?"

"Hey, Coop," Flynn greeted him with a wide grin. "Come on in. Maybe you can figure out a way to stop Susannah before she robs us blind."

The others greeted Cooper like a long lost friend, calling out teasing comments to him and making room for him at the table without a moment's hesitation, as if it wasn't at all unusual for the Rawlings brothers to sit in on an occasional game of poker with their own ranch hands. Watching him slap some of them on the shoulder and grin at their jokes, Susannah felt emotion clutch her heart and tried to convince herself that it wasn't guilt. If she wanted to continue her research without his help, that was her business. He had no right to look at her as if she'd just stabbed him in the back.

But as she slapped the deck of cards down on the table in front of him, her gaze couldn't quite meet his. "Your deal, *Coop*."

By the time the game broke up hours later, it was well past midnight. Susannah—along with everyone else—had lost a sizable number of her pennies to Cooper, and she had more than enough information from the storytelling cowboys to write ten books. She couldn't remember the last time she'd laughed so much . . . or so thoroughly enjoyed herself.

"Thanks, guys, for letting me join the game," she told them as she pushed away from the table and retrieved her jacket from the row of pegs by the door. "It was fun."

"Aw, you're just saying that 'cause you're walking away with enough of our money to start your own mint," Red retorted, his blue eyes crinkling at her. "Give us a chance to win our money back, and you can join us anytime."

"You got a deal." She chuckled. Seeing Flynn in conversation with Cooper, she called to him, "I'll wait outside for you, Flynn. Take your time."

She slipped out into a night that was clear and cool and awash with the not unpleasant scents of cattle and dew-dampened earth. Her head thrown back so she could get her fill of the stars scattered like diamonds in the black sky, she heard the door open behind her and smiled. "You know, I used to think the only place you could really appreciate the stars was from the deck of a ship in the middle of the ocean. I was wrong."

"We Rawlingses aim to please," Cooper drawled in a voice as dark as the moonless night. "You ready to go?"

Surprised, she whirled, her heart in her throat, to find him standing right behind her, his familiar figure bathed in shadows. "Flynn—"

"Suggested I take you home since I'm staying over there anyway," he finished for her easily. "No sense both of us making the trip."

He was right, of course—it was late and she'd feel like a shrew if she insisted that the man who brought her take her home, especially when she and Flynn hadn't been out on a date to begin with. But Lord, she dreaded riding even the short distance back to her ranch with him. Not that she intended to let him know that, she added silently, drawing her pride around her like a cloak. Her voice as cool as the pro-verbial cucumber, she said, "I should have thought of that myself. Let's go."

His eyes on the road he could have driven blindfolded, Cooper didn't say a word, letting silence fill the cab like a cold fog, until Susannah couldn't stand it. Her shoulders stiff with tension, she started chattering and couldn't seem to stop herself. "I'll have to call Flynn tomorrow and thank him for taking me tonight. The guys were great, and the stories they told were hysterical. I'll probably be up the rest of the night just writing them down—"

"You should have told me you wanted to sit in on a poker game," he cut in quietly. "I would have arranged it for you."

She shifted on the seat at his softly chiding tone. How could she tell him she hadn't asked for his help because of a kiss that refused to be forgotten? With Flynn, there hadn't been the slimmest chance that the evening would turn out to be anything but a few hours of innocent fun with the boys. There was no way she could make the same claim about Cooper.

"You were busy," she said stiffly. "I didn't want to bother you, and anyway, I didn't know anything about the poker game until I asked Flynn about visiting the bunkhouse last night." Her house came into view then, the porch light she'd left on a welcome glow in the darkness, and she sighed in relief. Before he'd braked to a stop in the drive, she was reaching for the door handle. "Thanks for the ride—"

"I'm coming in," he said flatly, his tone daring her to argue with him. "Just to make sure there aren't any surprises waiting for you."

She froze. She had no wish to walk in on any more unpleasant welcome home greetings from the man who was terrorizing her. But letting Cooper into her home at this hour of the night, when she was already so aware of him her heart was beating double time, could be nothing but a mistake. But what choice did she have?

"Fine," she said shortly, accepting the inevitable even while she fought the need to run. Without another word, she pushed open the passenger door before he could come around to help her.

Cooper's eyes narrowed at the way she avoided his touch, but he let it pass without comment and followed her up the steps to the porch, where Sammy waited for them, his tail wagging wildly. A wide grin split his canine face as Susannah stopped to greet him softly and give him a scratch behind the ears.

Chuckling at the dog's ecstatic expression, Cooper moved forward to ruffle his fur. "You old reprobate," he teased. "You're supposed to be guarding the place, not taking it easy on the front porch."

"Obviously everything's okay," Susannah said, stepping past Sammy to unlock the door. "He wouldn't be so relaxed if someone had been here."

"Probably not," he agreed. "But I'm going to check the place out, just the same. Stay here," he ordered, pushing the door open and stepping over the threshold. "I'll be right back."

He was gone before she could object, striding through her house as if he owned it, turning on lights as he went from room to room on the ground floor, then moving to the stairs and starting up without once checking to see if she had obeyed his order and stayed on the porch. As if she wouldn't dare disobey him, Susannah thought resentfully, and defiantly stepped inside.

The minute the front door closed behind her, she knew no one had been there. The house was too quiet, too peaceful, and she could see in a glance that everything seemed to be just as she'd left it. The sinister vibes that had raised the fine hairs at the back of her neck when she'd come home to the mess in her kitchen were noticeably absent, and with a sigh of relief, she released the breath she hadn't realized she'd been holding.

There had been no attacks against her or the ranch in days. No phone calls, no alarmed barking by Sammy in the middle of the night. Nothing. Which meant the man terrorizing her had grown tired of the game or had been scared off by Cooper's constant presence on the ranch, she concluded as she hung up her jacket. Either way, the taunting seemed to be over, and for that, she could only be grateful.

"I thought I told you to stay outside until I was sure the house was safe."

Caught up in her thoughts, she jumped and whirled to find Cooper right behind her. He made no attempt to touch her, but her pulse started to skip anyway. For days, she'd kept her distance and told herself it was what she wanted. Now she wasn't so sure and that rattled her more than she dared let him see.

Struggling for a nonchalance that just wasn't there, she arched a mocking brow at him. "Apparently I don't take orders well."

"Defiance always has a price," he warned huskily. His eyes suddenly gleaming with a decidedly sensuous fire, he reached out to trace the curve of her cheek. "If I remember correctly, I warned you that if you got within reach again, I just might have to kiss you. And look where you are...right here under my hand."

Trapped in his gaze, Susannah felt her heart kick into an erratic rhythm and her mouth go dry. She had to get him out of the house before she did something stupid, she told herself. But she couldn't seem to drag herself away from the hot promise of his gaze. A woman could lose her soul in his eyes and never regret the loss. "I don't think that would be a very good idea . . . kissing me, I mean."

One corner of his mouth curled mockingly. "Oh, I don't doubt that it's a bad idea," he murmured in a voice that was whisper-soft and rough as sandpaper. "But that doesn't seem to mean a hell of a lot where you're concerned. There are just some things a man's got to do."

"No—"

"Yes," he growled, his eyes devouring her as he lowered his mouth to hers. "Oh, yes."

He meant to take a kiss, just one single soul-destroying kiss that would teach her just how easy it was to get burned when she played with fire. It was a lesson a stubborn woman who was always challenging men badly needed to know, and Susannah was definitely that. With every breath that she took, every flash of her stormy gray eyes, every rebellious set of her chin, she dared him to just try and tame her.

The men she'd dealt with in the past might have let her get away with such defiance, he thought, his eyes burning into hers as he drew her arms around his neck and molded her close. But it was high time she realized that she wasn't dealing with other men now. She was dealing with him, and he didn't walk away from a dare ... especially one as maddeningly beautiful as the slip of a woman in his arms.

He thought he had it all worked out in his mind, just how he would woo her and seduce her into bending to his will. But at the first taste of her mouth, of her hot sweetness, all his fine resolves evaporated in a puff of thick, mind-numbing smoke. Frustrations that had been driving him crazy for days rose like a breaking tidal wave, swamping him with a hunger that threatened to send him to his knees. Blindly clutching her closer, he deepened the kiss, his tongue hungry and seeking, a desperation unlike any he had ever known driving him.

It wasn't enough. With a muttered curse, he raised his head only enough to change the angle of the kiss, then he was taking her mouth again and again, until needs, like his ragged breath, were tearing through him.

Feeling as if she were drowning, the thunder of her heartbeat echoing in her ears, Susannah clung to him and tried to hang on to rational thought. But he touched her and her heart skipped a beat; he kissed her and she melted. And he only had to murmur her name in that low, raspy, bewildered growl of his—as if he wasn't any surer of how they had come to this than she was—and she burned for him in a way she had for no man.

Stop him, she thought dazedly, her hands roaming over the broad width of his shoulders, blindly noting the way the well-worn leather of his jacket lovingly hugged his frame. She should stop him before things got out of hand. After all, it wasn't as if he hadn't kissed her before, she tried to reason. She knew from personal experience that the man was dynamite in boots and a cowboy hat, a potent force no woman in her right mind would take lightly. She should have braced herself for the wildness he stirred in her blood, the need that he ignited deep in the core of her.

But this was different somehow... hotter, stronger, and flavored with a possessiveness that set her heart clamoring fiercely in her breast and stole all the air from her lungs. He didn't ask, he took. As if he had every right. As if there wasn't a doubt in his mind that she was in perfect agreement with him. As if he wanted her with every fiber of his being, and he somehow knew that she wanted him with a passion that was just as deep, just as all-consuming.

And she did, God help her. She did.

The admission, like a thief in the night, sneaked up on her and jerked her back to reality. What was she doing?

"Wait." Her senses swimming, her legs weak, she brought her hands to his chest but couldn't bring herself to push him away. Shuddering, she whispered, "I need to think."

His mouth buried in the pulse pounding in her throat, he muttered, "God, that's all I've been doing, thinking about you...about this..." His fingers curved around her breast, the stroke of his thumb teasing the peak to a tight bud.

She gasped, heat, like a jolt of electricity, streaking right to the core of her. "No—"

Nearly mindless, he heard the rising panic in her voice and started to drag her closer, right into the heart of him, but it was already too late. One second he was holding a hot, willing woman, and the next she was slipping from his arms. "Dammit, Susannah!"

She stopped him from reaching for her with nothing more than a look. Her eyes were defiant, but beneath the blush that tinged her cheeks, her skin was pale. Wanting to touch her, to hold her, Cooper was suddenly afraid she would shatter if he made the wrong move. "What is it? What's wrong?"

Her heart racing madly, she could only shake her head. "This—" she gestured helplessly "—everything. I didn't come here for this."

His eyes sharpened. "Here? You mean New Mexico?"

"I couldn't write," she explained, swallowing the tears that welled in her throat. "My mother died two months ago, and the words just wouldn't come."

But they did now. Agitated, she turned away to pace, the ragged, disjointed sentences tripping over her tongue as she told him how she'd come home to find a father she could hardly remember. "There's so much I'd forgotten. His laughter. I opened the drawer to his desk and suddenly there it was in a bunch of jacks. How could I have forgotten that?"

Watching her wander around the room, Cooper almost told her that she'd probably forgotten it because Joe Patterson wasn't a man prone to laughter. But caught up in her musings, she spoke more to herself than to him. Frowning, he said, "So coming back must have been the right decision. You're remembering."

"Some things," she agreed.

"And when you remember the rest?"

The question brought her to a stop halfway across the room from him. Her eyes met his unblinkingly. "I'll leave." It wasn't a threat, just a statement of fact. "I need to scout out Tombstone and some other places, then I'll go back to Dallas to write the book. Which is why I can't . . . can't . . ."

For the first time, she floundered, her eyes skittering away from his. "Get involved?" he finished for her, his voice hard. "Is that what you're trying to say?"

She flinched at his accusing tone, but she didn't back down. "I've got enough to handle already. I don't need regrets, too."

So now he was a regret, he thought cynically. The label hurt, surprisingly more than he cared to admit. His mouth compressed, he said coolly, "In other words, back off. Right? Relax, sweetheart, I don't have to be told twice."

He was gone before she could open her mouth, his face a rigid mask as he jerked the door open and strode outside to his truck. Seconds later, the spinning wheels of the pickup angrily spit out gravel as he shifted into first and raced toward the foreman's cottage. Fool! he berated himself savagely. From the very beginning, he'd known that Susannah Patterson was a woman to be avoided at all cost, but had he listened? Hell, no! He'd come rushing to her rescue like some type of modern-day Don Quixote tilting at windmills, only to get kicked in the teeth. A regret. She thought of him as nothing but a damn regret.

Swearing a blue streak, he pulled up before the darkened cottage and glared at it, half-tempted to return to the Double R right now. The lady had been taking care of herself just fine before he came along, and since she obviously wanted nothing to do with him, she'd no doubt be glad to see the last of him. They could both go their separate ways and forget they'd ever had the misfortune to run into each other . . . let alone be attracted to each other . . . want each other. . . .

But he couldn't leave her there alone, unprotected.

He muttered a curse, wanting to deny it, but he knew there was no way in hell he could walk out on her when she was in trouble. He was stuck there until whoever was harassing her was caught. And if she didn't like it, that was too damn bad. Not that she had anything to worry about where he was concerned, he thought grimly. He didn't care if this crazy need he had for her kept him pacing the floor nights, he wasn't touching her again.

Over the next week, Cooper's eyes were like black ice every time he looked at Susannah. Whatever friendliness they'd managed to share in the past was gone, irretrievably lost, replaced by a coldness that Susannah would have sworn left frost on her heart. The lessons they'd agreed on continued, but only, she suspected, because they'd made a deal and he was determined to stick with it, come hell or high water. Making the lessons fun hadn't been part of the bargain, however. With the aloofness of a near stranger, he taught her the rudiments of riding and roping a calf from horseback. In a businesslike tone that didn't encourage questions, he explained the hard, backbreaking work involved in spring roundup—the branding, castrating and inoculating. Not once did he touch her or, God forbid, smile. At the end of each day, he walked away from her without a second glance, as if he couldn't wait for the damn lessons to end so he could also end his uncomfortable association with her.

Susannah tried to convince herself she didn't care, but still, his coldness hurt. When they finished another roping lesson at the end of the week, all she could think about was getting inside and licking her wounds. As soon as Paintbrush was brushed and groomed and back in his stall, she headed for the house.

Grooming George, the big bay gelding he'd brought over from the Double R, Cooper stopped her before she'd taken two steps. "Would you like to go to the Crossroads with me tonight?"

Taken aback, she stuttered, "You mean for a date? You're asking me out?"

"You said you wanted to know everything about a cowboy's life," he reminded her stiffly, sidestepping her question. "After a hard day, a lot of them go to the Crossroads for a couple of beers and a game or two of pool. It's the only bar between here and Lordsburg, and I thought you'd like to see it in person rather than just hear about it. But if you're not interested—"

When he started to turn away, a smart woman would have let him go. But the past week had been hell, and she'd never been very smart where he was concerned. She couldn't stand the hostility between them, the coldness, and if a few hours at the Crossroads would bring an end to it, then she was going to grab it with both hands.

"I've got a few things to do around the house, but I should be finished by eight," she said quickly. "Is that all right?"

He nodded, his expression shuttered. "I'll pick you up. Don't dress up. There's nothing fancy about the Crossroads."

Seeing it for the first time, Susannah had to agree with him. The Crossroads was one of those generic bars the West was full of. Hardly bigger than a cracker box, with a long, scarred wooden bar running down the length of one wall, it was dark and smoke-filled and crowded with jeans-clad cowboys who preferred their beer in a long-neck bottle and their liquor straight up. Anyone wanting wine or fancy mixed drinks would have to look elsewhere.

"Hey, Coop! Susannah!" Red caught their attention with a wave of his hand from the spot he'd claimed for himself at the busy bar. "Me and the boys were just talking about the poker game the other night. Come on over and join us. How 'bout a beer? You do drink beer, don't you, Susannah?"

"Aw, she don't want a drink," Shag said as the other cowboys from the poker game greeted them and made room for them at the bar. "Can't you see her foot's tapping? Wanna take a couple of turns around the dance floor, Susannah? I'm a real good two-stepper. Ask anyone. They'll tell you I'm the best dancer in the county."

"I don't know about that," Mike snorted. "From what I've seen, you're more like a bull in a china shop. Now me, I'm smooth. How 'bout it, Susannah? Let's show him how it's done."

She had to laugh. They were all so competitive! "I'm not exactly Ginger Rogers, guys." Aware of Cooper's silent, tense figure beside her, she glanced at him, wanting, more than anything, for him to ask her to dance. But he merely lifted a dark brow at her, as if to say the choice was hers. Disappointed, she turned back to the men patiently waiting for her answer. "Shag asked first," she reminded Mike with a grin as he started to grab her and haul her off to the post-age-stamp size dance floor by the jukebox. "No cutting in line."

"Yeah," Shag retorted, reaching around his friend to take Susannah's hand, the grin he shot Mike broad and triumphant. "No cutting. Try not to forget you're supposed to be a gentleman. Come on, Susannah, I believe they're playing our song."

Chuckling, she went willingly and was quickly swept into a lively two-step that soon had her laughing and hanging onto Shag for dear life. The song was hardly over, her heart still hammering in her ears, when Mike stepped in front of her. "*Now* it's my turn. Go sit down, Shag, so you can watch some real dancing."

For the first time in her life, Susannah knew what it was like to be the belle of the ball. Breathless and laughing, she was swept from Shag to Mike to Red and back to Shag again, spun around the little dance floor until her head was reeling and her feet were aching. The men, quick to try to outdo one another, practiced their fanciest steps with her and filled her ears with ribald comments about her other partners that had her eyes dancing with amusement.

But it wasn't until Cooper unexpectedly stepped in front of her, cutting out Mike, that she realized that, as much fun as the others had been, it was the long tall cowboy before her whom she really wanted to dance with. She'd felt his eyes on her all evening, his dark, brooding gaze watching her every move like a hawk. But he'd made no move to leave his seat at the bar and had seemed content to watch her with his ranch hands. Until now.

"I believe it's my turn," he said in a low, husky voice that slid down her spine like a hot caress. "Or didn't you plan to dance with the guy that brought you?"

She wanted to tell him that she'd been just waiting for him to ask her, but her throat was tight and she couldn't manage so much as a squeak. Without a word, knowing it was a mistake and not caring in the least, she went into his arms just as a slow, haunting love song purred from the jukebox.

The minute he felt her softness against him, Cooper knew he'd lost the battle he'd been fighting all evening. Watching her dance with his ranch hands, smiling up at them, had been pure hell. He'd tried telling himself he didn't give a damn, but inside, he'd found it harder and harder to hang on to the coldness he wanted to feel for her. Song after song, he'd burned to be the one whirling her around that ridiculous excuse for a dance floor until she was clinging to him as if she would never let him go.

Still, he'd silently sworn he wasn't going to go near her. No one had been more surprised than he when he'd found himself standing in front of her, waiting for her to step into his arms.

And now holding her, the tantalizing scent of her perfume intoxicating him, her body melting against his as she lost herself in the music, he knew he needed more than a dance or two with her, more than a few hours with her at a bar surrounded by noise, cigarette smoke and a bunch of rowdy cowboys who would have liked nothing better than to steal her away from him. He wanted her alone, preferably somewhere quiet and dark, with a bed close by. Hours, he thought with a groan, his arms tightening around her until she was pressed close. He wanted hours with her, days, between the sheets, with no one around for miles and all the time in the world to indulge himself in learning every inch of her delectable body.

She had bewitched him, he thought in wonder, accepting the inevitable. Old Joe Patterson's daughter. And he didn't even know how the hell it had happened. He just knew he wasn't letting her go anytime soon.

The rest of the evening was a blur for Susannah. She knew Red, Shag and Mike tried to claim another dance with her, but Cooper only grinned at them, hugged her closer and told them to bug off. She was dreaming, she thought dazedly, forgetting the research she'd come to do and everything else but the man who held her so close. She'd stepped into a dream and she was never going back to the real world.

But all too soon, Cooper was murmuring in her ear, telling her it was late and time they headed back to the ranch. She wanted to protest—she wasn't ready for the evening to end. Once they went home, they would part company as if the past few hours had never happened, each going to their separate beds to spend the night alone and aching. But before she could find the words—and the courage to say them—he was telling his men good-night, helping her into her jacket and guiding her outside to his truck.

Disappointed, she braced herself for the ride home, expecting it to be a repeat of the one from her ranch to the Crossroads, a tense, never-ending drive in which they each seemed to cling to their sides of the pickup while the silence thickened and grew until it was cold and unbreakable. But instead of escorting her to the passenger side of his truck, Cooper took her hand the minute they stepped into the cold night air and pulled her with him to the driver's side.

At her look of surprise, he admitted with a husky honesty that made her pulse skip, "I'm not ready to let go of you yet. Okay?"

Her heart flip-flopping in her breast, she couldn't have objected if her life had depended on it. Mutely, she nodded and scooted across the seat until she was in the middle. Seconds later, he was crawling in beside her, the long length of his leg pressed against hers.

For what seemed like an eternity, neither of them moved, let alone seemed to breathe. His eyes black and intense in the darkness, Cooper stared down at her searchingly until Susannah was sure he could see into her very soul. Something flashed in his eyes, a heat, a promise, that stole all the moisture from her mouth. She swallowed, but it didn't help. Then he was fitting the key into the ignition, and she couldn't be sure if the moment had been real or imagined.

The silence was back, just as tense as before, but this time it was colored with an anticipation that had her heart thumping like mad. Aware of nothing but Cooper, the heat of him against her, the way he skillfully handled the steering wheel and gearshift, she wasn't aware of anything wrong until he suddenly swore viciously and sent the accelerator to the floor.

Unprepared for the way the truck leapt forward, her head snapped back. "What is it?" she cried, alarmed.

His face grim, he nodded toward her ranch in the distance. "Look."

She glanced forward and gasped. "Oh, my God!"

A mile down the road where she knew her ranch sat, flames shot high into the night sky.

Chapter 9

It was the barn, not the house, as Cooper had first feared, that burned like a bonfire in the night. His curses scorching the air, he pulled up with a flourish, slamming on the brakes so quickly he almost stood the truck on its nose. He was reaching for the door handle before the vehicle had even shuddered to a stop. "Call my brothers," he barked over his shoulder at Susannah. "And the volunteer fire department. Hurry!"

Her eyes locked in horror on the flames dancing on the roof of the barn, Susannah hardly heard him. "The horses!" she cried, fumbling for her own door handle. "Oh, God, they're in there! We've got to get them out!"

Swearing, Cooper bolted around to the front of the truck and caught her as she ran full tilt into him. Over the roar of the fire, they both heard the wild cry of the animals.

"Let me go! Paintbrush—"

"I'll get him," Cooper snapped, shaking her. "Dammit, Susannah, do as I say! Do you hear me? Call the fire department and my brothers. Now!"

Turning her ruthlessly from the burning building, he shoved her toward the house, then took off running for the barn. He didn't turn around to see if she'd obeyed him for once in her life—there wasn't time. The fire, like something wicked in the night, was already creeping down from the loft, spreading insidiously, the licking tongues of flame consuming everything in their path. Minutes, Cooper gauged, his heart pounding like a sledge hammer. He only had minutes, at the most, before the whole building was ablaze.

Sammy rushed up to him, barking hoarsely, as if demanding he do something, and with a curt order, he told him to stay back. He already had two animals to worry about; he didn't want a third. Seconds later, he plunged into the thick black smoke that billowed out of the open barn door.

The heat hit him like a blast furnace, the hot, heavy air choking him and squeezing his lungs until he could hardly breathe. Coughing, his eyes streaming with tears, he spied a horse blanket hanging on a stall door and grabbed it.

The horses were wild with terror, kicking at their stalls. Reaching Paintbrush first, Cooper knew he'd hear their high whinnying cries in his nightmares for weeks to come. "Come on, boy," he called hoarsely. "Let's get you out of here."

He reached for the catch on the stall door, only to swear as the hot metal singed his skin. Gritting his teeth against the pain, he forced the latch open and jerked the door wide. "Go on," he urged, waving the blanket at him. "Get!"

The paint didn't need to be told twice. His ears back and eyes rolling, he ran for his life. Cooper hurriedly reached for the latch to the next stall. "Okay, George, your turn."

But the big bay wasn't as lucky. He shot from the stall the second he was freed, only to rear up in fright as a burning beam came crashing down from the loft, missing him by inches and blocking the way out. Muttering under his breath, Cooper made a grab at his halter and quickly threw the blanket over the horse's head. "Easy, boy, easy," he said coughing as smoke billowed around them. "I'm going to get you out of here. Just trust me a second, okay?"

His eyes stinging, he murmured soothingly to the quivering animal and led him away from the burning timber to the opening at the opposite end of the barn. Fire raged like an inferno around them, and from under the blanket, he could hear George snorting in fright. "Just a few more feet, boy," he promised huskily. "A few more feet and we're home free."

The gelding, catching the scent of fresh clean air from the open doorway just ahead, strained to be free of the hold on his halter. With a sweep of his hand, Cooper sent the blanket flying at the same time he released the halter, and, in the next instant, the horse was flying out into the night with Cooper right on his heels.

The falling beam seemed to come out of nowhere. One minute he was running full stride toward the cold dark night waiting just beyond the open barn entrance, and the next, fire was raining down on him like a shower from hell. He jerked his head up just in time to see the railing of the hay-loft falling toward him and could do nothing but throw up his hands.

The blow staggered him and nearly drove him to his knees. But all he felt was the white-hot pain in his hands. Crying out a hoarse curse, he shoved the fiery railing aside and stumbled outside, his breath tearing through his singed lungs as he dropped to his knees halfway between the house and the blazing barn.

"Cooper!"

Dazed and gasping, he looked up to find Susannah rushing toward him from the house, her face alabaster white in the bright glare of the fire. "It's just my hands." he coughed. "Did you call—"

She nodded. "Help's on the way."

Casting a glance over his shoulder at the inferno blazing behind them, he swore and struggled to his feet. "C'mon, we've got to get back. The whole thing's going to come crashing down any second."

But when he tried to urge her toward the house, she ignored him and took his hands in hers, turning them over so she could examine his palms. Cooper wasn't surprised when her breath hissed through her teeth at the sight of his raw, red, blistered skin. He didn't need to see them to know that his hands weren't a pretty sight. They hurt like hell.

"Oh, Lord, your poor hands!" Susannah murmured. "Come inside and let me put something on them."

"I don't have time now. The wind's too high—"

He pulled away, but in the next instant a string of trucks raced into the ranch compound. Before it had rolled to a complete stop, Gable, Flynn and Josey spilled from the first truck, and within seconds, the yard was full of Double R cowboys running toward the burning barn. Shouting orders, Gable and Flynn hurried to help before the flames spread out to the rest of the outbuildings and the house.

But the wind was rising, feeding the fire, catching the sparks and sending them flying into dry winter grass that was as volatile as kindling. "Over here!" Cooper yelled, sprinting to where a spark smoldered near the foreman's cottage. Ignoring his throbbing hands, he stomped out the burning ember with his boots, but within seconds, another one landed a short distance away, and then another. Susannah and Josey rushed over to help, but the situation was already getting out of control when the wail of a siren cut through the roar of the fire. A heartbeat later, the county's only fire truck turned through the ranch entrance and barreled toward them.

It was nearly two long hours later before the crisis was over. The flames were extinguished under a heavy stream of water, every spark killed in spite of the wind that refused to die. When all the smoke cleared, a black skeleton was all that was left of the barn, the burnt frame standing like a dark sentinel in the night, a mere shadow of the structure that had stood there as long as Susannah could remember.

The house had been spared, however, as well as the outbuildings, and for that she was grateful. Exhausted, dirty and smelling of smoke, emotions backing up in her tight throat, she thanked the men of the volunteer fire department when they finally packed up and left, then expressed her thanks to the cowboys of the Double R who had rushed to her aid. Without their help, she knew she would have lost everything.

And she hadn't realized, until she'd almost lost it, just how much the ranch meant to her, how much it had always meant to her. She'd tried denying it for years, but her roots were here, her memories, her childhood, everything that made her what she was.

Swallowing the tears that threatened to clog her throat, she hunched her shoulders against the cold and faced the Rawlingses. "I don't know how to thank you all for your help. If you hadn't come when you had—"

"We'd be lousy neighbors," Gable finished for her.

"Yeah," Flynn added with a self-effacing grin, totally unconcerned by the soot that smudged his face. "We all help each other around here, Susannah. That's just the way it is."

If they'd been normal neighbors, she would have agreed with him. But their families had never been friends. For decades, they'd shared a common property line and little else but antagonism. A Patterson didn't come to a Rawlings's aid, and vice versa. Or at least that was the way her father had recorded events in his journals.

How could she continue to consider these people her enemy when they rushed to help her whenever she needed help? she wondered. How could she distrust them when they welcomed her into their home without hesitation, when they risked their lives to save her ranch?

Disturbed, no longer as sure of her feelings as she had once been, she turned to Cooper and immediately forgot everything else when she saw him unobtrusively blowing on his hands. "Oh, God, your hands!" Until the last ember had been put out, he'd flatly refused first aid, but now that the adrenaline of fighting the fire had passed, the burns had to be killing him. "Now will you let Josey look at them?"

"He will or I'll have his brothers hog-tie him and hold him down for me," Josey retorted, retrieving her medical bag from the truck. "Come on, tough guy, let's go inside and check you out."

He grimaced, but gave in gracefully and took the steps up to the back porch. "Okay, okay. You don't have to bring in the big guns. I'll go peacefully. But you're making a fuss over nothing but a couple of small burns."

Remembering the blisters that had started to rise on his raw palms two hours ago, Susannah could just imagine what they looked like now. Turning to his brothers, she urged them inside, too. "Please, come in and clean up. I'll make some coffee while Josey's tending Cooper."

With the fire out and the wind growing colder with every passing second, they didn't need a second urging. "You got any snacks to go with that?" Flynn asked, grinning as he held the back door open for her. "Cookies? Cake? Ham sandwiches? I didn't realizing fighting fires was such tough work. I'm starving!"

For what seemed like the first time in hours, Susannah laughed. "I'll see what I can rustle up."

While Gable and Flynn cleaned up at the kitchen sink, Josey had Cooper sit at the table so she could examine his hands under the light that hung directly overhead. Hustling up sandwiches and coffee, Susannah couldn't help but marvel at the sight of the Rawlings family gathered in her kitchen as comfortably as if it were their own. They took over the room with their sheer size and laughter and held back the loneliness that usually waited for her in the silence of the empty house.

The phone rang, shattering her musings and startling her so that she spilled the coffee she was measuring into the coffeemaker. Muttering a curse, she quickly snatched up the receiver and cradled it between her ear and shoulder as she wiped up the mess. "Hello?"

Silence greeted her, the cold, threatening kind that drained the blood from her face and had her thundering heart jumping into her throat. She hadn't had a threatening call in days, but she knew it was *him,* the man who was terrorizing her, stalking her, watching her out there somewhere in the darkness. She could practically feel the hostility vibrating across the phone line, chilling her all the way to the bone.

Her fingers started to shake. "Who's there?" she whispered hoarsely.

"This time it was the barn," a harsh voice right out of her nightmares growled in her ear. "Next time it'll be the house. And you'll be in it."

"No!"

"Then you'd better leave, lady, 'cause your time is running out."

The line went dead before she could say another word, buzzing mockingly in her ear. Fighting the need to yell, to scream, to throw something, anything, she carefully replaced the receiver in its cradle. Cold. God, suddenly she was so cold.

"Susannah?"

She was pale, ashen in fact, standing frozen by the phone, her hand still on the receiver. Cooper hadn't been able to hear her side of the conversation, but something in her very stillness had him jumping up from the chair he'd pulled out from the table. Crossing to her, ignoring the bandages Josey had wrapped around his hands, he reached out and gripped her shoulders to turn her toward him, the weathered lines of his rugged face deepening into a scowl. "What is it? Who was on the phone?"

Lost in the horror that engulfed her, she glanced up and found him so close she only had to lean into him to feel his strength. "He said the house would be next if I—I didn't leave. And I would be in it."

Cooper swore a short, crude curse he rarely used and reached for her. He hadn't meant to touch her, but suddenly she was in his arms and pressed close, right where she belonged. At the feel of her trembling, a muscle twitched in his jaw. Over her head, his gaze met the interested eyes of his family. "Call Riley Whitaker," he told Gable grimly. "I know he's off duty by now, but he needs to know about this. Call him at home."

* * *

Riley arrived less than an hour later. Dressed in wrinkled jeans, a T-shirt and leather jacket, his jaw darkened with a night's worth of whiskers, he looked as if he'd just crawled out of bed. But at the sight of the charred skeleton of what had once been Susannah's barn, his mouth tightened. Grabbing a flashlight from his patrol car, he inspected the blackened remains for what seemed like hours, pushing through the ashes with a stick, lingering over them like a scientist examining a slide under a microscope.

When he finally walked away from the smoldering ruins and joined Susannah and Cooper on the back porch, where they waited with the rest of the Rawlingses, he was carrying a jagged piece of glass that looked as if it had once been part of a beer bottle. "Do you drink beer in your barn, Susannah?"

"No, of course not."

He smiled at her indignant response. "I didn't think so, but I had to ask. Have you ever seen this before?" he asked, holding up the innocent-looking piece of glass in front of the porch light so she could see it clearly. At the shake of her head, the grim lines around his mouth deepened. "I can't be sure without having the lab examine it, but I think this was used in a Molotov cocktail. Whoever did this could have pulled right up to the barn in their car, tossed this into the hayloft, then driven off before the flames were high enough to notice. And in a car, he wouldn't have had to contend with Sammy."

The last of the color drained from Susannah's face, already pale. It could have been the house, she thought, shaken, just as the fiend tormenting her had taunted her on the phone. Instead of attacking the ranch while she was gone, he could have just as easily thrown the bomb through her bedroom window in the middle of the night. Sound asleep and unaware of the danger she was in, she never would have stood a chance.

Suddenly more afraid than she'd ever been in her life, she started to tremble. "He's not playing games anymore, is he?"

"No," Riley said flatly. "With every attack, this bastard has grown bolder and more dangerous. He obviously means business, and for your own safety, I have to recommend that you find somewhere else to stay."

"You can stay with us," Josey volunteered immediately. "We have plenty of room, and we'd love to have you."

Susannah wanted to hug her, wanted to jump at the offer she so generously held out to her. Safe. She would be safe at the Double R, surrounded by the Rawlings family and their ranch hands, protected. She wouldn't have to jump every time the phone rang; she wouldn't have to sleep with one eye open, waiting and wondering where the next attack was coming from. It sounded like heaven.

But if her attacker could get to her at her place, couldn't he track her down at the Double R?

Even as the thought chilled her blood, Susannah was regretfully shaking her head. "I couldn't."

"Why the hell not?" Cooper growled. "Dammit, Susannah, didn't you hear what Riley said? This bastard's run out of patience. If you insist on staying here, you're going to wind up getting hurt."

"I know. But if I go to the Double R, how do I know he won't just follow me?"

"What if he does?" he retorted, scowling. "We can handle him."

"But that's the whole point," she argued. "*You* shouldn't have to. This is my problem, and running away won't solve it. This man—for whatever reason—wants me gone, and he's not going to stop threatening me just because I go to the

Double R for a few days. He could burn your barn, your house, and I won't be responsible for that."

"But that's not going to happen," Flynn replied. "You're pretty isolated here, but we've got cowboys swarming all over the Double R. The minute the bastard set foot on our place, somebody would see him and stop him. He'd never be allowed to get close enough to you to hurt you."

With all her heart, Susannah wanted to believe him. But she'd seen what the man stalking her was capable of, and after tonight, she would never underestimate him again. For reasons she couldn't begin to guess at, he was after her, and he would go through whoever he had to to get to her. She couldn't take a chance that he would hurt one of the Rawlingses because of her.

"I didn't think he'd be able to get into my house, either," she pointed out, "but he did. I'm sorry, but I think it would be best if I went somewhere else."

She made the explanation to Flynn, but it was to Cooper that she spoke, her eyes unconsciously pleading with him to understand. Clenching his teeth on an oath, he wanted to shake her, to drag her into his arms, to hold her close so no one could get to her. But she had her chin set at that stubborn angle that told him she'd made up her mind and nothing he could say would change it. Infuriating woman! Why did she have to be so damn independent?

Behind shuttered eyes, Gable watched the silent messages being passed between Susannah and his brother and bit back a smile at Cooper's obvious frustration. "There's an old cabin by the springs," he told Susannah. "It hasn't been used in years and it's pretty secluded. If you slipped over there tonight, you could hide out there, and no one would even know you were using the place but the five of us. There's nothing fancy about it, but you'd be safer there than you are here."

Safe. Susannah's eyes drifted to the charred remains of the barn and she felt a shudder whisper through her. Would she ever again be able to crawl into bed at night without worrying whether there was a nut case out there somewhere, watching her, waiting to strike out at her when she least expected it? "I'll pack a bag," she said quietly, and pulled open the back door.

"I'll help you," Josey said, following her inside. "You'll need to take as much as you can so you won't have to come back for anything."

It was a daunting thought—not knowing when she would return. It could be days, weeks, months. Pulling two suitcases from her bedroom closet, Susannah laid them on the bed and stared at them blankly, not knowing where to begin.

"God, I hate this!" She choked, her fingers bunching into fists. "What kind of man hides in the shadows and terrorizes an innocent woman? I don't even know what he wants from me!"

"A worm," Josey retorted without hesitation. "Only someone who crawls on his belly could be this low. There's no doubt about it—the man slid right out from under a rock."

Susannah had to laugh; Josey was so calm, so matter-of-fact, as if there wasn't a doubt in her mind that the man was the scum of the earth. The tension in her suddenly draining away, she grinned. "I couldn't have said it better myself. Thanks, Josey."

"For what?" she asked with a smile.

"For just being here. After everything that's happened, I didn't expect us to be friends."

"Why ever not?"

Surprised she even had to ask, Susannah said, "Because the Rawlingses sent my father to prison."

Josey's smile faded. "You make it sound as if we had a vendetta against your father," she said quietly. "But it wasn't like that at all. Your father was the one with the vendetta."

"No—"

"Yes," Josey said firmly. She saw Susannah pale and wished she could say something to ease her pain, but all she had was the truth. Sinking down onto the side of the bed, she sighed. "I wish I could make this easier for you, but the truth is that your father was plotting with some of the other ranchers around here to try to steal the Double R away from the Rawlingses. He and the others hoped to make them miss a balloon payment on a loan and lose the ranch to the bank. Then they'd buy it at auction."

Cooper had tried to tell her the same thing, but she hadn't wanted to listen, let alone believe him. Even when a voice in her head had reminded her that she'd always known her father was a driven man capable of desperate acts, she'd rationalized that Cooper would say anything to defend himself and his family. But try as she might, she could no longer bury her head in the sand and pretend that her father hadn't had feet of clay. All she had to do was look at Josey Rawlings's face to know that she spoke nothing less than the truth. Her eyes were clouded with memories and an outrage that hadn't faded with the passage of time.

"It was just talk," she said desperately. "I know my father was no saint. He was a hard man to like, let alone love. But talking about something like that and actually doing it are two separate things. He obviously didn't do anything but spout off at the mouth. The Rawlingses are still at the Double R. Nothing happened."

"Gable was shot in the back," Josey retorted bluntly. "He almost died, and your father was the one who pulled the trigger. I know. I was there. I saw it with my own eyes."

Susannah flinched. Somewhere deep inside, she'd known something like this had happened. She hadn't seen her father in more than a decade, but she hadn't forgotten what he could be like. Rigid. Jealous. *But to actually shoot Gable!*

Dear God, how could he? How could he have shot an innocent man simply because he had something he wanted? And in the back, no less! No wonder Cooper had bristled every time she mentioned her father's name. No wonder he'd been suspicious of her simply because she was her father's daughter. He had no reason to trust a Patterson.

Stricken, she sank down to the side of the bed. "I should have known—"

"Why? Because he was your father?" Josey asked, giving her a chiding look. "I know you must have loved him, but you hadn't seen him in years. How were you supposed to know what he was capable of?"

"I was his daughter—"

"And Gable was his neighbor for all of his life, but he still didn't suspect Joe until the very end. It's not your fault, Susannah," she said gently. "I didn't tell you to lay a guilt trip on you. You're not responsible for what your father did. You weren't here, you didn't pull the trigger. I just thought you should know."

With one part of her brain, Susannah knew Josey was right—her father had obviously had some serious problems, and anyone who had ever seen him in one of his moods knew that he could be impossible to reason with when he'd made up his mind about something. She was only his daughter, not his keeper, and not accountable for his irrational behavior. But knowing that did nothing to ease her conscience when she thought of the accusations she had thrown at Cooper. She'd actually suspected him of trying to trick her to get his hands on her ranch. God, how she must have sounded like her father!

Mortified, she finished packing, wondering how she was going to face him now that she knew the truth. But when she walked out of her bedroom with Josey at her side and set her suitcases by the front door, she discovered there were more immediate worries—how she was going to get to the cabin at the Rawlings's springs without being followed. It was dark as pitch outside, and for all they knew, the man terrorizing her could be sitting out there in the night, hiding out like a snake in the grass, watching her every move.

"I'll take Susannah in my truck and hit some of the back roads," Cooper suggested. "If anyone follows us, I'll be able to see him for miles. I won't head for the cabin until I'm sure it's clear."

The sheriff nodded and walked over to the switch near the front door. With a flick of his hand, he turned out the floodlights that still illuminated every inch of the ranch compound. "Everybody load up in the dark, and he won't know which vehicle Susannah is in. When you get to the highway, split up. I'm going to hang back here for a while and keep watch, so even if the bastard tries to follow you without turning on his lights, I should be able to see his brakelights. Everybody ready? Then let's go."

The plan worked perfectly, and within seconds, they were all headed in different directions, racing off into the dark, along twisting, winding dirt roads they could all have driven with their eyes closed. Making it impossible for anyone to guess their different destinations, the Rawlings brothers took unexpected turns without rhyme or reason or turn signals, crazily crisscrossing the countryside like teenagers out for a joyride.

But there was nothing joyful about the experience. His gaze bouncing between the darkness reflected in the rearview mirror and the narrow dirt road in front of him, Cooper was aware of the tense set of Susannah's shoulders, the silence that hung like a pall in the air. He'd tried talking to her, tried assuring her that everything was going to be fine, but she'd hardly spared him a glance, let alone responded. And who the hell could blame her? She was safe now, not because of anything he had done, but because the man stalking her had decided to warn her that next time she wouldn't be so lucky.

A muscle working in his clenched jaw, he cast one final glance in the mirror to make sure the road was empty behind them before turning abruptly into a little-used back entrance to the Double R. A few minutes later, the rest of the world was left behind as they eased into the rocky canyon the springs bubbled out of.

Caught in the beam of the headlights, the log cabin was small and dark and as rough-hewn as the canyon that huddled protectively around it. A rock fireplace climbed one wall, and a comfortable-looking porch stretched invitingly across the front. Within easy reach of the cottonwood-lined creek that bubbled in the distance, it was quaint and secluded, welcoming.

Susannah took one look at it and knew she would be safe here. After all, she was miles from her own ranch and back in a canyon that could have been trapped in time. The land was too rocky for grazing, so there was little likelihood that any of the Double R cowboys ever came back here; and no one else but the Rawlingses and the sheriff knew where she was. The chances of her tormentor thinking to look for her in such a remote place were slim to none.

Pulling up before the front porch, Cooper cut the lights and the ignition. "I know it looks pretty rough, but it's really not that bad," he said in the sudden silence, his husky voice reaching out of the darkness to wrap around her. "My father had indoor plumbing put in years ago, and the fireplace keeps it plenty warm. There's no electricity, though. Dad wanted to put in a generator once, but Mom talked him out of it. She said it would ruin the atmosphere."

"She was right," Susannah said softly, the primitiveness of the structure calling out to the romantic in her. "This is the kind of place that needs kerosene lamps and candles. I'm sure it'll be perfect."

She pushed open her door and reached in the back for the lighter of her two suitcases, and within seconds, Cooper was joining her on the porch and pushing open the unlocked door. It was black as tar inside and so quiet the silence seemed to echo, but he strode across the threshold without hesitation and headed right for the old pine table that had sat to the right of the front door for as long as he could remember. Setting down the suitcases he carried, his fingers blindly closed around the kerosene lamp that was right where it was supposed to be. Seconds later, a match flared, hissing to life as he struck it along the scarred tabletop.

The minute he held the dancing flame to the wick of the lamp, light seemed to rush into the cabin like a breath of fresh air, pushing back the shadows. Standing just inside the doorway, Susannah caught her breath in appreciation.

The inside of the cabin was every bit as rugged as the outside, and just as appealing. It was one large room, with no interior walls or dividers, just pockets of comfort that formed a kitchen, living room and bedroom, all within easy reach of the fireplace's heat. Her eyes taking in the woodburning cookstove against one wall, the old brass bed cozily situated in an opposite corner and the rocking chair pulled up before the hearth, Susannah felt the tension that had knotted her muscles for the past two hours gradually drain away. Peace. If she could find it anywhere, she knew it would be here.

Then her gaze fell to the suitcases Cooper had dropped near the table and she felt herself stiffening. She still held one of the two she'd packed, but there were two setting on the floor. And one of them wasn't hers. Her eyes flew to his. "You're not staying here."

It was a statement of fact, not a question, but if he noticed, he gave no sign of it. "Oh, yes, I am," he said easily, moving to the fireplace to build a fire with the wood stacked at the end of the hearth. "Come on in and shut the door. It won't take any time to warm this place up once I get the fire going."

Because it was as small as a matchbox, Susannah thought, reluctantly shutting the door. Fighting the sudden claustrophobia that squeezed her throat, she had to force herself to step farther into the cabin, her gaze straying like a voyeur's to the corner that comprised the bedroom. One double bed—more than enough room for one, adequate for two.

Images, quick and unbidden, hot and steamy, flashed before her eyes, teasing her, tempting her. Her heart jerked in her breast, setting her pulse pounding and alarm bells clanging. She couldn't do this, she realized with sudden clarity. Having him in the foreman's cottage on her ranch was one thing; sharing this small, intimate one-bed cabin was quite another.

She wanted him too much. And now that she knew the truth about her father and that the Rawlingses weren't the ruthless, land-grabbing monsters she'd tried to convince herself they were, she had to face the feelings she'd been denying for days now. She was only a heartbeat away from falling in love with Cooper. Staying with him in this cabin, spending all of her days and nights with him, would only push her over the edge. And she wouldn't let that happen.

Because he was still a strong, domineering cowboy, and she was a woman who wouldn't be dominated.

Her throat dry as sandpaper, she watched the fire flare to life in the fireplace and could take no comfort in it. For a moment, a brief flash of insanity, she toyed with the idea of trying to be the kind of woman he needed, the kind of woman who was content to love and care for him and let him be the king of his castle, the lord of the manor, the decision maker who always knew where his woman was—at home where she belonged. But as sure as she was that she could make a fool of herself over him, she knew she couldn't be that woman. From her earliest memories, she'd been struggling against the strong hand of a man, and the instinct was too deeply ingrained for her to stop now. She'd make him miserable, and she couldn't do that to him.

Loneliness tugged at her, squeezing her heart. "You can't stay here," she said more harshly than she'd intended. "There's no reason to. We weren't followed and no one but your family and the sheriff knows where I am."

Incredulous, Cooper straightened to face her, unable to believe he had heard her correctly. "Is this some kind of a joke? Or do you really think I'm such a jerk that I'd go off and leave you here alone after that bastard threatened you and damn near burned your barn to the ground?"

"No, of course not—"

"No, this isn't a joke? Or no, you don't think I'm a jerk?"

"Of course you're not a jerk!"

She threw the words at him in exasperation, fairly shouting them in a silence that was suddenly tense and crackling with awareness. Stunned, his brown eyes searched hers. "Since when?" he asked softly. "I would have sworn you thought I was lower than dirt."

Heart pounding, knees shaking, she backed up before she could stop herself. "I never said that."

"Not in so many words, no," he agreed. "But you got your point across. So what changed your mind?"

His gaze pinned her to the floor in front of him, demanding an answer she knew he wasn't going to let her sidestep. "I was wrong," she admitted stiffly. "About you. And about my father."

Before she realized she was close to tears, her eyes flooded, horrifying her. Why, after all the times she needed to cry and couldn't, did she pick now to let the tears come? Muttering an exclamation, she turned away, wiping furiously at her cheeks. "I'm the jerk, not you," she choked. "That's why you can't stay here. I misjudged you, and I have no right to keep taking advantage of your generosity."

From three feet behind her, Cooper stared at her, struck dumb by her honesty. Just when he thought he was figuring her out, she threw him a curve that knocked him for a loop, and all he could think about was reaching for her. But nothing had changed, he reminded himself. He was still a regret she didn't want.

Determined to keep his hands to himself, he said quietly, "I'm a grown man and I know when a woman is trying to take advantage of me. You're not, so relax. I'm staying."

Chapter 10

She tried, she really tried, to casually accept his decision and act as if sharing living quarters with him was nothing out of the ordinary. After all, they weren't teenagers at the mercy of raging hormones. They could control themselves . . . or so she thought until her eyes fell on the bed.

She couldn't, she thought, heat flushing her cheeks. She couldn't share a bed with him. Not without tumbling over the edge and falling hopelessly in love with him.

She didn't remember making a conscious decision, but the next moment, she was stepping around Cooper and reaching for one of the down sleeping bags on the bed. Aware of his eyes on her, she moved past him to the hearth and, without sparing him a glance, spread the sleeping bag on the wooden floor in front of the fire.

"What do you think you're doing?"

"Getting ready for bed," she said huskily. "It's late, and I'm bushed."

"Don't be ridiculous," he growled. "There's no need for you to sleep on the floor."

He sounded so irritated, she would have laughed—if her heart hadn't been thumping to beat the band. "Yes, there is," she said lightly. "I get cold easily, so I'll be warmer here by the fire." Without another word, she slipped out of her shoes and snuggled down into the sleeping bag until she was covered all the way to her ears.

Cooper had no idea how long he stood there, scowling down at her, wanting to shake her. What kind of cretin did she think he was to let her take the floor while he stretched out on the bed? For two cents, he'd snatch her up, sleeping bag and all, and put an end to this nonsense before it went any further.

Images played before his eyes at the thought...Susannah in his arms, arguing with him, her gray eyes spitting fire, then her hands reaching for him as he lowered her to the bed, her fingers sweetly clinging to him as she abruptly gave in and dragged him down with her.

Unprintable curses echoing in his head, he clenched his teeth on an oath, fighting the sudden need that clawed at him while the night grew darker, more intimate. Every time he'd kissed her, she nearly went up in flames in his arms, a wicked voice in his head reminded him, tempting him. All he had to do was touch her—

To feel like the lowest life form on earth, he thought furiously, disgusted with himself. The lady was on his property, under his protection, and she'd made it clear she didn't want to share a bed with him. She didn't have to hit him over the head with a piece of firewood for him to get the message. Swearing under his breath at the heat burning in his loins, he turned away to the cold, empty bed.

Every muscle in her body tight with tension, Susannah knew the second he lost the silent argument with himself and gave up the fight. One moment she could practically feel his indecision, his frustration, and the next, he was making the bed with an occasional grumbled curse not meant for her ears. Even then, she still wasn't convinced he'd accepted the situation until she heard his boots hit the floor, then the bed springs squeak as he stretched out on the mattress.

An eternity later, he sighed heavily and lay still. Cautiously sneaking a peak, she saw that he was flat on his stomach, as fully clothed as she, with his face turned away from her. Only then did she silently release the breath she hadn't known she was holding. With a sigh that echoed his, she closed her eyes and courted sleep. Still, it was a long time coming.

Susannah truly thought things would be better the next day. She'd brought some of the research material from her attic with her, as well as paper and pencil since there was no electricity for her computer, so she could while away the time working. She'd be able to forget Cooper's presence in the cabin for hours at a time.

And pigs could fly.

Much to her dismay, nothing changed with the rising of the sun. The close confines of the cabin made any kind of privacy except for the bare necessities nonexistent, and Cooper couldn't even scratch without her being aware of his every movement. And he was just as conscious of her presence as she was his.

Oh, he didn't say anything, but she could feel the tension building between them like a storm gathering force on the horizon, and there didn't seem to be anything either of them could do but wait for it to break. And it took hours.

They had breakfast, then lunch, meals Cooper prepared since she didn't have the slightest idea how to cook on a wood stove without burning everything to cinders. As polite as two strangers who suddenly found themselves trapped in an elevator, they skirted around each other without touching, their conversation stilted, avoiding eye contact as if they were afraid of what they would see in the other's eyes.

By late afternoon, Susannah was going quietly out of her mind. Cooper sat in the rocking chair by the hearth, ignoring her, all his attention focused on the pocketknife he sharpened with a whetstone. For what seemed like hours, he dragged the edge of the knife across the stone with slow, even strokes, over and over again in a steady, ceaseless rhythm that scraped along her nerve endings like sandpaper on an open wound. Then, just when she thought she was going to scream in frustration, he'd pause, carefully test the sharpness of the blade with his thumb, then start all over again.

And she couldn't stand it!

Staring at the sentence she'd been trying without success to write for the past fifteen minutes, she threw down her pencil with a hastily swallowed expletive and surged to her feet. "I need some air," she announced. "I'm going for a walk."

His eyes on the blade he was testing, Cooper didn't even glance up. "Not right now. It's too risky."

Susannah almost laughed at that, the emotion darkening her eyes anything but humorous. If he wanted to see risky, just let him try and keep her cooped up five more seconds! "I won't go far," she assured him, heading for the door. "Just to the springs."

She never saw him move, never saw him drop the knife and whetstone and rise from the rocking chair, but suddenly he was there, right behind her, his bandaged hand moving past her shoulder to land with a sharp slap flat against the door. "I told you no," he growled, his breath hot and moist in her ear. "We haven't even been here a day yet. It's not safe."

She wanted to cry, her heart starting to thud. This wasn't safe. *He* wasn't safe. "Please," she choked. "Let me go. I've got to get out of here."

He'd only been thinking of her safety, but at the sound of her broken, husky whisper, the awareness that he'd had the devil's own time ignoring all afternoon was stronger than ever. And just that quickly, the air in the cabin was thick and hot and humming. *Let her go?* Caution murmured in his ear like a jealous mistress, telling him not to be a fool. If he could fight his need for her in the dark of night, when temptation was strong and strength of will weak, he sure as hell could keep his hands to himself in the light of day.

But last night, he'd been smart enough to keep his distance and she'd been wise enough not to let him hear the longing in her voice.

With a will of their own, his hands moved to her shoulders. "No," he said thickly. "I can't. You're asking too much."

She felt his fingers tighten, his hands turn her, and there didn't seem to be anything she could do to stop him. One minute she was stubbornly facing the door, clinging to the thought that it wasn't too late to slip outside, and the next she was facing him and being scorched by the burning heat and promise in his eyes.

The ground shifted beneath her feet, and she knew she was in trouble. "This isn't very smart," she began hoarsely, panicking. "We don't even like each other—"

"Oh, I like you, honey," he murmured in a voice that was suddenly as rough as sandpaper. "That's the whole problem." Purposefully, he drew her nearer. "Come here."

With the ease of a man who finally knew exactly what he wanted, he wrapped her close, covered her mouth with his and dared her to protest. For all of two seconds, she seriously considered it. Then she felt the wild, thundering beat of his heart, tasted the blind, searching hunger of his mouth and felt the need of the arms that held her as if they would never let her go. And suddenly, she couldn't think, couldn't reason, couldn't do anything but give in to the longing that had become an ache in her heart that wouldn't go away. With a sigh that could have been his name, a promise, a whisper of contentment, she closed her eyes and forgot everything but the madness of wanting Cooper.

Somewhere in the back of her mind, a voice that refused to be muzzled warned her it shouldn't have been that easy to let go. But giving herself permission to kiss him without caution, she discovered, was as simple as giving in to an unbearable craving for chocolate. Without a single thought of resisting, she closed her eyes and just let herself enjoy.

Craving. She was a craving in his gut, a burning in his blood, a fire in his loins that made rational thought impossible. He knew he should slow down, *think, for pity's sake!* When he'd stopped her from charging out the door, he really hadn't intended to do anything but shake a little sense in her. But this . . . there was nothing sensible about this, nothing sensible about the wildness she stirred in him, the need. When she was this close, her softness right there under his hands, the enticing scent of her driving him out of his mind, all he could think about was her. Touching her, tasting her, seducing her until all she could think of was . . . him.

A groan tearing through his lungs, he wrenched his mouth from hers, but only to scatter kisses over the curve of her cheeks, the stubborn jut of her chin, the silky spot where her pulse hammered wildly at the base of her throat. Sweet. She was so sweet! He could spend hours just tasting her. Giving in to temptation, he touched his tongue to her, stroked her with his wet heat . . . and almost lost it when she whimpered and clutched at him, her hands latching on to his shoulders as if she'd dissolve at his feet if she didn't have him to hold on to.

Naked, he thought, dragging her closer. He wanted her naked and under him on the bed in the corner, her hands moving over him, her cries and his ragged breathing the only sounds in the stillness as the shadows grew long and time slowed to a crawl. Before he gave himself time to think, he was reaching for the hem of her sweater.

"I want you," he growled hoarsely. He hadn't meant to admit it, but the words were out before he could stop them and what was the point, anyway? He held her so close, his hips snug against hers, there was no denying his arousal. The fingers at her waist stilled, his free hand lifted to her face and cupped her cheek. Tilting her head back until he could see all the way to her soul, he slowly rubbed a callused thumb back and forth across her bottom lip. "Let me touch you, sweetheart ... don't say no...."

Her eyes wide, she stared up at him, saw the desire sharpening the angles and planes of his rugged face. He wanted to make love to her, but he had no intention of sweeping her off her feet without giving her time to think. There would be no regrets later, no claims from either of them that they'd been caught up in the moment and hadn't realized what they were doing. A yes, and they would end up in bed; a no, and he would set her free and probably never touch her again.

It was that simple.

Her gaze trapped in the heat of his, she knew it was only a matter of time before she would be forced to walk away from him, forced to deal with the emotions that she hadn't expected to have to deal with. But not today, dear God. Not today.

Her heart in her eyes, she lifted her fingers to his hand, to where his thumb rubbed lazy circles against the fullness of her bottom lip. Pressing a kiss to his warm, gauze-covered palm, she gave him his answer without saying a word.

Heat shafted through him like a flaming arrow. His breath caught in his throat, his eyes turned black as coals. With a groan that could have been her name, he swooped down and replaced his thumb with his hungry, seeking mouth.

A practiced, cunning woman he could have handled without losing his head. But there was no artifice to her, no holding back. She leaned against him and gave and gave and gave, and he was lost before he ever knew what hit him.

He didn't remember reaching for her sweater again, but suddenly, it was on the floor and she was standing in his arms wearing nothing but her bra and jeans. Before the thought registered, before she could do anything but gasp, he had her bare and was reaching for the fastenings of his own clothes.

But her hands were there first. "My turn," she whispered huskily.

When her fingers moved to the buttons of his shirt, he went absolutely still. Suddenly afraid he had changed his mind, her eyes, smoky and vulnerable, flew to his. "Cooper?"

He would have had to be deaf to miss the sudden confusion that shaped the sound of his name on her tongue. His fingers closed around hers. "Oh, honey, you don't know what you're asking," he murmured thickly. "My patience isn't very good at the best of times where you're concerned, and right now, I want you like hell. Come here."

Pulling her close for a sizzling kiss, he fought the restrictions of his clothes, battling buttons and the fastening of his jeans without once letting her up for air. But it wasn't enough. Suddenly desperate for the feel of her under him, surrounding him, he muttered a curse against her mouth and sent the last stubborn buttons of his shirt pinging across the floor of the cabin.

Susannah laughed, she couldn't help it, but he only grinned and dragged her against him as he shed the last of his clothes. Her smile fled, her breath hitched. Heat. Skin against skin. Pounding heart against pounding heart. With a moan that came from low in her throat, she melted against him.

In the next instant, she was caught up in his arms and being carried to the bed. And nothing had ever felt so right as when he followed her down, his weight settling over her, his arms surrounding hers, his mouth hard and hungry on hers. Crushing her to the hard length of his body, he drank from her mouth as if his very existence depended on the sustenance only she could give him. And just that easily, he made her burn. With every sweep of his tongue, with every slow brush of his bandaged hands over her hips and thighs and breasts, he sent the fires climbing higher.

And then his mouth was following his hands, stringing kisses over her hot skin with increasing urgency. Charting a course down her body, he bathed a beaded nipple with his tongue, nipped at the tantalizing indentation of her waist, trailed liquid heat over her stomach and abdomen to the dark curls at the juncture of her thighs. With nothing more than a kiss, he had her arching toward him, her hands frantically clutching at him, her startled cry echoing in the heavy silence. "Cooper!"

Up until then, he'd have sworn he was in control. He'd intended to draw out the pleasure until she was mad with it, until she was so desperate for him that she burned as he did, but at the sound of his name on her lips, at the feel of her small hands rushing over him, pulling him closer, he was stunned to feel himself losing it, his control unraveling, the need tearing at him, fogging his brain until all he could think of was being buried deep inside her.

A fierce frown of concentration gathering on his brow, he tried to slow down. But it was too late. Hot, driving need made his hands impatient, his mouth hungry. No woman had ever driven him to this, pushed him to this, and there wasn't a damn thing he could do about it. His passion breaking over them both like a storm, he moved over her, parting her thighs, his fingers searching for the slick, hot, secret heat of her.

Caught up in the maelstrom, Susannah shuddered, a moan tearing from her throat. She wanted to tell him to hurry, but she couldn't manage the words. Then he was moving over her, his wicked, knowing fingers stroking her, seducing her, stealing her breath and tightening every nerve ending in her body.

Even then, she wasn't prepared for the first rush of passion. With nothing but the driving rhythm of his fingers, he took her to the edge and over before she could do anything but gasp. She was still shuddering when he made a place for himself between her thighs and surged into her welcoming warmth, filling her.

In the long shadows that gathered around them, her gaze met his. His eyes were black with emotion, hard with desire, backlit with something that tugged at her heart and set her aglow. And just that quickly, she knew that whatever happened in the future, she wouldn't regret this moment.

Then he moved, and she couldn't think at all. He stroked her from the inside out, setting her body pulsing with the rhythm of his lean hips, driving her higher and higher, until the last rays of sun that spilled across the bed were somehow inside her, streaking through her like heat lightning. Her body drawn tight, she gasped. A heartbeat later, the fireball building inside her burst without warning, sending a shower of stardust cascading through her. His name a fractured cry on her lips, she tightened her hold on him and dragged him after her into the ecstasy.

This was all they had, all they could ever have, Susannah thought as she lay wrapped close in his arms and solemnly watched the first rays of the morning sun peek through the cabin windows. Moments stolen out of time, nothing else.

Yesterday, she'd convinced herself it would be enough. But yesterday, she hadn't been thinking clearly. Caught up in the magic they'd found in each other, they'd made love again and again, like two insatiable teenagers just discovering the glory of their sexuality, stopping only long enough to eat supper before tumbling back onto the bed. It had been crazy, wild, wonderful.

She'd known it was only a matter of time before reality returned to send her crashing back to earth, but she'd hoped it would be later rather than sooner. So much for wishing, she thought, blinking back tears. The future was there before her, staring her in the face, and from where she lay now, it looked like a dark and lonely place.

But it couldn't be any other way. Not with a cowboy like Cooper Rawlings. Not with an independent woman like her.

So they had today. Tomorrow. A week, maybe more. But eventually, the man terrorizing her would be caught and there would no longer be any reason for the two of them to hide out at the cabin. She would go her way and Cooper his, and if they ever ran into each other again in the years to come, it would just be by chance.

No! she wanted to cry. It wasn't enough. But deep in her heart, she knew it would have to be. She could either accept that and make the most of their time together or ruin the present by worrying about the loneliness of the future before she had to.

Put that way, the choice was a simple one. Swallowing the lump that threatened to choke her, she hugged the masculine arms that held her cradled spoon fashion and willed herself to pretend, just for a little while, that there was no other world outside the cabin, no other time but the here and now.

Later that evening, Cooper stood at the open front door and stared out at the gathering darkness that blanketed the canyon. In the distance, he could hear the gurgle of the springs, sounding for all the world like the murmur of Susannah's soft laughter. It was a sound he knew he would remember a year from now, a lifetime from now. And it was too late to do anything about it. The damage had been done.

The day had passed like a dream, a dream no man in his right mind would ever want to wake up from. Susannah had been sweet and loving and so damn sexy he couldn't look at her without wanting her. Like lovers marooned on a desert island, they'd whiled away the long hours touching, kissing, making love.

She thought he hadn't noticed, but he'd seen the shadows that pushed their way into her eyes at odd times during the day. He'd caught her staring off into space and he'd known that reality was intruding into her thoughts in spite of her best efforts to ignore it. And all he'd wanted to do was drag her back into his arms and make her forget the world that existed beyond the rocky boundaries of the springs.

And that, more than anything, scared him spitless. Because in making her forget, he couldn't stop himself from falling into the fantasy, too. Caution had whispered in his ear that he was making a mistake—she was vulnerable and scared. Any woman in her position would turn with gratitude to the man who came charging to her rescue. But that fact no longer seemed as important as it should have.

Staring out at the colors painting the western sky, he knew he had to have some space...to clear his head, to remember that he had a real talent for misreading a woman's feelings for him. He'd made that mistake with Mary Lou, and it wasn't one he cared to repeat. Especially with Susannah, who could drag emotions out of him Mary Lou had never even tapped.

Swearing, he stepped out onto the porch. "I'm going for a walk," he tossed back over his shoulder in a rough growl. "I need some air."

He was gone before Susannah could open her mouth, disappearing into the darkening shadows beyond the doorway like a phantom in the night. Her heart thudding, she stared after him, fighting the need to follow. She hadn't missed his restlessness, the brooding, speculative looks he'd sent her when he thought she wasn't watching, the words that seemed to hum in the air, waiting to be spoken. Everything had changed, yet nothing had. They had given in to the demands of the passion that had been sparking between them for what seemed like decades, but the future was still just as dark, just as nebulous, just as *lonely,* as it had been from the moment they first stumbled across each other.

Emptiness spilling into her heart, she told herself to let it go, let *him* go. But from where she sat, she could feel the coolness of early evening creeping in through the open door. It had been a warm day for early February, the kind that held a tantalizing hint of spring, but now that the sun was down, the temperature was quickly dropping. And Cooper hadn't taken his jacket. Not caring that she was looking for an excuse to go after him, she rose and grabbed her jacket and his from the pegs near the door, then followed him outside.

Pausing a moment on the porch, she gave her eyes time to adjust to the darkening twilight, then glanced toward the springs. Nothing moved in the night that she could see, but instinctively she knew that Cooper had gone there. The soft murmur of the water as it tumbled over the rocks was like a temptress's call to the troubled and discontent, and she couldn't resist it any more than she sensed he had. Slipping into her own jacket, she draped his over her arm, buried her hands in her pockets and started walking.

Still, it was another fifteen minutes before she found him. Following the rough, rock-laden bank of the springs, she had left the cabin around a curve and out of sight when she suddenly saw his dark silhouette near the far end of the small canyon that surrounded them like a fortress. Like a deer caught in the scope of a hunter's rifle, he stood unmoving and still as stone.

It wasn't until she drew near that she realized he was gazing off into the distance, toward the entrance to the canyon. Was he already regretting his insistence on staying with her? she wondered, her breath catching painfully in her throat.

Hesitating, she was seriously considering slipping soundlessly back to the cabin and leaving him to his silent reflections when he spoke in a low voice that wouldn't carry beyond the canyon walls. "I've been standing here racking my brains trying to figure out why anyone would want you to leave your ranch so badly that they resorted to threatening you. And I think I just may have gotten my answer. Look."

He gestured to where her land lay in the distance. Frowning, she took the final few steps that brought her even with him and studied the concealing darkness that lay before her. Nothing moved.

"What? What is it?" she began, only to freeze as she suddenly saw what he wanted her to see. "A light! My God, someone's on my ranch!"

If the light had been at the house, she would have seen it immediately, but it was miles from the ranch headquarters, close to the rocky ridge that formed the western boundary of the property and extended all the way south to the Double R. The most barren part of the ranch, there was nothing there but a dry creek bed of rocks and dust and an occasional cactus or two.

Confused, she glanced back at Cooper. "Why would anyone be out there in the middle of nowhere? What are they doing?"

"I don't know, but I mean to find out," he said grimly. "Come on."

All the way back to the cabin, Susannah tried to reason with him. She was just as anxious as he to find out who was out there, but not like this, not alone, just the two of them, skulking around in the dark, tracking a man whom she didn't doubt for a minute was armed and dangerous. It was too risky. If Cooper was really serious about surprising the man in the act of whatever he was doing, then they needed to get his brothers and the sheriff to go with them.

But he vetoed that idea immediately. You couldn't sneak up on anyone with a whole army at your back, and he wasn't taking a chance on scaring the guy off before he even got a look at him. But he did understand Susannah's reluctance and suggested she wait for him at the cabin. She just looked at him and climbed into his truck.

Knowing his headlights carried just as far as the other man's did, Cooper cut the lights before cautiously driving out of the canyon. He saw in an instant he could have saved himself the trouble. The Patterson place was dark as pitch again, the light extinguished. "Damn!"

At his softly muttered expletive, Susannah followed his gaze to where the light had been and didn't know whether to be relieved or disappointed that it was no longer there. "Do you think he's gone?"

"Looks like it, but I'm still going to check it out," he said as he rolled over the cattle guard that formed a little-used entrance to her ranch. "Hang on, I'm going cross-country."

With that warning, he cut away from the rough road that led to her house and headed for the spot where he had seen the light. For the sake of caution, he left his own headlights off. There was nothing to hit but an occasional cactus, and he was able to dodge those in the dark. Bouncing and swearing over the uneven terrain, they drew closer and closer to the rocky ridge.

Any hope that the trespasser might still be there died the moment Cooper braked to a stop at the spot where he estimated he'd seen the light. The place was deserted. Littered with boulders, some of which were as large as the truck, there was no sign that there'd been any life there for decades.

"Well, hell!" Pulling on his headlights, he pushed open his door. "This is probably a wild goose chase, but since we're here, we might as well look around," he told Susannah grimly. "There had to be a reason for the bastard to come to this particular spot. He didn't just pick it out of thin air on a whim."

Joining him in front of the truck, Susannah had to agree. "Well, it's miles from the highway," she offered. "And you can't see it from the house. In fact, you can't see it from anywhere except the springs at the Double R, and nobody goes there after dark."

"Which meant he was doing something that he didn't want anyone else to see," Cooper concluded, searching the ground for tire tracks. "Now we've just got to figure out what."

By mutual agreement, they divided up the area illuminated by the truck headlights, with Cooper taking the left side and Susannah the right. Heads down, eyes trained unrelentingly on the ground, they were so caught up in searching what was directly in front of their feet that neither of them saw the opening chiseled out of the rock cliff until Susannah almost stumbled into it.

At her gasp, his head snapped up. "What is it? Did you find something?"

"A mine," she said, her eyes wide with surprise as she glanced over her shoulder at him. "There's an old mine here."

He was at her side in an instant. "Son of a gun," he swore, frowning at the old timbers that formed the entrance to the mine shaft. "I knew there had to be something here. I knew it!"

Stunned, Susannah couldn't drag her eyes away from the dark, shadowy interior that eluded the illuminating glare of the truck headlights. "I had no idea there was ever any mining done on the ranch. If my father knew, he never said anything. Let's check it out—"

"Oh, no," he growled, grabbing her. "We're not going anywhere near it until we know it's safe."

"But someone's already been here. Look, there's a footprint right there in the dirt."

His gaze followed her pointing finger, and sure enough, there was the clear outline of a boot print in the soft dirt. Whoever had been there earlier had gone into the mine, for what reason he couldn't imagine. Mining in that area had been abandoned decades ago, so there was little chance of any ore being found at this late date.

"Maybe so," he retorted, "but I don't even have a flashlight with me, so you can forget about going in there tonight. We'll come back tomorrow when we're better prepared."

At any other time, she would have taken exception to his autocratic tone, but just the thought of a cave-in crashing down upon their heads was enough to turn her throat to dust. "You're right," she agreed. "There's no use taking any chances."

But when they returned to the cabin, Cooper discovered that the danger wasn't in the mine they would inspect in the morning but in the long hours they had to get through until then. He'd promised himself he wasn't going to touch Susannah again. He couldn't, dammit, not if he was going to be able to let her go when this was all over with. And that moment was drawing closer and closer with every passing day.

The thought gnawed at him, eating a hole in his gut. He was half tempted to go outside for another walk until she went to bed, but then she announced she was going to take a bath. Relieved, he turned to the cold fireplace. "I'll build a fire."

It took all his concentration just to strike the match once he heard the water running from the solar-powered hot water heater in the bathroom. He watched the flames take hold, but it was Susannah's image that danced in the fire. All too easily, he could see her sliding out of her clothes, piece by piece, slowly dropping her jeans, sweater and underclothes to the floor, until she was beautifully, completely bare....

Before he could draw a sharp breath, he was hard and aching. His fingers curling into a fist, he turned the air blue with a series of curses that would have done a sailor proud. He wasn't surprised when it didn't help.

The only solution was to be in bed before she got out of the bathroom, he decided grimly. Then he wouldn't be tempted to reach for her. His face set in hard, unyielding lines, he rose from the hearth.

When she stepped out of the bathroom a few minutes later, the sleeping bag she'd claimed for herself last night was laid out in front of the roaring fire and Cooper was sitting at the table in nothing but his jeans, tugging off his boots. He glanced up at the sound of the door opening and felt his heart stop.

She was dressed in a navy-blue nightshirt that covered her from neck to midthigh and successfully concealed almost every curve she had. With her hair damp and tousled, her face scrubbed free of makeup and her feet bare, Cooper tried to tell himself there was nothing the least bit sexy about her. She could have passed for a fourteen-year-old at a slumber party. But in his heart he knew she could have worn rags and still stopped traffic.

And there was no way in hell he was going to be able to resist her.

He saw her gaze drop to the sleeping bag on the floor, then shift to the covers turned back on the bed. He didn't have to read her mind to know that she'd instantly guessed his intentions—the knowledge was there in her steady gaze as her eyes lifted to his.

"I'm going to have a hard time letting you go when this is over with," he said bluntly, without apology.

"So you're letting me go now? Is that it?"

Her tone was accusing, her eyes reproachful. Swearing, he pulled off his boots and pushed to his feet. "What if I am? I don't want to hurt you."

Standing tall and straight before him, her eyes locked with his. "Then don't."

She was pushing him and they both knew it, right into what they both wanted. "Dammit, Susannah...." Even as he cursed the pull she had on him, he reached for her.

A log shifted in the fireplace, sending a shower of sparks shooting up the chimney. But the heat that radiated from the dancing flames was nothing compared to the fire that Cooper built in Susannah with nothing more than his hands. She never knew how it happened, but suddenly she was naked and flat on her back on the sleeping bag, with her lover bending over her, his sure fingers trailing liquid heat as they moved slowly over her, wooing her, seducing her, turning her to putty in his hands.

He was as bare as she, his skin golden in the firelight and stretched taut over muscles that were lean and hard from a lifetime of physical labor. She'd seen him before, touched him before, loved him until she was weak with it, but there was something in his narrowed eyes, an intensity, a determination that would not be denied, that reminded her of a pagan god claiming what was his. Shuddering at the feel of his hands on her, she wanted, *needed,* to touch him, but when she reached for him, his fingers clamped around her wrists to draw them above her head, staking her to the floor in a gentle, unbreakable hold.

Her heart jerked in her breast; her mouth went dry. Suddenly her breathing was ragged and she could only lick her lips and gasp, "Cooper, please..."

"I intend to," he growled, his gaze dark with promise as he slid his free hand slowly up her body and captured her breast, his thumb lazily tracing a circle around her already pouting nipple. At her instinctive cry of pleasure, satisfaction gleamed in his eyes. "I'm going to please you until you go up in flames in my arms. Do you hear me, sweetheart? I'm going to make you burn."

"No—"

"Oh, yes," he rasped, replacing the hand at her breast with his hot, nuzzling mouth. "I need to touch the fire in you."

With no more warning than that, he teased her with his tongue and sent flames streaking from her breast to the hot, secret core of her. Whimpering, she arched up off the sleeping bag, pushing her nipple deeper into his mouth, blindly offering herself to him, her arms tensing, straining to be free.

"Please . . . let me touch you. . . ."

"In a minute," he promised thickly. "Just a minute."

He moved over her like a hot summer wind, breezy and bold and playful, skimming the dips and curves of her body with his hands and mouth and tongue, never staying anywhere too long, always tasting, always loving. And everywhere he touched, he left behind little embers that smoldered like coals just waiting for the right conditions to flare into an inferno.

Pressed close, his legs tangling with hers, her ragged breathing driving him wild, he felt the heat bloom under her skin, the need clawing at her. But it wasn't enough. He wanted to steep her in pleasure, drown her in it, drag her with him down into the depths of a passion unlike anything she had ever known before. Because when this was all over, when he had to let her go, this was all she would have of him to remember.

"Beautiful," he murmured, trailing kisses down the very center of her, loving the silky softness of skin that was as pale as ivory beneath his tongue, the curve of a hip that seemed specially made for his hands, the sensitive spot high on the inside of her thigh that he was sure no man but him had ever tasted. "You're so damn beautiful."

She wanted to tell him she wasn't—her looks weren't anything special, just average, nothing more. But he had a way of telling her she was drop-dead gorgeous, then making her believe it. Because no man had ever worshiped her as if she were a gift sent down from heaven just for him.

"My hands," she moaned, sensuously moving under him, *for* him. "Let me go. I need to touch you."

He was hotter than a firecracker with a lit fuse, ready to explode any second, but right then and there, he couldn't have denied her the moon if she'd wanted it for a night-light. His hold on her wrists eased, but only long enough to drag her fingers down to his hard arousal. "Touch me, baby. Yes, like that. Oh..."

His control, what was left of it, disintegrated at the feel of her hand closing around him, and suddenly he was the one burning like a house on fire. He stood it for as long as he could—all of ten seconds—before he groaned, "Enough!" and pulled her hand from him. Before she could blink, before she could catch her breath, he was between her thighs, gentling her, testing her readiness, sliding into her with a moan that seemed to come from the very depths of his being.

In the span of a heartbeat, the heat in her blood was a wildfire raging out of control. With every touch of his sure, knowing hands, with every mind-drugging kiss, with every stroke of his hips against hers, he fanned the flames higher and higher, greedily adding fuel to the fire like a pyromaniac with a pocketful of matches and a can of gasoline. And when he finally sent her shooting over the edge into the showering sparks of passion, there wasn't a doubt in either of their minds that he'd kept his promise. He'd made her burn.

Chapter 11

One end of the coiled rope tied around a heavy boulder just outside the entrance of the mine and the rest slung over his shoulder, Cooper tested the flashlight he carried to make sure the batteries were working properly, then glanced over his shoulder at Susannah with a frown. Dressed in faded jeans and a black turtleneck, she stood patiently at the entrance, her own flashlight at the ready, a spare coil of rope on her slim shoulder.

Ever since he'd woken up this morning with her in his arms, he'd tried his best to talk her out of coming with him to the mine, but the woman could be as stubborn as a mule. Nothing he could say had fazed her, not even warnings about the danger. He'd wanted to throttle her and had even thought about taking the truck and slipping off without her before she realized his intentions. But knowing her as he now did, he wouldn't have put it past her to walk to the mine and go in by herself.

His blood ran cold just at the thought of her doing something so reckless.

"Are you sure you want to do this?" he asked her again, his brown eyes dark with a mixture of worry and irritation. "It's not going to be a picnic, you know. There could be all sorts of bugs and spiders in there, not to mention snakes."

Susannah smiled slightly, touched in spite of herself by his concern. "I'm not afraid of snakes, Cooper. There shouldn't be any around at this time of year, anyway. It'll be cold down in the mine shaft. Any snake with any brains is going to be outside sunning himself on a rock. So will you relax? Everything is going to be fine."

He gave her a look that told her she was asking for too much, then turned toward the mine. "I'll relax when we come out," he said grimly. "Stay close. I don't want to lose you in there."

The sunlight that spilled through the mine entrance was quickly left behind, and within moments they were swallowed whole by a darkness that looked as if it came straight from the pits of hell. They both already had their flashlights on, but the beams that had seemed overpowering outside the mine hardly made a dent in the opaque blackness that engulfed them.

Muttering a curse, Cooper stopped in his tracks and felt Susannah bump into him from behind. "Easy," he murmured, studying the shadows that waited for them, concealing all kinds of hazards. "We're going to take it nice and easy. This shaft's going to take a downhill slant any minute now and if we go too fast, we're going to be in big trouble."

Susannah peeked around his broad shoulders to see the black curved walls of the tunnel hovering over them threateningly. A shiver slid down her spine. "Can you see anything?'' she said in a whisper that sounded like a shout in the tense silence.

''Nothing. But Jack the Ripper could be standing behind one of these old support posts and we wouldn't see him until he was standing over us with a knife.''

''Geez, Cooper, I really needed to hear that,'' she drawled, shooting him a reproachful look. ''Any more pearls of wisdom you want to lay on me before we get any deeper into this thing?''

He chuckled. ''Keep your head down. The ceiling gets real low up ahead.''

Moving farther into the bowels of the earth, they glided forward as if they were walking on glass and each step could be their last. But the ground remained, thankfully, firm beneath their feet, though it did, as Cooper had predicted, start to drop off at a sharp angle.

Slowing their pace to a crawl, Cooper directed the beam of the flashlight down the dark tunnel that waited for them like a black hole. If he lost his footing, it was going to be a hell of a slide to who knew what. His jaw clenched on an oath, he started down.

He'd hardly taken a step when Susannah gasped behind him. ''What's that?''

He froze. ''What?''

''That,'' she retorted, shining her flashlight to the left. ''It looks like another shaft.''

Surprised that another tunnel would start so close to the surface, Cooper swung toward her and added the power of his light to hers. ''It could be a shaft,'' he agreed, studying the tight opening that didn't seem to be much wider than his shoulders, ''but I don't think so. It's too narrow. Let's check it out.''

Ducking his head, he carefully eased through the roughly chiseled entrance that he wouldn't even have noticed if it hadn't been for Susannah. For a moment, it seemed as if the walls were closing in on him. Scowling, he was beginning to wonder if the shaft was nothing more than a dead end when it suddenly opened up into a large, cavernlike room.

"Son of a bitch!" he hissed between his teeth, stopping in his tracks.

Right behind him, Susannah stepped to his side and caught her breath in surprise. "My God, it looks like a department-store warehouse!"

His narrowed eyes trained on the electronics piled haphazardly on the dirt floor, Cooper had to agree with her. There were enough television sets, VCRs, camcorders and cameras stored there to supply a small army. But unlike the merchandise found in a department store, none of it appeared to be new. In fact, unless he missed his guess, it was all stolen.

And suddenly, like the sudden appearance of a bolt of lightning in a clear sky, the pieces fell into place. "Damn." Why hadn't he seen it sooner?

"What?" Susannah demanded, glancing at him sharply. "What is it?"

"The thief Riley told us about," he replied. "Remember? He's been hitting ranches all over the county for months now, stealing everything that's not nailed down. Riley's had every deputy he's got on the case, but evidently the bastard's as slippery as an eel. Every time Riley thinks he's on to him, he hits a different part of the county, then slips away in the dark."

Susannah paled. "And you think this is the stuff he's stolen? Some two-bit thief is using my ranch to hide his loot?"

"He's been doing a hell of a lot more than that," he said grimly. "Unless I'm way off base—and I don't think I am— he and the bastard who's been threatening you are one and the same man. It's the only thing that makes sense. This place was deserted for two years, so it was the perfect place for him to stash his loot until he could fence it in El Paso or Tucson. Then you came home unexpectedly—"

"And threatened to ruin everything just by being here," she said, startled. "My God, no wonder he tried to scare me into leaving! If I stumbled across the operation by accident—"

"He could kiss this little setup goodbye," he finished for her.

Her eyes drifted back to the stolen goods that had been snatched from ranches all over the county. "We've got to get out of here and call the sheriff. He can get some men out here, set up a trap...."

"We'll call him from your house. Let's go."

They hurried back into the mine's main shaft, the caution they'd had to use earlier no longer necessary now that they knew there were no dangerous pitfalls between them and the entrance. In the distance, daylight gleamed like a diamond, beckoning them forward.

Her heart in her throat, Susannah lengthened her stride to keep up with Cooper, all the while feeling as if she was rushing pell-mell toward disaster. It was over, she thought, blinking back stupid tears. She should have been happy. As soon as the sheriff was filled in on what they'd discovered, it was only a matter of time before the thug terrorizing her was under lock and key. Then her life could return to normal. She could go home, sleep nights without having to keep one eye open, finish the work she had to do here, then get on with the rest of the research she needed to do before she could actually sit down to write Diego Kelly's story.

Which meant she would be leaving soon, she acknowledged, despair clutching her heart. And these past few weeks she'd had at the ranch with Cooper, stolen moments out of time, would be left behind like forgotten mementos gathering dust on a closet shelf.

No! she wanted to cry. It couldn't be over so soon. But she knew it was. They'd been thrown together because of the threats against her, but now it was time to return to the real world. No matter how much it hurt.

The need to weep almost more than she could bear, she struggled for control as they finally reached the mine entrance, but the minute she rushed from the blackness of the mine into the sunlit day, her eyes began to tear. It was just the glare, she told herself, wiping furiously at the moisture that leaked out from beneath her lashes. That was all it could be.

"Well, well, what do we have here? Two busybodies who don't know how to mind their own business."

At the sound of the familiar chilling voice she'd heard too many times to ever forget, Susannah stumbled to a halt, shocked. Behind her, Cooper cursed savagely, but she never took her eyes from the man who lounged negligently against one of the huge boulders right outside the mine. He was a big man, tall and broad shouldered, with a face that was good-ol'-boy friendly. But there was nothing friendly about the gun he pointed right at her heart.

Cooper spit out a vehement curse and immediately stepped protectively in front of her. "Denkins," he said with loathing. "God, I should have known it was you. Only the scum of the earth would threaten an innocent woman."

"Denkins?" Susannah choked, her gaze fastened in dawning horror on the other man. She knew of only one man with that name, but this couldn't be him. "Dwayne Denkins, the ex-sheriff?"

Cooper nodded grimly, his brown eyes black with a contempt he made no attempt to hide. "That's right, sweetheart. The man who threatened to burn down your house with you in it is evidently none other than our infamous former sheriff. He's a real prize, isn't he? Now you know why he didn't get reelected. He's got this problem with a thing called honesty. He hasn't got much use for it."

Denkins flushed hotly. "You and your whole bunch always did think you were holier than thou," he snarled. "You sit out there on that fancy spread of yours and look down your noses at the rest of us poor souls just trying to make a decent living."

"Oh, please, spare me." Cooper snorted. "Since when does taking kickbacks qualify as making a decent living? You knew what Joe Patterson and the others were doing two years ago, but did you put a stop to the conspiracy before it got out of hand? Hell, no. All they had to do was pay you to look the other way, and you nearly snapped your neck falling in with them."

"That was a loan, dammit! I told you and your family that at the time, but you wouldn't listen. No! You were looking for someone to blame for Gable getting shot, and you weren't content with just sending Patterson up the river. You had to ruin my life, too." So furious he could hardly speak, he glared at Cooper as if he would like nothing better than to put a bullet in him. "I didn't just lose the election, I lost everything—my job, my house, my standing in the community. People looked at me like I was dirt, and the only work I could get was as a janitor."

"So what is this?" Cooper taunted, jerking his head back toward the mine. "Your side job?"

For the first time, Denkins smiled, his close-set eyes alight with an unholy glee. "Oh, no. This is nothing but sweet revenge. I promised myself when I lost the election that I was going to make the whole county pay, and that's just what I've done.

"Then you had to come along and ruin everything," he said accusingly, his gaze abruptly shifting to Susannah, who stood half-concealed behind Cooper. "You just couldn't take a hint, could you? I tried to warn you away, but you wouldn't listen. So now you both have to die. And you've got no one to blame but yourselves."

He meant it, Susannah thought, horrified, her heart jerking to a stop in her breast. He made the announcement without an ounce of inflection in his voice, as if he were announcing what shirt he'd decided to wear for the day. "Cooper's family knows where we are," she said quickly. "If we're not back in an hour, they'll come looking for us."

"Save it," he jeered. "Gable and Flynn don't know anything or they'd be right here with you." With a sharp gesture of the gun, he motioned to Cooper. "Tie him up," he told her.

"What?"

"You heard me. Tie him up. *Now.*"

Susannah blanched, fear battling with the outrage that suddenly burned deep in her gut. No, she thought furiously. She wasn't going to do it. If this bastard was going to kill them, he wasn't going to get any help from her.

But before she could open her mouth to tell him to go to the devil, Cooper said quietly, "Do it."

"But—"

"Don't argue with him, sweetheart. I know him. He'd just as soon shoot you as look at you if you give him any flak."

"You'd better listen to him," Denkins added silkily. "He knows what he's talking about."

Susannah ignored him. Her heart in her eyes, she turned to Cooper, silently begging him not to make her do this. He couldn't know what he was asking of her. To tie him up, to leave him defenseless against a madman with a gun—she couldn't do it.

But something in his eyes told her she could.

Pain clawing at her, she did.

The second the rope settled on his wrists, Cooper had to steel himself to stand still. Every ounce of self-preservation he possessed urged him to break free, then go for Denkins's throat and stop him before he had a chance to hurt Susannah. But that was just what the other man was waiting for—he could see the expectation gleaming in his eyes. The minute he took a step toward Denkins, the lowlife would shoot him.

Cooper was damned if he'd give him the satisfaction.

"Don't try any tricks," Denkins warned Susannah. "If that rope isn't tight enough to keep him from escaping, I just might have to put a bullet in him so he doesn't wander off when I'm not looking."

Behind him, Cooper felt Susannah's shaking fingers fumble at his wrists. Denkins would pay for this, he promised himself, his eyes hard with fury as he glared at the other man's smug face. He didn't know how the hell he was going to accomplish it, but somehow, some way, he was going to make the bastard wish he'd never been born.

The rope snapped tight, biting into his skin. He didn't so much as flinch, but Susannah knew his wrists had to sting. "I'm sorry," she whispered.

"It's all right, sweetheart. Just do as he says."

"Yeah, *sweetheart,* just do as I say and we'll all get along just fine," Denkins drawled. Pushing himself up from the rock where he lounged, he strolled toward them, as relaxed as if he were taking a walk in the park. But the gun clutched tightly in his hand never wavered.

With a sharp movement of the weapon, he waved Susannah away from Cooper, then checked the ropes that securely bound his wrists behind his back. "Not bad," he praised, pleased. But when he turned to Susannah, he wasn't smiling. "Now your turn."

"No!" Cooper growled, whirling. "Leave her alone, dammit. She can't hurt you—"

In the blink of an eye, Denkins moved, snatching Susannah in front of him and jerking the gun up to her head before she could do anything but gasp. "Not if she's dead," he agreed harshly. "So what's it going to be? Tie her up or shoot her? The choice is yours."

Choice? Cooper raged silently. There was no choice and they both knew it. Denkins was going to kill them both, and the only chance Cooper had of stopping him was to buy them some time. Hatred boiling in him, he shot the other man a cold look that condemned him to burn in the fires of hell. "Tie her up."

Bound and virtually helpless, Cooper stood as close to Susannah as he could get and watched Denkins load the stolen goods from the mine into his pickup. Denkins wasn't going to get away with it, she told herself. He couldn't drive down the highway with a truckload of stolen goods without drawing attention to himself, and someone was bound to start asking questions. And even if no one noticed his unusual behavior, the Rawlingses would eventually show up at the cabin by the springs and start an all-out search for them when they couldn't find them. She only prayed it was sooner rather than later because they were running out of options real quick.

Tossing the last of the items into the truck, Denkins dusted his hands and tossed a tarp over the bed of the pickup, concealing the whole load. "All right, that's it," he said in satisfaction, snapping the tarp into place. "Now for a little unfinished business." He turned toward them, the gun once again in his hand. "Come on, into the mine."

"The mine! But—"

"But nothing," he growled, and shoved Susannah in the back to send her stumbling toward the entrance. At Cooper's angry snarl, he rammed the pistol against his ribs. "I didn't ask for your comments. Now, move it. When I came out here to get a load to take to El Paso, I didn't expect to run into you two, and I'm behind schedule."

His jaw like granite, Cooper did as he was told, but all the while, his narrowed eyes were searching for a way out. But there was none. Darkness closed around them, cold and bottomless, and as they left the entrance behind, they had only the thin stream of light that came from the flashlight Denkins held to guide them deeper into the mine. And with every step they took, the danger grew. The ground started to slope downward, the tunnel grew narrower, and air that had never touched the light of day turned as icy as the Arctic.

"That's far enough," Denkins grunted. "Stop right there."

Cooper froze, his blood running cold as he realized they had just run out of time. He wanted to tell Susannah to run, but he never got the chance. As they turned, Denkins raised the gun and aimed it right at him. A second later, the deafening report of a shot being fired reverberated through the mine.

"Oh, God, no!"

The bullet ripped through Cooper's leg like a jagged bolt of hot lightning. Crying out in agony, he barely heard Susannah's horrified scream. He stumbled, but with his hands tied, he couldn't catch himself. He hit the ground hard, a low groan rolling from his throat.

"Cooper!" Tears welling in her eyes, Susannah dropped to her knees beside him, but she was bound, too, and there was nothing she could do to stop the blood spilling through the ugly hole just above his knee.

"Untie me," she whimpered to Denkins, tugging at the ropes that cut into her wrists. "You've got to untie me and let me help him."

For an answer, the stark light illuminating the shaft vanished abruptly, plunging the narrow tunnel into blackness.

Cooper cursed, damning Denkins to hell, as Susannah whirled on her knees to confront the bastard. But he was already heading for the entrance, taking the last of the light with him. "Wait! Where are you going? You can't just walk away and leave us here like this!"

His laugh was mocking and unrepentant. "I can do anything I want. Haven't you figured that out yet?"

"But Cooper will die!"

"So will you, lady. Neither one of you is ever going to see the light of day again. When I get through barricading the entrance, nothing short of a bulldozer will get you out of here."

He was gone, then, disappearing into the darkness without a backward glance, leaving behind a darkness that was thick as ink, cold, and all-consuming.

"Don't panic, honey," Cooper gritted out through clenched teeth, breaking the sudden, tomblike silence that engulfed them. "That's just what that jerk wants you to do, and you're tougher than that."

Strangling on a hysterical laugh, she choked, "Thanks for the vote of confidence, but I think you should know that I'm not especially fond of small, tight places."

He swore, a short, pithy comment that bounced off the closely hovering walls. "Then why the devil did you insist on coming down here with me in the first place?"

"Because I knew we weren't going to be in here very long. I didn't plan on dying here."

"We're not going to," he retorted flatly. "But first we've got to get untied. How tight did he bind you?"

Her hands were numb, her wrists burning from the rope that cut deep into her tender skin. But he was lying there on the cold ground, bleeding from a bullet in his thigh, and she'd have bitten off her tongue before complaining. "Just tight enough that I can't pull my hands free," she lied. "Maybe I can snag the rope on a rock and work out the knot. Hang on and let me see what I can do."

Gritting her teeth, she managed to awkwardly push to her feet, but not without a price. White hot heat streaked through her shoulders, setting them afire, and it took every ounce of determination she possessed to silently swallow the groan that rose in her throat. Sweat popping out on her brow, she drew in a swift, healing breath, and waited for the pain to ease. But it was still several moments before she could find the strength to move.

"Hey, you okay?"

With nothing more than his voice, he reached out of the darkness and touched her, soothing her. Swallowing the sudden lump in her throat, she laughed shakily and backed up against the rough-hewn wall, her fingers blindly searching for a jagged edge she could use to saw through the rope. "Oh, yeah. I'm fine. Well, at least as fine as I can be considering the fact that we've been buried alive."

Behind her, her fingers scraped against a jutting lance of stone that almost took the skin off her knuckles. Her heart stumbled, jerking into a ragged rhythm. "I've found something, a sharp edge that might cut the rope," she told him.

Groping awkwardly, she eased her hands into position over the bladelike edge until the rope was snug against it. At the first sawing motion of her hands, the sharp rock ground indiscriminately into rope and skin. Tears welled in her eyes, but she didn't stop. She couldn't, not even when she felt blood trickling down her fingers and the black walls closing in on her. "Talk to me," she whispered hoarsely, desperate for something to distract her. "Tell me about spring roundup again. What's it like?"

He heard the pain in her voice that she tried so hard to hide from him, the fear that had his gut clenching and his hands fighting against his bonds. But the draining wound in his thigh sucked the strength from him, and even if he could have managed to break free, he couldn't have found her in the dark without falling flat on his face.

So, aching to hold her, he talked. In a low, husky voice, he told her about the roundup and how all the cowboys looked forward to it after the inactivity of the winter months. It was a time to cut loose, a time to test their skills, a time to throw themselves into work that was hard and tiring and satisfying. With the eloquence of a master craftsman, he painted pictures with words, drawing images in the dark of dust and heat and glaring sun, blood and sweat, bawling cattle and the thunder of galloping hooves.

The low, soothing tone of his voice washed over her, calming her as nothing else could, effortlessly defusing the panic threatening to shatter her control. Clinging to his words, she sawed away at the rope shackling her, only to jump in surprise when it suddenly gave way. "Got it." She sighed in relief. "Thank God!"

"Atta girl," he praised her thickly. "I knew you could do it."

Pain and a faintness that had her heart pounding in alarm laced his words. He was weakening. Fast. Stripping the offending rope from her raw, throbbing wrists, she made her way to his side as quickly as she dared in the blackness, her arms outstretched and her hands blindly reaching for him as she dropped to her knees. "How badly are you bleeding?" she began, only to gasp when her fingers encountered the soaked material of his jeans. "Oh, God!"

"That bad, huh?" he said tightly. "Then we better find a way to get out of here in a hurry. Untie me, sweetheart, and help me up."

"First I've got to get this bleeding stopped," she said, and removed her turtleneck.

In the all-concealing darkness, he couldn't see a thing, but there was nothing wrong with his ears. "What the devil are you doing? Put your sweater back on. It's colder than hell in here."

"If I do, you'll bleed to death. Hold still."

Ignoring his muttered curses, she folded the body of the sweater into a thick pad and then gingerly searched for the wound on his thigh. When she found it, her fingers told her it was every bit as bad as she feared. She felt him stiffen like a poker, heard his muffled groan and had to squeeze back tears.

"I'm sorry."

"Just do what you have to do," he said between his teeth.

With shaking fingers, she carefully placed the makeshift bandage over the wound, then used the arms of the sweater to tie it tightly into place. "Can you turn over on your side so I can untie you?" she asked huskily when she was finished. "Easy. Let me help you...."

Weak as a baby, he had no choice. His jaw locked tight, he let her gently roll him to his side, then waited while she fumbled with the ropes holding him hostage. His arms had long since gone numb, which was probably a blessing in disguise considering the fact that he'd been lying on them. But then Susannah managed to loosen his bindings and a thousand ants seemed to be swarming under his skin at once, crawling out of his shoulder joints and down his arms as the feeling gradually returned.

"Aaargh!"

"I know. It stings, doesn't it? Here, let me help you." In the darkness, her hands found his arms and worked up them, kneading the soreness out. Only when he sighed in relief did she stop. "Better?"

He nodded, then realized she couldn't see him. "Yeah," he growled, taking one of her hands and twining his fingers with hers. "Thanks, sweetheart. You ready to get out of here?"

She laughed, she couldn't help it. Eyes straining in the darkness, she glanced around and saw nothing but the blackness that was so thick she couldn't even see her fingers when she held them right at the bridge of her nose. "How? You heard Denkins. He was going to block the entrance."

"Then we won't go out the entrance," he said simply. "Feel that breeze?"

Standing there in nothing but her jeans and bra, she'd felt the cold wind whisper through the shaft the minute she'd pulled off her sweater. "I'm trying not to," she retorted in a voice laced with rueful amusement. "In case you've forgotten, you're wearing my sweater."

He hadn't forgotten. How could he? In spite of the burning ache in his leg, it was driving him crazy that she was standing before him half-naked and he couldn't even see her. His fingers tightened around hers. "It's not coming from the entrance, so there's got to be an air shaft around here somewhere that will lead us right to the surface. All we have to do is find it."

He made it sound easy. A piece of cake. The only problem was they were working in the dark, the blind leading the blind, without a single match between them to show them the way.

Chapter 12

Later, Susannah was sure it was pure dumb luck that led them to the air shaft. They stumbled around in the dark for what seemed like hours, going deeper and deeper into the mine, their noses raised to the air like hounds catching a scent. Cooper had long since given up holding her hand and had slipped his arm around her shoulders, and with every step, he grew weaker, his weight against her heavier. He was slipping away from her—she could feel it—and it took every ounce of strength she had not to dissolve in tears. Fear choking her, she was rattling on about anything and everything, pretending that everything was peachy-keen, when the tunnel suddenly intersected another one and fresh air swirled around them teasingly.

"Here," she said, stopping in her tracks. "Feel it? It's got to be here somewhere, on the wall to the right."

At her side, Cooper silently cursed his rapidly dwindling strength and forced himself to move away from her. "Some of the air shafts in these old mines were used for escape routes in case of cave-ins," he said thickly, turning to run his hands blindly over the rough wall. "The miners chiseled handholds in the rock...."

He really hadn't expected that to be the case here, but then his fingers swept over an indentation that just fit his hand. Surprised, he doubled back and took a moment to investigate it, then slid his other hand up the wall to the spot where another handhold would logically be. "Well, I'll be damned."

At his soft exclamation of surprise, Susannah's heart started to pound. "You found it?"

In the darkness, his hand searched for and found hers. "Here," he said, guiding her fingers to the chiseled-out depression in the cold, stone wall. "Don't forget, these handholds were designed for miners, so they may be spaced pretty far apart for you. Take your time and don't panic. I'll be right behind you."

He urged her in front of him, but she hesitated. "What about your leg? How can you climb—"

"Don't worry about me," he replied grimly. "Nothing's keeping me in this hellhole, sweetheart. I'll make it even if I have to pull myself out by my fingernails." His hands settling about her waist, he boosted her up to the handholds. "Up you go."

The going was slow and torturous and downright hairy at times. Once they left the solid footing of the ground, there was no going back. Clinging to their handholds, they were stuck to the side of the cold wall like flies. One slip of the fingers, one misjudged grip, and they could both go crashing down to the mine far below.

Her heart in her throat, Susannah felt sweat pop out on her palms and brow in spite of the fact that the temperature had to be hovering somewhere around forty degrees. Every instinct she possessed urged her to hurry, but even if it had been safe to do so, nothing, not even her own screaming need to breathe freely in the wide-open spaces outside the mine, could have made her leave Cooper. He was right behind her, and in the utter stillness that embraced them, his breathing was ragged and labored, his movements slow.

She could practically feel his pain, the agony that he refused to give in to, and her heart wanted to break for him. She wanted to tell him not to be a hero. She wanted to tell him to curse the fire she knew was burning in his thigh—groan, dammit!—but she was afraid he was going to need every ounce of that steely self-control of his to make it out of the air shaft. If he gave in to the pain, even for a second, he could be in trouble. Biting her tongue, she kept climbing.

The light, when it spilled over her like stardust, caught her completely by surprise. One minute, she could see nothing but a blackness that was as dense as the darkest night, and the next, the shaft took a sharp turn and suddenly she was blinking at the sight of her hands curled into the niches in the rock wall. Startled, she snapped up her head.

And there, in the distance, the light of day gleamed, the sun at the end of the tunnel.

And just that quickly, her eyes were flooded with tears. "Cooper..."

"I see, honey," he said in a voice that was as gruff as hers. "We're home free. What do you say we blow this joint? I don't know about you, but I've had just about all of this mine that I can stand."

She didn't need a second urging. And with the light to guide them, the handholds they'd had to blindly search for in the darkness were much easier to find. Within moments, they had reached the end of the air shaft and were scrambling out onto the rocky ground to freedom.

Susannah tried to convince him to stay right there and let her go for help, but Cooper stubbornly refused to let her out of his sight. He wouldn't put anything past Denkins, and he was taking no chances that the ex-sheriff might come back. Wherever she was going, he would be right there with her every step of the way.

She'd wanted to shake him, to cry out for him to take a good hard look at himself. He was pale and drawn, his face carved in deep lines of agony. The bandage she'd fashioned from her sweater was holding and had at least slowed down the bleeding, but he was still in no shape to walk the half mile to her house. She could make the trek twice as fast alone and be back with help before he even knew she was gone.

But had he listened? No, of course not! His eyes had dropped to her breasts, to the simple cotton bra covering them, reminding her that she was almost topless, and he'd flatly announced that he was going to stick to her like glue. Her skin scorching from the touch of his eyes, her protests had dried up like so much dust and blown away.

Somehow they made it back to her house, but it seemed to take forever. The sudden burst of adrenaline that had shot through them both at having escaped the mine didn't last long, and soon Cooper's steps were dragging, the arm he'd slung around her shoulder a heavy weight. Worried by his pallor, she was horribly afraid his wound had begun to bleed again, but there was nothing she could do about it until she got him home. Tightening her grip on his waist, she focused her gaze on the house once it came in view, and urged him forward.

She'd planned to call Josey and the sheriff just as soon as she got Cooper inside. Retrieving the spare key she kept in a flowerpot on the porch, she opened the door and waited only until she had Cooper on the couch with a blanket spread over him before reaching for the phone. But the minute she raised it to her ear, she knew Denkins had covered his bases just in case they found a way to escape. The phone was deader than a doornail.

From the couch, Cooper watched the anger flare in her eyes seconds before she slammed the phone down. "Denkins's been here, hasn't he?"

She nodded, wanting to throw something. "Come on, let's go. I've got to get you to Josey. We'll take my car."

Too tired to move, Cooper could only lie there, a crooked grin pulling at his lips as his gaze swept over her. "Don't you think you should put a shirt on first? Not that I don't appreciate the view," he assured her, chuckling. "But I'd just as soon my brothers didn't see you walking around like that."

Blushing, she laughed and turned toward her bedroom. "Good point. I'll be right back."

She took only a second to pull on a red flannel shirt, and then she was rushing back to his side and helping him out to her car. It wasn't until she was seated behind the wheel that she realized she didn't have the keys. Muttering a curse, she reached under the dash.

At her side, Cooper frowned. "What are you doing?"

"Hot-wiring it," she retorted, grunting in satisfaction when the motor roared to life. Shooting him a triumphant grin, she explained, "I learned how for one of my Ace MacKenzie books. It's a neat trick, don't you think?"

Unable to hold back a grin, he could only shake his head at her as she put the car in gear and headed for the Double R. He didn't know why he was so surprised at her resourcefulness. She'd been hitting him with one surprise after another from the day they'd met.

The minute they arrived at the Double R and Susannah helped Cooper inside, pandemonium broke out. The whole family had been seated at the dining room table, lingering over a late lunch, when they looked up to find Cooper swaying in the doorway, his face white as parchment and blood seeping out from the rough bandage tied around his thigh. He looking as if he'd have slid right down to the floor if Susannah hadn't been clinging to his waist, shoring him up.

"Good God, what the hell happened to you?"

At Gable's sharp question, the shock holding the others frozen in their seats snapped, and suddenly they were all rushing forward, shouting questions, hands outstretched to help.

"Gable, Flynn, carry him into the den to the couch," Josey said, throwing out orders. "Alice, get my medical bag from the hall closet. Easy," she cautioned. "Don't jostle that leg."

Within minutes, they had him on the couch, and Josey was bending over him, using her scissors to cut off his jeans high on his thigh. She took one look at the oozing wound and announced flatly, "You need to be in the hospital."

"It'll have to wait," he retorted, his mouth tight with pain. "We've got to go after Denkins."

"Denkins?" Flynn exploded. "What the hell does Denkins have to do with this?"

"He's the one who shot me." He gave his brothers a short, concise accounting of the ex-sheriff's illegal activities and his run-in with them. "The bastard left us to die and just took off. He's probably halfway to Mexico by now, and we've got to stop him."

Gable moved to the phone on the table at the end of the couch. "I'm calling Riley."

"And you're going to the hospital," Alice added, shooting Cooper a look that just dared him to argue with her. "If Josey says that's where you need to be, that's where you're going."

Flynn stepped forward, his jaw set at a stubborn angle. "That's right. So don't even think about vetoing the idea. You're outnumbered."

Cooper's eyes glittered. "Oh, yeah?"

"Yeah," Gable retorted, adding his two cents with a grin as he finished his call to the sheriff and hung up. "Give in gracefully, little brother. You're beaten and you know it."

He did, but that didn't mean he had to be happy about it. Just the thought of being fussed over in a hospital had him grinding his teeth in frustration. "That's the trouble with this family," he grumbled, his mouth twitching in spite of his best efforts to hang on to a frown. "You wait until a man has a bum leg, then gang up on him." Glancing over to where Susannah stood at the far end of the couch, he arched a brow at her. "I suppose you're throwing in your lot with the rest of these worrywarts."

"We can take my car," she said without blinking an eye. "It's right out front."

By nightfall, it was all over. The doctor in the emergency room at the hospital in Silver City had taken one look at Cooper's wound and had him wheeled into surgery. The family was nervously pacing the waiting room when Kat rushed in an hour later from school, white as a sheet and terrified. Cooper came out of the operating room soon after that, grumbling that he wasn't spending the night in the hospital, but he was so woozy that he could barely keep his eyes open. Not even the news that Denkins had been apprehended in El Paso while trying to slip over the border into Mexico had been able to keep him awake.

There had been no reason for anyone to stay after that—the doctor had warned them that Cooper would sleep straight through till morning—but leaving him had been the hardest thing Susannah had ever done. Politely declining the

Rawlingses' invitation to spend the night at the Double R, she'd gone home instead. Alone.

The empty silence hit her in the face the minute she walked through the front door. Agitated, too unsettled to do anything but prowl around the living room, absently inspecting her father's things as if she'd never seen them before, she finally forced herself to stand still and face the truth.

She loved Cooper Rawlings. Totally, completely, heart and soul.

Another place, another time, she might have gloried in the realization. But here in her father's house, surrounded by memories that were just as painful today as they had been in her childhood, the truth was untenable, unacceptable. She couldn't love a man like Cooper. She simply couldn't.

Part of her wanted to believe he wasn't like her father. Just because he was a strong, stubborn cowboy with a take-charge attitude didn't mean that he would try to keep her under his thumb as her father had her mother. He wouldn't do that. He wasn't like that. He wouldn't use her love for him as a weapon to control her. Would he?

With all her heart, she wanted to cry out an unequivocal *No!* But she couldn't be sure and that was what terrified her.

She'd stayed too long, she thought, swallowing a sob. And now she had to pay the price. She had to leave.

Cooper waited all day for Susannah to show up at the hospital. When she still hadn't put in an appearance by four that afternoon, he called her, but the phone was evidently still out and all he got was a recording. Disgusted, he hung up and called the Double R instead. When Kat told him none of the family had seen Susannah since last night, when she'd insisted on going home instead of staying at the Double R, every instinct he possessed told him something was wrong.

"Get somebody over here to pick me up," he growled. "I'm getting out of here."

"But I thought you were staying another couple of days," she said, bewildered. "The doctor said—"

Cooper clenched his teeth on an oath and struggled to hang onto his patience while somewhere deep inside a voice whispered, *Hurry. Hurry.* "Kat, honey, the doctor's an old woman. So will you quit worrying about me and just come and get me? And bring me some clothes. If I spend another night in here, I'm going to go crazy."

For a long moment, he was sure she was going to turn him down flat and claim it was for his own good. But then she sighed in defeat. "Okay, okay, you big baby. Keep your pants on. I'll be there as soon as I can."

"Cute, sis. Real cute," he drawled, grimacing down at the bandage that made it impossible to get his jeans on without cutting up the left leg. "I love you, too. Now would you cut the chatter and get a move on it?"

"I'm already on my way."

"Good. Just try to keep the speedometer under seventy, okay? You hear me? *Don't speed.*"

For an answer, she only laughed and hung up.

The next two hours were the longest of Cooper's life. Something was wrong—he could feel it in his bones—but all he could do was wait. And patience had never been his strong suit. When Kat finally strolled into his hospital room with a pair of jeans that she'd already split high up the thigh, he was ready to chew nails.

Leaving wasn't as easy as simply walking out, but once the hospital staff realized he had every intention of doing just that, they were more cooperative. Twenty minutes later, he was crawling into the pickup Kat had brought from the ranch and cursing the unexpected tiredness that hit him during the short walk from his room to the hospital's front entrance.

In spite of that, he still insisted on driving himself to Susannah's once they reached the Double R. Kat had a fit, of course, and bluntly pointed out that he was as weak as a baby and had no business getting behind the wheel of a car. But he threatened to walk if she didn't give him the keys. With the bluntness of a sister who had been holding her own with three older brothers longer than any of them could remember, she told him exactly what she thought of his stubborn stupidity and gave him the keys.

It wasn't until he saw the lights burning at the Patterson homestead that he realized he'd expected her to be gone.

Stunned by the strength of the relief that shuddered through him, he braked to a stop in her drive and just sat there in the gathering darkness, staring at her house, his thoughts reeling. When had she ceased to be Joe Patterson's daughter and become, instead, a woman he couldn't imagine life without?

He loved her.

The knowledge came to him slowly, quietly, spilling into his heart like a phantom lover sliding into his dreams. Shaken, he couldn't have denied it if he'd wanted to. Without him even knowing how it had happened, she'd taken over his every thought, waking and sleeping, and a man didn't let a woman do that to him unless he was crazy about her.

And it was high time he told her.

His lips twitched just at the thought of how she would react to that little announcement. She'd give him an argument if for no other reason than she was an independent woman who wouldn't give up her freedom without a show of token resistance—he expected no less of her. But they belonged together, and she knew that as well as he did. Now all he had to do was find a way to make her admit it.

Grinning like an idiot at the possibilities that flooded his thoughts at that, he pushed open the pickup door and bounded up the porch steps, hardly noticing the steady throb in his thigh.

When she opened the door at his knock, he'd expected her surprise, even shock, since he wasn't scheduled to be released from the hospital for at least another day or two. What he wasn't prepared for was the dismay that flashed like lightning in her gray eyes before she could stop it.

The greeting that hovered on his tongue withered and died, unspoken. His gaze slipped past her shoulder to the living room beyond. At the sight of the cardboard boxes stacked there, he started to ask her what was going on. Then he saw the suitcases at the foot of the stairs.

His eyes snapped back to hers. "You're leaving?"

His tone was harsh, accusing. Susannah winced, the guilty color that flooded her cheeks telling him everything he needed to know. Fighting the need to hug herself, she lifted her chin and gave him a level look that offered no apologies. "Yes. I've done all I can here. It's time to move on."

"Just like that, huh?" he retorted, snapping his fingers in front of her nose, his eyes as hard and unyielding as black diamonds. He glared at her. "And when were you going to get around to letting me know what you were planning? Or were you just going to slip off in the dead of night and let me find out for myself when I got out of the hospital?"

She paled. "It wasn't like that—"

"Oh, really?" he growled, pushing his way past her. "That's sure as hell the way it looks to me."

A month ago, weeks ago, she would have heard nothing but the biting anger in his voice. But she knew him better now, and she didn't miss the pain in his eyes, in the words that lashed at her like a whip. She wanted to reach for him, to just go into his arms and try to make him understand, but if she touched him now, if she made the mistake of letting him hold her, it would be all too easy to forget why she had to leave.

Forcing herself to stay where she was, she closed the front door, then leaned back against it as she faced him. "I wasn't trying to sneak out without telling you goodbye," she said stiffly. "I just thought it would be easier this way."

"Why?"

"Because I have to leave—"

"Why?"

She expelled her breath in a huff, wanting to shake him. She should have known he wouldn't make it easy for her. "I would think that would be pretty obvious," she retorted. "I'm a writer. I've got a book to write."

If she'd hoped to get through to him, she might as well have saved her breath. His only response was to lean back against the newel post and cross his arms across his chest. "So? What does what you do for a living have to do with this?"

"Being a writer isn't what I do. It's what I *am,*" she said. Struggling for words, she tried to explain and knew from his scowl that she was doing a poor job of it. "I don't walk away from a book at the end of the day like most people do their jobs. I can't. All my attention is focused on my characters and their story. And if I need more research to tell that story, then I go wherever I have to to get the information I need...even if that means dropping everything and going halfway across the country."

His narrowed gaze pinned her to the door. "I see. So what you're saying is that you turn your back on everything, *everyone,* and just walk away. Right? Because your book, your writing, is all that's important to you."

His soft, sharp words had an edge like a knife and sliced to the bone. Blinking back tears, she just stood there without once opening her mouth to defend herself. She could have told him that walking away in the past had been easy because all she'd walked away from had been an empty apartment. Leaving him was a whole other ball game. She hadn't even gotten in the car yet, and the pain was already more than she could bear.

Blinking back tears, she swallowed thickly. "My mother had to answer to my father every day of their married life. She couldn't so much as go to town for groceries without okaying it with him first." Standing straight and tall before him, she forced herself to say the words that had to be said. "From the time I was old enough to know what was going on, I promised myself that I would never ask permission of any man to do what I wanted to do. So the answer to your question is yes. Nothing else matters."

A muscle working in his jaw, Cooper could only stare at her, betrayal twisting in his gut. If he'd wanted to know where he stood, she'd just told him. She wasn't letting him or anyone else get in her way. Now that she was no longer in trouble, now that she no longer needed him, she was going back to her old life—just like Mary Lou. All the stuff about her parents and answering to a man was just so much crap. He'd never once expected her to ask permission from him to do anything, and she knew it.

Idiot! he raged at himself. Fool! Once again, he found himself in the unenviable position of listening to the woman he was crazy about tell him why she was walking away from him. And he had nobody to blame but himself.

Pride stamping his face in rigid lines, he said curtly, "Then don't let me stand in your way. Since you've already learned all you can about cowboys, I presume you're now going to scout out locales for the story. Where did you plan on going?"

Afraid he would come after her, she didn't want to tell him. But something in his eyes warned her he wasn't leaving until she did. "Santa Fe," she said stiffly. "Then Tombstone and Jerome."

Without a word, he jotted down names, addresses and telephone numbers on a sheet of paper he tore from the notepad she kept by the phone. "We've got friends in Santa Fe and Jerome. And the Montgomerys don't live too far from Tombstone," he said as he handed her the list. "Your phone's still out, so I'll have to call them from home to square it with them, but I'm sure they'll be more than happy to help you with your research. Just give them a call when you get into town. Have you decided what you're going to do with Paintbrush?"

Surprised by the sudden shift in subjects, she blinked. "No. Actually, I'd forgotten about him since he's been at the Double R since the fire."

"You don't need to make any decisions today or tomorrow—we'll keep him for you as long as you want. But if you decide to sell him, I'd like first crack at him. I'll give you a good price for him."

"Yes, of course." Frowning, her eyes searched his. "Why? Why are you doing this?"

He could understand her confusion; he was just as confounded by his behavior as she was. Self-mockery glittering in his eyes, his mouth curled cynically. "Damned if I know. When I figure it out, I'll let you know." Without another word, he headed for the door.

Seconds later, the sound of his truck rumbling to life broke the silence. Staring blindly down at the list of friends he'd given her, Susannah heard him drive away and told herself she'd done the right thing. She should have been relieved. Instead, she'd never been more miserable in her life.

In the end, leaving turned out to be far more difficult than she had expected. She found a dozen reasons not to go, a dozen justifications why it would be all right for her to stay. After all, the ranch was hers, and after she finished her research, the only other place she had to go was her apartment in Dallas. It had served as her home base for years, the place she always came back to when it was time to sit down and actually write the book she had been researching for months. She was comfortable there; it was home.

But just the thought of leaving New Mexico for good, of returning to the city, brought the sting of tears to her eyes. She told herself it was because she'd learned to love the ranch, the constant murmur of the wind, the rippling waves of yellowed buffalo grass that stretched for as far as the eye could see. She'd found a freedom here she'd never expected to find, a peace that she hadn't even known she was searching for.

She left, but she didn't go far and she wasn't gone long. She justified her actions as a career move, and not necessarily a permanent one at that. She had research to do in that part of the country, a Western to write when she had all the information she needed to tell Diego Kelly's story. And what better place to do that than right in the middle of an area that epitomized the West? She could use her father's place as a base, make the side trips she needed to make, settle down for another four or five months with her computer, and then decide where she was going from there. It was that simple.

Or at least it would have been that simple if Cooper had cooperated. She'd thought she'd made it clear that there was no room in her life for him, but evidently he hadn't gotten the message. When she came home from Santa Fe, she found a package from him that he'd somehow managed to leave on her kitchen table. Under the wrapping was a small, cloth-covered volume with an attached note that told her the book was his great-grandmother's journal. He'd thought she might be able to use some of the old lady's stories in her writing.

Touched, she'd carefully turned the yellowed pages, entranced. And all the while, a voice in her head had warned her that she couldn't accept the loan of the book if she was really serious about cutting Cooper out of her life. But she hadn't been able to return it, which was no doubt just what he'd expected.

What was a woman supposed to do with a man who knew her so well?

A week later she returned from Jerome, and once again he had a surprise waiting for her. This time it was some family pictures and tintypes from the 1800s and several old maps that gave the locations of little-known towns and villages that hadn't been in existence since the turn of the century and had long since faded from modern-day maps. Fascinated, she hadn't even considered sending those back.

But it was the letter waiting for her in her mailbox the afternoon when she got back from an overnight trip to Tombstone that stopped her in her tracks. In it, Kyle Elkins, a rancher in Wyoming who just happened to be godfather to the entire Rawlings bunch, invited her to visit him and his wife in Jackson Hole and stay through the spring and summer while she wrote her book.

Cooper had arranged this for her, she thought, stunned, as she sank down onto the couch in her living room and read the letter again. She'd never told him how just being in the same setting as her book inspired her, but he'd obviously realized that living at a ranch would make it easier for her to capture the mood of a Western. And since she'd made it clear she didn't intend to stay in New Mexico, he'd made it possible for her to do her writing somewhere else.

Why? she cried silently. All this time she'd been trying to convince herself that he was like her father, a rough, tough, chauvinistic cowboy who thought of a woman as a possession he kept close at hand. But time and time again, he'd gone out of his way to help her with her career, and now he was giving her the means to leave so she could do what she loved, what she'd told him meant more to her than any-thing.

And that was something her father would never have done. For as far back as she could remember, he had ruth-lessly ignored her mother's tearful pleading to go to col-lege, claiming that she was his wife and that should be enough for her. He'd forced her mother to divorce him rather than give in.

And she'd thought Cooper would be just like him, threatened by a woman's independence.

Shaken, needing to think, she laid Kyle Elkins's letter on the coffee table and rose jerkily to her feet, too agitated to sit still. Without any conscious decision on her part, she found herself in her father's study, reaching for his last di-ary, which had been returned to her by prison officials af-ter his death. Up until now she'd put off reading it simply because she hadn't been able to stand the thought of her fa-ther locked up in a cage like some kind of wild animal. She hadn't wanted to face what that must have been like for him, but now she desperately needed a way to reach him and that was all she had left of him. Dropping into the chair behind the desk, she opened the journal and began to read.

An hour later, she finished. Stunned, she stared unsee-ingly down at the diary. Whenever she'd let herself think about her father in prison, she'd assumed he'd spent his days hating the Rawlingses and life in general, blaming everyone but himself. Instead, he had, much to her sur-prise, done a lot of soul-searching, not only about the events that had led to his arrest and imprisonment, but also about the past.

Her father had been a man haunted by fears. She'd al-ways thought he was so strong, so invincible. But he'd been so afraid of losing his wife that he hadn't trusted her out of his sight. And in trying to hang on to what he loved the most, he'd only accomplished what he'd been trying to prevent . . . he'd driven her mother away.

If only she'd known, Susannah thought, blinking back tears. *This* man, the one who wasn't afraid to face his own insecurities, she could have loved the way she'd always longed to love her father. Just knowing that his actions were motivated by fear would have changed everything—not only in her relationship with him, but with other men. With Cooper.

Realization rippled through her, stripping away the blinders that had kept her in the dark about her own feelings. In her own way, she'd been just as insecure as her father. She'd run, using her writing as an excuse, because she'd been afraid. Afraid to let down her guard, afraid to let Cooper into her life, afraid to trust. And like her father, she'd nearly lost the one person in the world who meant more to her than anything.

At the thought, images flashed before her eyes, stark, lonely projections of what her future would be like without Cooper. Pain squeezed her heart, and just that quickly she knew she couldn't let another night pass without telling him what he meant to her. She wouldn't lose him the way her father had lost her mother. She couldn't! She had to see him, she thought, jumping to her feet. Now. Before it was too late.

When the knock came at the door, Cooper was lost in an Ace MacKenzie book and cursing himself for being an idiot. He could hear Susannah's voice in every word, see her hand in every fine plot twist, all too easily picture her throwing herself into the research with reckless abandon. He'd thought if he stepped back and gave her the room she so obviously needed, she'd realize he was nothing like her father and eventually come home to him. But he hadn't heard a word from her, and he missed her, dammit! But did he put the book down and quit torturing himself? Hell, no.

When the knock came again, he seriously considered ignoring it. It was probably Flynn again, or Gable, there to cheer him up. But he didn't want to be cheered up. He was enjoying his misery just fine all by himself and he'd thank everyone if they'd just leave him alone.

Deciding to tell his unwanted visitor just that, he set the book down and strode over to the door and jerked it open, harsh words already forming on his tongue. But at the sight of Susannah standing on the porch, her fist raised to knock again, he was struck dumb. He could only stare at her, unable to believe she was finally there after he'd spent days aching to just see her.

"Josey told me I'd find you here," she said huskily. "Can I come in?"

He opened the door without a word, wondering if Josey had also told her that the reason he was staying at the spring cabin was because he'd been a bear to live with ever since she'd run off to do that damn research of hers. Not wanting to inflict his foul mood on the family, he'd withdrawn to the cabin to lick his wounds.

"Have a seat," he growled. "You want a cup of coffee or something?"

"No... thank you." Jumpy as an ant on a hot rock, she moved jerkily around the cabin, struggling for words. Why was it suddenly so hard to say what she knew had to be said? "I guess you're wondering why I'm here," she began.

He merely lifted a brow and pulled out a chair from the table and straddled it. "The thought crossed my mind. I thought you'd be halfway to Wyoming by now."

"I couldn't. I tried... I thought it was for the best. But I was running and I didn't even know it." Driving her fingers through hair with an impatient gesture, she tried to offer a logical explanation, but the thoughts whirling in her head were flying by at the speed of sound. "No man has ever meant as much to me as my writing. I was scared...my father...I found his diary."

Hot tears suddenly flooded her eyes and spilled over her lashes. With a muffled, impatient exclamation, she tried to brush them away but they just kept coming. "I-I never knew how afraid h-he was. He was crazy about my mother, but he was so afraid of losing her, he drove h-her away. I won't do that," she warned him, her gray eyes suddenly snapping. "I'm not going to let fear ruin my life the way it did my parents'."

His heart starting to pound in his chest, Cooper sat as if turned to stone and told himself not to jump to conclusions. She was obviously upset, jumping all around whatever it was that she'd come there to say. As much as he'd like to, he couldn't put words in her mouth. "What is it you're trying to say?" he asked tersely. "Just spit it out and get it over with."

He made it sound so easy. Stopping in her tracks, she stared at him, her eyes searching his for the courage she didn't think she had. Then something in his expression softened and warmed and suddenly the words were there on her tongue, begging to be spoken.

"I've been so afraid to love you," she admitted with a simple honesty that, had she but known it, almost brought him to his knees. "That's why I couldn't stay after Denkins was captured, why I ran. I knew I was falling in love with you and that terrified me. How could we possibly have a future together? I wasn't the type of woman you needed, and you were like my father. Or at least I thought you were."

Unable to sit there another moment and watch her bare her soul, he surged to his feet and swept the chair out of the way. "Honey—"

Knowing she would be lost the second he touched her, she hurriedly took a step back. "You let me go," she said in wonder. "And just when I was close to convincing myself it was because you didn't care, I'd come home and find a present waiting from you. And every time I left, it was harder to go."

He took another step toward her, heat flaring in his eyes. "Good. That's what I was hoping for."

Her heart stumbled into a wild, erratic beat as she retreated another step, only to feel the wall at her back. "Then I read my father's last journal," she said quickly. "The one he wrote in prison. He was so afraid of losing my mother that he kept her under his thumb all the time, until she just couldn't stand it any longer."

"So that's why she divorced him," he said softly, closing his fingers over her shoulders. "I always wondered."

Her eyes lifted to his. "He lost everything because he was afraid. I'm not going to make that mistake. I'm not scared to tell you I love you. Not that I expect anything in return," she added quickly. "I'm responsible for my own feelings. I mean I didn't lay this on you so you'd be obligated to... to tell me—"

A grin tugging at his mouth, Cooper pulled her closer and slowly lowered his head. "Honey?"

Her gaze trained on the sensuous line of his descending mouth, she swayed closer. "Hmm?"

"I love you," he murmured. "I was just waiting for you to stand still long enough so I could tell you."

Her eyes wide, her throat tight with emotion, she only had time for a surprised "Oh!" before he chuckled and covered her mouth with his. When he finally let her up for air, it was his time to talk.

"I never wanted to keep you under my thumb," he rasped, dropping kisses across her cheeks. "I never wanted you to be anything but what you are."

"I can't give up my writing—"

"You're damn right," he agreed promptly. "I've been reading *Night of the Hunter,* and I haven't been able to put the damn thing down. You're good, sweetheart. And I can see how important your research is to you. I would never do anything to stand in the way of that. Hell, I'll go with you after we're married, and help you. After all, the ranch is back on its feet now, and Gable and Flynn can take up the slack while I'm gone. It'll be—" He broke off abruptly at the sudden arching of her brow. "What?" he asked. "What's wrong?"

Her heart singing, Susannah struggled to hold back a smile. *"After we're married?"* she echoed.

For a moment, he froze. God, had he misread her that badly? Then he saw the amusement dancing in her eyes. His own lips twitching, he pulled her closer. "Oh, didn't I mention that?"

"No, I don't believe you did."

"Then maybe I'd better correct that right now." Before she could guess his intentions, he was down on one knee, his eyes steady and full of love as they met her startled ones. "I love you with all my heart, Susannah Patterson. Will you marry me?"

Her eyes flooded. "Oh, Cooper!"

* * * * *

Keep on the lookout for flirting Flynn Rawlings's story in the next exciting installment in the Wild West Series. Only from Intimate Moments!

HE'S AN

AMERICAN HERO

He's a man's man, and every woman's dream.
Strong, sensitive and so irresistible—he's an
American Hero.

For April: KEEPER, by Patricia Gardner Evans:
From the moment Cleese Starrett encountered
Laurel Drew fishing in his river, he was hooked.
But reeling in this lovely lady might prove harder
than he thought.

For May: MICHAEL'S FATHER, by Dallas Schulze:
Kel Bryan needed a housekeeper—fast. And
Megan Roarke did more than fit the bill; she fit
snugly into his open arms. Then she told him
her news....

For June: SIMPLE GIFTS, by Kathleen Korbel: For
too long Rock O'Connor had fought the good
fight to no avail. Then Lee Kendall entered his
jaded world, her zest for life rekindling his former
passion—as well as a new one.

AMERICAN HEROES: Men who give all they've
got for their country, their work—the women they
love.

Only from

IMHER08

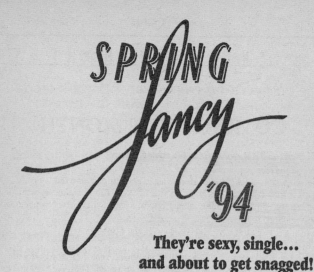

SPRING fancy '94

**They're sexy, single...
and about to get snagged!**

Passion is in full bloom as love catches
the fancy of three brash bachelors. You won't
want to miss these stories by three of
Silhouette's hottest authors:

CAIT LONDON
DIXIE BROWNING
PEPPER ADAMS

Spring fever is in the air this March—
and there's no avoiding it!

Only from

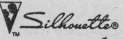 *Silhouette*®

where passion lives.

SF94

COMING NEXT MONTH

#559 KEEPER—Patricia Gardner Evans
American Hero
From the moment American Hero Cleese Starrett encountered
Laurel Drew fishing in his river, he was hooked. But this alluring woman
had a tortured past and a threatened future, a future that Cleese wanted to
share—at any cost.

#560 TRY TO REMEMBER—Carla Cassidy
Romantic Traditions
"Jane Smith's" memory had vanished, so when Frank Longford offered
her a safe haven and a strong shoulder, she accepted. Then the nightmares
began, with remembrance proving scarier than amnesia, and Jane feared
losing the one man she truly loved.

#561 FULL OF SURPRISES—Maura Seger
Chas Howell's life changed irrevocably the day he laid eyes on
Annalise Johannsen. This feisty lady rancher needed help and protection,
and Chas knew the job would suit him just fine—and so would
the employer....

#562 STRANGER IN TOWN—Laura Parker
Jo Spencer thought she'd seen a ghost, so strongly did Gus Thornton
resemble the forbidden love of her past. But even though Gus claimed to
be new to town, Jo swore she glimpsed familiar desire—and haunted
memories—in this stranger's eyes.

#563 LAWYERS, GUNS AND MONEY—Rebecca Daniels
With the conviction of a major crime boss to her credit, federal prosecu-
tor Gillian Hughes became a red-hot target. Undercover agent Ash Cain
vowed to keep her safe. Yet soon he found himself in over his head,
because tough-guy Ash had fallen head over heels....

#564 HARD EVIDENCE—Laurie Walker
Pursuing the evidence that would clear her of a manslaughter charge,
Sergeant Laurel Tanner found herself with an unlikely ally, the dead
man's brother. But she soon feared that Scott Delany's helpful intentions
stemmed not from desire—but from double cross.

It's those rambunctious Rawlings brothers again!
You met Gable and Cooper Rawlings in IM #523
and IM #553. Now meet their youngest brother,
Flynn Rawlings, in

by Linda Turner

Fun-loving rodeo cowboy Flynn Rawlings
couldn't believe it. From the moment he'd
approached beautiful barrel racer Tate Baxter,
she'd been intent on freezing him out. But Tate
was the woman he'd been waiting for all his life,
and he wasn't about to take no for an answer!

Don't miss FLYNN (IM #572), available in June.
And look for his sister, Kat's, story as
Linda Turner's thrilling saga concludes in

THE WILD WEST

Coming to you throughout 1994...only from
Silhouette Intimate Moments.

If you missed the first two books in THE WILD WEST series, *Gable's Lady* (IM #523) or *Cooper* (IM #553), order your copy now by sending your name, address, zip or postal code, along with a check or money order (please do not send cash) for $3.50, plus 75¢ postage and handling ($1.00 in Canada), payable to Silhouette Books, to:

In the U.S.	In Canada
Silhouette Books	Silhouette Books
3010 Walden Ave.	P. O. Box 636
P. O. Box 9077	Fort Erie, Ontario
Buffalo, NY 14269-9077	L2A 5X3

Please specify book titles with order.
Canadian residents add applicable federal and provincial taxes.

WILD3

SILHOUETTE... Where Passion Lives

Don't miss these Silhouette favorites by some of our most distinguished authors! And now you can receive a discount by ordering two or more titles!

SD	#05772	FOUND FATHER by Justine Davis	$2.89 ☐
SD	#05783	DEVIL OR ANGEL by Audra Adams	$2.89 ☐
SD	#05786	QUICKSAND by Jennifer Greene	$2.89 ☐
SD	#05796	CAMERON by Beverly Barton	$2.99 ☐
IM	#07481	FIREBRAND by Paula Detmer Riggs	$3.39 ☐
IM	#07502	CLOUD MAN by Barbara Faith	$3.50 ☐
IM	#07505	HELL ON WHEELS by Naomi Horton	$3.50 ☐
IM	#07512	SWEET ANNIE'S PASS by Marilyn Pappano	$3.50 ☐
SE	#09791	THE CAT THAT LIVED ON PARK AVENUE by Tracy Sinclair	$3.39 ☐
SE	#09793	FULL OF GRACE by Ginna Ferris	$3.39 ☐
SE	#09822	WHEN SOMEBODY WANTS by Trisha Alexander	$3.50 ☐
SE	#09841	ON HER OWN by Pat Warren	$3.50 ☐
SR	#08866	PALACE CITY PRINCE by Arlene James	$2.69 ☐
SR	#08916	UNCLE DADDY by Kasey Michaels	$2.69 ☐
SR	#08948	MORE THAN YOU KNOW by Phyllis Halldorson	$2.75 ☐
SR	#08954	HERO IN DISGUISE by Stella Bagwell	$2.75 ☐
SS	#27006	NIGHT MIST by Helen R. Myers	$3.50 ☐
SS	#27010	IMMINENT THUNDER by Rachel Lee	$3.50 ☐
SS	#27015	FOOTSTEPS IN THE NIGHT by Lee Karr	$3.50 ☐
SS	#27020	DREAM A DEADLY DREAM by Allie Harrison	$3.50 ☐

(limited quantities available on certain titles)

	AMOUNT	$
DEDUCT:	10% DISCOUNT FOR 2+ BOOKS	$
	POSTAGE & HANDLING	$_____
	($1.00 for one book, 50¢ for each additional)	
	APPLICABLE TAXES*	$_____
	TOTAL PAYABLE	$_____
	(check or money order—please do not send cash)	

To order, complete this form and send it, along with a check or money order for the total above, payable to Silhouette Books, to: **In the U.S.:** 3010 Walden Avenue, P.O. Box 9077, Buffalo, NY 14269-9077; **In Canada:** P.O. Box 636, Fort Erie, Ontario, L2A 5X3.

Name: _____

Address: _____ City: _____

State/Prov.: _____ Zip/Postal Code: _____

*New York residents remit applicable sales taxes.
Canadian residents remit applicable GST and provincial taxes.   SBACK-JM

Silhouette®